Vanguard:

Stephen Novak

Acropolis Series: Book One

STEPHEN NOVAK

Vanguard, © January, 2021

ISBN 978-0-6450823-0-2

VANGUARD

Dedication

Dedicated to my parents, whose unwavering support has always helped me achieve my goals.

STEPHEN NOVAK

Chapter One

Taj

Taj's breath came in harsh pants as he sprinted down the long dark tunnel of the Labyrinth. The only sound in the quiet tomb like passage was his rough leather boots slapping against the cold hard granite, reverberating his footsteps in all directions. Halfway down the tunnel, he stopped, released the clip from his ramshackle automatic rifle and quickly shoved another in the weapon.

Wiping the sweat from his brow, Taj shuffled forward, his eyes straining in the blackness. He slowly moved his rifle from left to right, scanning the surrounding area for his pursuer, but the small light on his gun barely illuminated the complete darkness.

"Listen and be aware of your surroundings," Tre always said. "The smallest sign could signal great danger." Often in dangerous situations, the voice of his unit's leader echoed in his head.

Taj cringed as something wet and cold dripped on his head, sending a chill down his spine. He looked up; water dripped off the rounded, algae covered roof of the tunnel, and slime oozed out of the thick concrete walls, pooling on the chipped and grimy granite tiles that covered the ground.

"Enough of this, where are you, ya ugly bastard," he challenged. "You were right behind me only two seconds ago."

Taj kept moving forward, his hands shuddering a little as he strafed the light back and forth, searching for the creature. The main tunnels of the Labyrinth were nearly twenty feet wide and at least fifteen high, making it impossible for him to light the whole area at once. He reached the end of the passage and put his back to the damp wall, glancing around the corner at one of the smaller side sections that branched off from the main path.

His heart raced, the small organ going into overdrive from a mix of fear and his recent exertion. He slowly inhaled the damp stale air, trying to tame his growing dread. Being alone in the underground was dangerous; a lifetime of experience had shown him what happened to those who strayed off alone for too long. Most were never seen alive again, their carcasses left to rot until a patrol stumbled upon the mangled remains in a forgotten corner of the ancient tunnel system.

Taj absentmindedly wiped his sweaty palms on the cloth shirt that was peeking through his armour. He hated this part, not knowing where it was, what it was doing — it could be anywhere. Tre's voice already started creeping back into his mind. He already knew what the commander would say if he returned without the creature. It wasn't the first time he had received a lengthy chastising lecture about his failure to complete his duties as a Vanguard, nor would it be the last.

Unable to tolerate the waiting anymore, Taj pushed himself off the wall, making a mental note to clean the slime off his back when they returned to the city. He started roaming, firing a few shots in front of him, sending the super-heated metal ploughing into the walls and scattering chips of concrete and dust.

"I'm here, come and get me," he yelled in one final attempt to goad the creature out from hiding. "Dinner time," Taj sprayed the last few shots from the hundred bullet rifle clip, arcing the weapon in front of him. "Must have given it the slip, just my luck, the onetime I want one of them to follow me."

A low growl came out of the pitch black behind him and his heart stopped; had it been there the whole time? *Watching me?* He turned and saw two big red bulbous eyes a few metres away, his light illuminating a vicious set of yellowed, knife-like teeth clenched in a silent snarl.

Taj swore and his legs turned to jelly as what little of his courage remained threatened to disappear. With shaking hands, he reloaded his weapon and took careful aim down the rifle sight. The creature let loose a blood-chilling roar and he opened fire, hammering his foe in the face and chest, the deafening sound echoing around him and assaulting his eardrums. The custom-made armour-piercing rounds cut into the creature's flesh, but it didn't fall.

Satisfied that would follow him, Taj exited into one of the many side passages that ran parallel to the main pathways, they were roughly half the size at eight feet high, and twelve wide, making it difficult for some of the larger creatures in the underground to squeeze inside. The Labyrinth had thousands of tunnels honeycombed all over the continent, the remnants of a long-dead civilisation. No one knew what the massive network had been designed for, but he doubted the original architects had envisioned their great masterwork would be used to house exiles and dangerous creatures.

The injured creature bellowed and gave chase, its bulk shaking the foundations as it ran after Taj. He followed the side path for a few metres and then made his way back into the main tunnel section, retreating the way he had come. He rounded a corner, checking every wall he passed, frantically searching for the symbol that would signal his salvation. A tingle ran down his spine as hot, rancid breath brushed against the back of his neck. He instinctively took the next left, feeling no small amount of satisfaction at the sound of something heavy hitting the ground, and the resulting shockwave.

"They're awful with tight corners," he muttered, a smile ghosting his face as he repeated the words that had often been barked at him during his training.

"That was too close, nearly had me." Taj continued his retreat down the main passage, silently hoping that the combination of wounds, and the subsequent fall would slow the creature long enough for him to stay out of danger. He stole a glance behind, spying the tell-tale bulbous red eyes still in hot pursuit. "Nearly there," he panted to himself, brushing the sweat out of his eyes.

Approaching a fork in the tunnel, Taj spied a familiar luminous symbol painted above the right path, two rifles crossed with a grinning human skull in the middle. The emblem was used to indicate when there was a friendly unit nearby and was the best friend of every Vanguard. He breathed a sigh of relief, which quickly gave way to anger as razor-sharp claws ripped through the armour on his back, digging deep into his flesh. Without looking behind him, he fired over his shoulder and increased his pace, fear giving him unnatural speed.

Something splattered on his mouth and Taj accidentally swallowed the bitter tasting substance, his inside churned and the contents of his stomach threatened to spew forth, but he clenched his jaw and kept running, forcing the bile back down. Near the end of the tunnel, bright lights flooded in from the next chamber banishing the dark.

"Finally," he whispered.

Chapter Two
Ambush at The Crossroads

Crossing over the threshold into the bright light, Taj shielded his eyes, scrunching up his face as pinpoints of red clouded his vision. He caught sight of the blurry outlines of six figures in the centre of the crossroads. Running directly at the group, he dropped to his knees and slid the last few metres, coming to rest at their feet.

The creature lumbered in after him and hit the carefully planned ambush, six guns exploded to life in an instant, spattering spent bullet casings on Taj's prone form. A loud roar of anger quickly turned into a low whine as the creature was gunned down. An almighty thud sent shockwaves through the granite tiles as the massive body hit the ground.

Taj sat up, a dull ringing in his ears; the other six men in his unit hadn't bothered to check on him, they were too focussed on their kill. They were all dressed as he was, in standard Vanguard armour: an iron chest piece, gauntlets, and leg guards, every man also had a sidearm or knife strapped to their belt. All their armour followed the same basic design and black colour scheme, but constant repairs, and customisation with extra coverings or markings ensured no one set was the same. Four tall, thin cylinders glowing with bright blinding light were set up a few metres apart in a square, illuminating the entire area.

A large gloved hand appeared in Taj's face, he grabbed it and winced as he was pulled up, the wound on his back throbbing in protest. He spat on the ground, rubbing his tongue on his arm to replace the acrid taste of whatever he had swallowed with something far less distasteful.

"Nearly got you," the young man who helped him up said, his amusement clear by the tone of his voice; a near permanent cheeky grin was plastered across his grime-covered features. "That would have been a poor end to your first culling mission as a Vanguard."

"Up yours, Dal," Taj snapped. "Next time you can be the bait, I think I got its blood in my mouth."

"Calm down, it's not the end of the world," Dal said as he casually flicked his long, blonde, dirty hair out of his striking blue eyes.

"It nearly caught me while I was searching for the Vanguard Symbol, terrible job by the way, it was in the worst possible spot."

"Well, I'm sorry that my humble paint job wasn't up to your high standards," Dal countered. "Maybe next time you should run faster."

The long-time friends burst out laughing; to an ignorant observer their banter might seem serious, but they had been playfully arguing all their lives and had never genuinely fought for long. Dal was twenty-one, a full two years older than Taj, however, the two had been like brothers since their mothers had left them to play together as babies.

"I don't know what you're complaining about anyway," Dal said when their laughter died down. "That scratch is nothing, I cut myself worse trimming my hair this morning, you're whining like a Surfacer."

Taj hid his grin, preparing a scathing comeback of a similar nature. They had only encountered the Surfacer civilisation a year ago, when the entrances that allowed access topside were reopened after being sealed thousands of years earlier. Only a handful of their people had been allowed to leave the underground since contact was re-established, the lucky few brought back stories of a great city that covered the entire continent above, and the spoilt, snobbish citizens who lived in the metropolis.

"Both of you, shut the hell up," thundered a loud clear voice with a tone of authority to it. Taj and Dal tensed in anticipation of another tirade about their constant arguing. "If I wanted to listen to fools bickering, I would go home to my family, now get over here."

Unwilling to attract further berating from Tre, Taj and Dal silently joined the rest of their unit, who were all still huddled around the dead creature. As he often did after a kill, Dal viciously kicked it, a look of pure hatred plastered on his face.

The creature lay on its back, mouth agape in a final snarl, a large part of its smooth, hairless head was missing, a result of the kill shot. The rest of its heavily muscled body had been riddled with bullets, all except the chest where mottled bits of dark red skin formed in thick clumps, acting as a natural type of armour that protected from all but the most determined attackers.

"Which one of the seven is this anyway?" Dal enquired, ceasing his post kill ritual for a moment.

A short stocky man swore loudly, a scowl forming on his rough features. Unlike the others, who had given up on teaching Dal due to his laziness, Ren always felt the need to push him to do better. At first Taj had thought it was out of dislike, but he had quickly begun to realise it was because the man genuinely cared

"You have been a Vanguard for nearly three years now, Dal," Ren growled, his voice low and gravelly from a lifetime of yelling orders. "You should know the names and weaknesses of the seven creatures that lurk in the underground."

"Settle down, old fella," Dal mocked. "You'll have a heart attack, and then who would nag me."

Ren clenched his jaw and ruffled his grey beard, he was the oldest in their unit at 55 and held the rank of second captain, most people showed him respect either for his decades of experience, or his rank. As always, Dal was flirting with danger, the older Vanguards weren't above handing out a beating to humble a rude subordinate.

Taj considered trying to defuse the situation to save his friend like he had done many times in the past, but decided against it. As

11

the newest member of the unit, his word didn't hold much sway. He often got the worst of the jobs, acting as bait to lure in creatures, checking the dead, carrying any extra equipment, serving as the rear-guard, speaking out of turn would most likely result in him receiving a far worse task.

Ren decided to drag him into the conversation anyway.

"I'd wager the young blood knows," the second captain said. "It's his first culling mission, but I bet his two years of training weren't wasted."

Dal shrugged, staring directly into the veteran's hard brown eyes as a sign of defiance.

"How about it, boy?" Ren barked, pointing a thick gnarled finger at Taj. "Do you know what this thing is?"

Taj swallowed, quickly trying to recall what he had been taught. He looked over the creature's beefy arms, which ended in three claws on each hand, then drifted upward to the head, catching sight of its slit like nostrils and flat face. *Damn thing would be at least seven feet tall when standing, that combined with the armour on the chest, I think I know what it is.*

"It's a Butcher, known for size and resilience," he guessed. "They are named after the way they dismember victims. Their natural body armour means a head shot is the easiest and most reliable way of killing them."

"That's exactly right, boy, good job," Ren complimented. "It's a good thing we killed this one as well, before it wandered too close to the city. It could have caused a great deal of trouble for the Watchers."

With his input no longer required, Taj ignored the remainder of Ren's lecture to Dal, and tried to take in every detail of the fallen Butcher. He hadn't fired the shot that killed it, but still felt his contribution was large enough to warrant pride at its demise. After examining it from its thick legs upwards, his eyes came to rest on five gouges out of the creature's chest that he hadn't noticed earlier. Whatever cut it, had sliced right through the rock hard, mottled armour like skin and the wounds appeared to be sizzling and widening before their eyes.

What could do that? he wondered.

"Boy, what happened here?" Tre growled, pointing to the mysterious claw marks with his unusually long fingers.

Taj gritted his teeth, he hated being called boy, but he held his tongue; Tre was a commander, the second highest rank in the Vanguards, and he didn't want to cause problems over a trivial matter.

"I'm not sure, Tre," he answered truthfully. "You sent me out to lure in a creature to the ambush, I found this Butcher lurking near an old generator station not far from here, I couldn't tell you if it received the wounds before or after it started chasing me."

Taj waited for Tre's rebuke; he knew exactly what the commander would say.

You always need to stay alert, even the slightest missed detail can cost lives.

It was one of the first things they were taught. When Tre failed to say anything, Taj was both relieved and worried; very few things got in the way of the Vanguard leader chastising those under his command.

Tre continued to stare at the corpse, his sunken dark eyes darting back and forth as he began to mutter indecipherable words under his breath.

Something must be amiss, Taj decided. They had been on the culling mission for nearly two weeks now, killing countless creatures, and they had never lingered at a corpse for so long. He burned with curiosity and hoped an explanation was coming, but he was to be disappointed.

Tre woke from his trance and beckoned Ren, who had finished arguing with Dal but was still visibly simmering after the exchange. Neither of them said a word, after years of working

13

together the two could have whole discussions without uttering anything out loud.

"Form up, our culling mission is done, we are going back to the city," Ren instructed after reaching a silent consensus with Tre. "You two," he pointed to twin brothers, Ace and Ash, the lean, brown-haired, elfin-faced scouts. "Take apart the spotlights and get them ready for transport, then check out the passages around us, make sure the area is clear, I don't want anything sneaking up on us."

The brothers nodded, their green eyes flashing as they moved to carry out the task with their usual unnerving efficiency.

"Wes, take the boy, and Dal, scratch the Vanguard symbol, we won't be needing it anymore," Ren continued. "We move in ten."

Wes patted his balding head and ran his twitching hands through the last vestiges of his snow-white hair. "Boy, you take the right-hand side, Dal the left," he said, his voice only just above a whisper. "I'll stay in the centre, if you see anything that doesn't look human, blast the damn thing until it stops moving."

The three Vanguards wandered back down the tunnel Taj had just lured the Butcher through, keeping a metre between them to avoid friendly fire if they were ambushed. Using his light in unison with Dal and Wes, all shadows were banished, affording Taj a much better view of the passage. Every crack and dark stain on the walls was visible, along with the long, thin air vents that dotted the underground tunnels at regular intervals. The vents were as ancient as the Labyrinth itself, nobody knew where the lifesaving air that drifted in came from, but along with the plants in their city, they were the only things that kept them from suffocating.

Taj kept his finger on the rifle trigger; he didn't relish more combat, the last few days had given him more than his fill of fighting, but it was one of the few constants in the underground. No matter how many creatures the Vanguards killed, there always seemed to be more around every corner. When they reached the symbol above the tunnel fork, Wes wasted no time issuing new orders.

"Boy, watch our backs, Dal, I'll give you a leg up to wipe out the emblem, I'm not going up there."

Taj accepted the duty with glee, it was by far the easiest job he'd been assigned since the start of the mission. He positioned himself in the centre of the passage leading to the fork in the path, his dark eyes darting between the three possible entrances, alert for any sign of movement.

"What have you been eating," Wes grunted to Dal. "I've lifted load bearing cinder blocks lighter than you."

"Well, if you weren't afraid of heights, we could swap," Dal teased. "I still remember how you squealed when Tre asked you to mark that nest we cleared a few months ago, it reminded me of my mum whenever she spots a spider."

Taj couldn't help but chuckle when Wes voiced an angry reply, Dal had a special talent for knowing exactly how to get under someone's skin. Even the usually stoic Wes was unable to resist the provocation. The two continued to trade insults, even as Wes handed Dal the foul-smelling rag that would remove the luminous paint.

Taj wanted to keep eavesdropping on the argument, but he was determined to keep his focus on the task at hand, an attack could come at any moment in the underground, and carelessness could get him, and his friends killed. He made sure to repeatedly check each of the entrances, one after another, dragging his light across the passages. On his fourth run through, he saw it, down the tunnel leading back to the old generator station where he had first found the Butcher.

"How did I miss that," he muttered, firing three quick bursts at the familiar shape leaning against the wall, waiting for a roar that would signal his shots hit the target. The creature didn't move. Wes and Dal appeared either side of him, their squabble forgotten for the moment.

"What is it?" Wes asked.

"I think it's another Butcher," Taj replied, keeping his gaze fixed on the shadowy shape. "Not sure if I hit it, the last one chased me almost immediately."

"Move up," Wes ordered. "If it so much as twitches, don't stop shooting until it's down."

Here we go again, Taj mused. The Butcher stayed motionless as the three Vanguards cautiously shuffled towards it. The smell of death greeted them when they found the creature propped up against the passage; it was nearly identical to the one they had just killed, except its skull had been cracked open, exposing a fist-sized, red brain dripping green ooze. The gore on the nearby wall gave the impression its head had been repeatedly rammed into the unforgiving concrete. Clusters of the sickly yellow mushrooms that frequently grew in the dark corners of the tunnels were either side of the macabre display.

"Ugh, does it smell like that because it's dead?" Dal groaned. "Or is it those damn mushrooms kicking up the stink?"

Taj considered the question before answering. "I don't think you want to be close enough to a live Butcher to find out."

"Agreed." Wes's small expert eyes raked over the mass of flesh. "Boy, I take it this wasn't here when you lured the other one past earlier?"

"No way, I would have seen this, it's definitely new," Taj replied.

I hope, or Tre will kill me for failing to notice it, he added to himself silently

"Very curious," Wes said after a few more moments of examination. "I have never seen a Butcher have its skull opened this way before. It also appears to have similar wounds to the other one." He pointed to a set of five distinct claw marks gouged into the creature's chest, unlike the other Butcher though, the marks

16

didn't appear to be widening.

Taj's back wounds twitched, sending out a stinging pain around the affected area. He used his left hand to feel where he had been mauled, finding five distinct cuts, his stomach dropped, Butchers only had three claws. *What if the same thing that killed these two creatures scratched me too.*

He gingerly poked at the injury, trying to determine if his flesh was melting away. *Doesn't feel like it,* he thought. A chorus of high-pitched echoing howls, and the pitter patter of dozens of little feet sounded in front of them. All three Vanguards sprang into action, aiming their weapons towards the dreaded noise, Wes took the centre position, while Taj and Dal stood either side of the more experienced fighter.

"Don't run," Wes commanded in his soft tones. "The scavengers are fast, you'll be torn to pieces before you get more than a few steps. Stand firm, wait for my signal to shoot, keep them from getting in close."

Taj fought the urge to run as his light raked over the frontrunners in the pack, their thin needle-like teeth and milky white eyes shining in the glare. The waist high, lithe creatures huddled together, elongated heads arched up, sniffing the air as they searched for prey.

The rest of the herd quickly followed, filling the entire passage. The blind creatures mulled around, swinging their long tails, waiting for the moment to swarm. Taj had never seen a pack of Lurkers in person before, but he had heard tales of veteran Vanguards being reduced to tears at the sight of them; the knowledge wasn't a comfort.

"Wait for the Alpha to signal the attack," Wes roared over the chorus of howls. "If we figure out which one it is, and kill it, the rest of them will pause while the Beta assumes control of the pack."

Taj gritted his teeth, using every ounce of willpower to stop himself from shooting. Luckily, he didn't need to wait long. A Lurker, standing a full head taller than the others, shoved its way to the front, hissing and slashing with its small dual claws at any of its brethren who were in the way.

"Drop it," Wes ordered.

The Vanguards opened fire, a hail of bullets catching the Alpha in the sternum, sending its bloodied body to the ground. The others went deathly still, sensing the demise of their leader.

"Alright, let them have it," Wes shouted. The three Vanguards peppered the Lurkers with a near constant stream of gunfire, only stopping to reload. None of the placid creatures reacted to the assault, even as they fell in droves. When there were no longer any live ones in sight, Wes lifted his arm to signal a stop.

"Is that it, did we get them all?" Taj inquired as he rubbed his ringing ears. He eyed his gun barrel, which was glowing red from the constant firing, if the fight had gone any longer, it might have jammed, or even melted.

"No," Wes stated.

Taj's jaw fell open. "How can there be more?" he exclaimed.

"I don't know, there hasn't been a Lurker pack this large outside of the sub-levels in nearly a decade," Wes explained. "Check your supplies and have your knives ready."

Dal laughed sardonically, drawing his eight-inch serrated blade from his belt. "Maybe they can use it to pick their teeth when they are done with us."

Taj had to agree, the prospect of fighting so many Lurkers in close quarters seemed insane, he didn't relish testing his reflexes against the notoriously fast and energetic creatures. Regardless of their odds of survival, he checked his twin six-inch curved knives were still strapped to his belt, then moved onto ammunition, finding three more clips for his rifle and five for his pistol.

"Ammo count?" Wes demanded. "I have four rifle clips left, and three pistol."

"I have three rifle, five pistol," Taj answered.

"Two rifle, four pistol," Dal added.

"Less than ten rifle clips left between us, this is bad," Taj muttered as the chorus of howls began again, steadily getting closer.

"Don't let any get behind us," Wes commanded. "Stay on your feet, once your guns are empty, switch to your blades, do not fall down, or you're dead."

A steady stream of new Lurkers flooded into view—some stopped to cannibalise their fallen kin—but most charged past the bodies, their placidness giving way to aggression now the Beta had taken charge.

The Vanguards fired, dropping the frontrunners, but each kill cost them precious ammunition. Their bullets were the only thing holding back the tide of ripping, tearing teeth and claws. Before long, Taj loaded his last rifle clip and his heart sank, the pack still showed no signs of relenting, and they were a long way from help. He unloaded his last hundred bullets, slung his rifle and then drew his pistol and a knife, one in each hand. Wes and Dal did the same, their last few rifle shots spent. A ripple went through the pack, and the lead creatures slowed, snarling, and baring their teeth, saliva dripping from their jaws, savouring the end of the struggle.

"Make them work for it," Wes thundered while throwing a sun flare, a device the size of an index finger into the air. The flare began to fizz, then exploded, bathing everything in a near blinding orange light as the heaving mass of Lurkers charged.

Taj fired his pistol until it was empty, killing several creatures and wounding a few others. Before he could reload, another member of the pack leapt ahead of its brethren forcing him to cut it down with a swift decapitating strike. He abandoned his gun and drew his second knife just in time to slay the next foe that launched itself at him.

He slew four more in quick succession, his knives a blur as

they sliced through flesh and bone. Then the pack surged, and he was overwhelmed by the bulk of bodies. Darkness enveloped him as the howling creatures knocked him to the ground and swarmed, their needle like teeth closing around his limbs and scraping against his armour. He closed his eyes and began wildly screaming and slashing with his knives; adrenalin numbing his body as he thrashed around like a newborn babe.

After a time, his blades were no longer meeting flesh and he peeked through slitted eyes, afraid of what he would see. Several Lurkers lay dead around him, stab wounds covering their lithe forms. The rest of the creatures were an arm's length away, standing together placidly like when the Alpha had died, many bore cuts and bruises from his frantic attacks. He pushed clear of the dead and slowly got to his feet, his knives held aloft in a defensive position.

"You alright?" Wes rasped from somewhere nearby.

"I'll live," Taj replied, keeping his eyes on the Lurkers, afraid the spell holding them back would break if he averted his gaze.

A shrill whining, which ended in a howl radiating with pain, came from somewhere behind the bulk of the pack. Then a noise unlike anything Taj had ever heard started. It began as a deep rumbling, then rose to a thundering roar that sounded like laughter. The noise suddenly ceased and was replaced by loud scraping as something sharp was dragged across concrete. The Vanguards used the lull in hostilities to move back a few metres, putting some distance between them and their enemies.

A howl went through the pack, and Taj lifted his blades, preparing himself for the next wave. To everyone's surprise, the Lurkers turned, running back the way they had come. The entire pack disappeared in seconds, the last few tails slipping over the piles of dead and back into the well of blackness.

"No one is going to believe this," Wes declared.

****

Wes gave his report to Tre back at the crossroads, Taj sat nearby, his muscles groaning in agony. Dal was next to him, sitting back and staring at the ceiling, hands behind his head as though he didn't have a care in the world. The rest of their unit stood around them, listening to Wes's story in silence. He detailed everything they had seen, the dead Butcher, the Lurker attack and their unexplained retreat. When he finished, a long silence followed while Tre considered the tale.

"A pack of that size hasn't been seen this close to the city in years," Ren said, breaking the quiet. "Vanguard Grandmaster Jye needs to be warned. If the Lurkers have left the sub-levels in such high numbers, we need to get a kill team mobilised as soon as possible. They can't be allowed to have free reign."

"What concerns me," Tre said, ignoring Ren's comments. "Is their behaviour. I've never known Lurkers to retreat, especially when there is food on offer. Could you have unintentionally done something to cause the sudden change?"

"No, Tre, it wasn't us," Wes insisted. "There was something else there. Those noises, I've never heard anything like it; whatever it was, the Lurkers were scared enough to leave."

"Perhaps," Tre answered slowly. "I think we need to be very careful, and not jump to any conclusions until we have all the facts."

Taj listened to the slow-paced conversation with impatience. After the Lurkers disappeared, Wes had them search the area, and they found nothing but piles of corpses. He had begun to suspect that whatever made the inhuman sounds and scared them away, killed the Butcher and scratched his back. Whatever it was, it had completely different characteristics to the other seven known creatures.

Something new is stalking the underground, but the

21

commander isn't willing to say that, at least out loud, maybe I can force the issue?

"Whatever is out there, it attacked me while I was luring the Butcher," Taj interrupted, pulling off his armour to show the marks on his back.

Ren and Tre cursed, while Wes fumbled for the medical supplies in his satchel.

"Why didn't you mention this earlier?" the medic scolded, examining the wounds.

"You're lucky, the cuts on the Butcher were eating away at the flesh," he eventually said. "You don't need stitching, Gilo should be enough to stop infection. You will need to keep this covered for a few days, just to be safe."

Taj tried not to flinch as the soothing, anti-bacterial gel-like substance was applied to his back. Afraid of appearing weak, he gritted his teeth and buried the pain.

"We need to get back and report to Jye," Tre announced to the group. "I don't know what we are dealing with here, but I already hate it. Ren, Dal, finish packing up the lights. Ace, Ash walk the perimeter, I don't want anything else lumbering in here unawares. When Wes has finished healing the boy, we are gone."

Everyone else went to work without a fuss; Dal grumbled loudly, and only undertook his assigned task after Ren loudly berated him. The four spotlights were taken apart, and the individual pieces were spread amongst the rest of the unit. Like most of their equipment, the devices were designed to be portable and easily carried. The crossroads returned to darkness, and the twins came back a moment later, reporting the surrounding area was clear of enemies.

Spare ammunition was then shared with Dal, Wes, and Taj, with each member of the unit sacrificing some from their stockpile.

"Alright, move out," Tre ordered. "Standard formation."

Unconsciously obeying the command, the twin scouts took up

their usual front positions. Ren took the right flank, while Wes took the left. Tre stood in the middle of the group ready to bark commands. Dal and Taj usually had the rear guard, and today was no different.

"Keep your eyes open. There is a massive Lurker pack nearby, and who knows what else."

When the rest of his unit left, Taj decided to linger a moment and see if there were any more clues about what attacked the Butchers; if he was quick, nobody would notice his absence. He returned to the dead creature and had a closer look, holding his light next to the strange wounds.

"Why are your cuts being eaten away, while mine aren't?" he questioned the body. "What did this?"

Taj recoiled as a rat scurried past, sinking its teeth into the meat, he wasn't necessarily afraid of the small rodents; they just made his skin crawl. Several more stormed out of the dark, and before long, the corpse was writhing from the attentions of the scavengers. Fresh meat rarely lasted long when left unattended, if creatures didn't eat it, the innumerable rats or other vermin would.

"What are you doing?" Dal whispered, prodding him in the back with his foot.

"Nothing," Taj lied. "Let's get back to the others."

Chapter Three

Acropolis

"Open up, Unit 17 back from the culling," Tre shouted to the Watchers, the dedicated guardians of the underground city.

Taj and the rest of the unit waited behind the commander in a loose skirmish formation at one of the four metal gates that allowed passage through the outer barricades. The defensive structure circling the city stood over twenty metres tall and had a healthy mix of scavenged steel and concrete used in its construction. Behind them a stone and dirt plain extended all the way back to a tunnel entrance that led back into the Labyrinth.

Their home, the city of Acropolis had been built two hundred metres beyond the fortifications and housed in a massive hollow. The walled settlement always had a glowing aura from the millions of lights attached to every building and street.

The Watchers scrambled into action; two-person teams loaded the short barrelled fixed machine guns that were positioned at ten metre intervals along the outer barricades. Every weapon in range was then aimed at the commander.

"Identify yourself," a man stammered from above. "Name, rank and unit number, or we will open fire with the big guns."

Tre glowered. "Has everyone lost their minds in our absence?" he yelled. "We are clearly not enemies, open the gates, now."

"As per the new security protocols, you have thirty seconds to comply," the man replied.

"If you shoot, you had better hit me enough times to make sure I don't get back up," Tre roared. "I have very little patience for fools today. Who is in charge of the watch?"

Taj warily eyed the big guns while the commander continued

to berate the grim-faced men and women operating the large
weapons.

Would they really shoot us? he wondered. *The Watchers are
resolute in their duty of guarding the city, but surely common sense
will prevail here, we aren't a threat.*

"Would they really gun us down?" Dal asked Ren, voicing
Taj's thoughts. "Should we get ready to shoot back?"

"No point," the second captain said calmly. "Did you see what
happened to the Berserker who broke through the ring of light last
year? The lumbering oaf was torn apart before it took two steps
towards the barricades, those cannons can fire one hundred rounds
a second."

The others all nodded, which prompted a snort of amusement
from Dal. "That's right, I heard the halfwits on duty hit it with over
fifty thousand rounds, wasn't much left to clean up. Talk about
overkill."

Taj couldn't help but grimace at the memory, unlike the rest of
his companions, he was not yet indifferent to the macabre things
they experienced while performing their duties.

*I don't know how they can be so calm at the prospect of a
grisly death. Is this what I'll be like after a few years as a
Vanguard?*

The rusted gate in front of them suddenly opened outward; the
old metal screaming as it ground against the granite. Standing at
the entrance was a heavily built man with cropped, grey tipped
hair. Every visible piece of his skin had scars of varying sizes and
shapes, and his red Watcher armour bore similar marks of combat.
A yellow pictograph of an eye with a knife through it adorned his
chest, identifying him as Lee, the Watcher Grandmaster.

"Hold fire, and stand down, Watchers," the grandmaster rasped
as he limped towards Tre. "Before someone gets hurt."

The city guardians obeyed the command without question,
lowering the big guns so they were pointed at the ground rather

than the Vanguards.

"Sorry about that commander," Lee apologised, extending his hand in a gesture of good will. "The last few days have seen problems from above and below, we are tightening security until further notice."

"Good to see you, Lee," Tre said, shaking the man's hand and strolling out of earshot.

The two leaders conversed for a moment before parting ways. When Tre returned, his back was bowed as though he had suddenly acquired a tremendous weight.

"Let's go home," he said. "Before something else tries to kill us."

Taj noted the change in the commander's demeanour, and he raged with curiosity. He stifled the urge to ask questions, knowing he wouldn't get any answers, and followed the rest of his unit through the gate. A group of Watchers waited for them on the other side, their only greeting was a slight incline of the head. Most of them were missing limbs or other appendages. The majority of the Watchers were those who had failed the Vanguard training, many were also too old or injured to fight in the tunnels.

Once past the outer barricades, it was a short hike up a dirt and garbage-covered incline to Acropolis. The double-doored city gate was already open, with a standard seven-person team of Watchers on guard.

Acropolis housed nearly one million people and was always a hive of activity as the cave-dwelling residents went about their business without being hindered by day and night cycles. Buildings of all shapes and sizes, constructed of metal, wood, stone or a combination of all three took up most of the space inside the walls. No two structures were the same, and many of the larger ones had four or five generations of families crammed into them.

"Ace, Ash, return the portable light pieces to the storage sheds by the city walls," Tre instructed. "Then come straight back. I have some news to share before we all part."

The twins quickly carried out the task while the rest of the unit waited. Taj doubted that it would be good news, he had quickly learned that all news was bad.

"No more units are being sent out," Tre announced when the identical brothers returned, "The surface has called off peace talks again, and Jye has scrubbed the rest of the creature cull. All Vanguards are being summoned to a muster in three days. I'm not sure if this is the prelude to war with the surface, but I can't rule it out."

"Are you going to tell Jye about the thing that attacked the Butchers?" Taj asked

All eyes turned to him and his face heated under the scrutiny. In truth, he hadn't meant to say it out loud, but the thought had been nagging at him throughout the entire return journey and finally burst out of its own accord.

Tre considered the question, and Taj was unsure whether he'd get an answer or a smack to the side of the head; both were distinct possibilities.

"Yes," the commander finally answered. "It seems he may already know, another unit returned with a story like ours an hour ago. I'm heading to the Vanguard compound now, if there is anything worth knowing, you will find out at the muster, so don't be late."

The older members of the unit dispersed without further words, leaving Taj and Dal. Tre and Ren went towards the inner city where they lived with their families. The twins left for their hut near the outer wall, Wes followed, he usually stayed with one of them, having no other family left alive.

"Tre's in a good mood, as always," Dal said when the commander was well out of earshot.

"What I wouldn't give to hear what he tells Jye," Taj said ignoring his friend's comment. "Something isn't right Dal, whatever new thing is out there, has Tre worried, and considering the man has a few decades of experience as a Vanguard, that is a cause for concern."

"One time out in the Labyrinth and you're already an expert?" Dal laughed. "There is always something weird going on out there, during the last cull six months ago, we found a Harpy and a Ticker hunting as a team."

"That is weird, but not the same thing, there are no creatures with five claws, Dal. Whatever attacked me, and the Butchers is not one of the creatures our people have been fighting for the last few thousand years."

"I don't think it matters. Whatever is coming, we will deal with it, like we always do, or we will die. Until it presents its ugly face to us, we can't do anything about it, so worrying is pointless."

Taj sighed, he both envied and hated his friend's matter of fact view on life. Dal was rarely curious and hated to talk about anything of a serious nature. Most of the time it seemed like he didn't have a worry in the world, it made him level-headed and reliable in a fight, but difficult to confide in.

"Might be a good time to see the family, I'd say we will be out for a long time after the muster," Dal said, changing the subject.

"You think we will go out again so soon?" Taj questioned, rubbing his itchy eyes.

"Do you remember the last time there was a Vanguard muster?"

"Yes, right after the fall of Agora, the day Acropolis became our last settlement in the underground, and everything changed for both of us."

"Exactly, my mother was made a widow, and you and your sister were made orphans, so what does that tell you?"

Dal didn't wait for a response and walked away, slapping Taj on the arm as he passed. "Congratulations on not dying, you should be proud," he called over his shoulder. "There are plenty of

Vanguards who don't survive their first time."

"I thought you said no one has ever died on their first mission," Taj said.

"I lied," Dal chuckled, raising his hand in goodbye.

"Cheeky," Taj muttered as he began his slow trudge home. The narrow streets snaked through the entire settlement and were nearly always choked with people. He gently pushed through the crowds, nodding to the few that offered a greeting. Most were shuffling through the street at a sedate pace, their basic cloth or denim clothing clinging to their malnourished bodies leaving folds of fabric that fluttered as they trudged to their destination.

At his feet were children playing in the dirt and gravel with whatever toys they could make from discarded tools and other garbage. Small homemade stalls were set up on the side of streets offering various goods, extra clothes, food and sometimes homemade weapons. Taj ignored the store owners screaming for customers, he didn't have anything to trade anyway.

"Step right up for fresh items from the boondocks," a distinctly cheery voice yelled from nearby. "Gather around and buy some of the latest equipment from the only trading quarter on the surface."

Taj stopped in his tracks, only a handful of people from Acropolis were allowed on the surface to trade, it had been one of the first things the two civilisations had agreed upon during initial negotiations. For the most part, everyone else remained oblivious of the world outside of the Labyrinth. Unable to tame his curiosity, he pushed his way to the front of the small crowd gathered in front of the man selling items from above.

The storeowner was unusually tall, at least a head taller than Taj, he wore no shirt or shoes, and his long blue denim pants were patched with mismatched fabric. His freshly shaven head had been tattooed with swirling black patterns, drawing whispers and pointing from some of the older people who had gathered to hear his sales pitch.

"Welcome, friends," the man boomed, donning a smile and revealing a full set of unnaturally white teeth. "I have for you here–" he gestured to a small array of odd shaped items on a table covered in an old, torn brown blanket "—some amazing devices from the surface, things that defy belief, machines that can create food at the snap of your fingers, creams that will prolong your life by decades, and even a device that will deter creature attacks. Roll up and barter, because they will sell out fast."

Taj looked over the items and couldn't help but laugh, prompting several observers to throw dirty looks at him. If he was any judge, the charlatan was selling a few different rocks, an old plastic container and several other useless objects.

Another scumbag taking advantage of desperate people, they're becoming more common, I should let the Watchers know to shut him down.

He turned to leave and narrowly avoided bumping into an elderly couple who slowly hobbled to the front, their gnarled hands holding a few meagre possessions, a hairbrush, reading glasses, and what looked like an old book. Trading was the only way to buy things in the underground, either goods or services.

That's probably everything they own, and this lying thief is going to take it from them.

Like all predators, the charlatan knew when he was close to catching new prey.

"Who knows what this is?" he yelled, brandishing a flat, grey rock. When no one was forthcoming with an answer, the trickster leaned forward. "This my friends," he whispered directly to the old couple, "Is a Surfacer weighting device, they use them to weigh things down, and it was procured at great expense."

Taj tensed, his anger rising as the charlatan lied through his perfectly white teeth.

How can he sell this crap and act like he is doing them a favour? It's as though all he cares about is himself.

30

"That's a rock, and you know it's useless," he interrupted when he'd finally had enough of the blatant lies spewing forth from the salesman's mouth. "There are literally thousands of them around."

"No, good sir, not like this," the charlatan countered. "This is from above, a Surfacer rock, its uses are many and varied."

"Why don't you show us one of these uses then?"

The man adopted a pained expression as he stared at the rock, almost like he was willing it to do something extraordinary. When nothing was forthcoming, the crowd began to disperse, some grumbled as they left.

"Wait, my friends, this is a once in a lifetime opportunity," the man pleaded, but the damage was already done. Nobody was listening anymore.

Taj smirked and continued his journey home, feeling a deep sense of satisfaction that he had foiled the scam.

The scum will probably be back tomorrow, at least everyone is safe from him today.

He passed by one of the thirty house-sized generators that powered the whole city, pausing when the nearby light buzzed and shot out sparks. Taj frowned, cautiously poking a nearby artificial sunlight globe with his finger.

Everything is falling apart in this place. Suddenly loud cursing, plumes of smoke and red sparks shot out from behind the concrete fence surrounding the nearby generators.

I know that voice.

"Nice one, Tig," he called over the barrier. Despite the solid wall, he could almost picture the lanky man wearing his grey Guild jacket, bent over the generator, a look of wonder on his face as he tinkered with it. They had known each other since they were very young, but Tig had been recruited by the Guild, the men and women responsible for manufacturing and maintaining all the equipment used in the city, while Taj had joined the Vanguards.

31

"Is that you, Taj?" Tig asked, his voice high-pitched and cheerful as always. "Didn't know you were back"

"Yeah, just got home. What are you doing back there? That smoke didn't look good."

"The council wants the generators working at eighty-five percent, but these damn things are so old they probably can't put out that much juice anymore."

"Well, don't break them, I don't fancy all the lights going out in the city."

"Not to worry, I have been made very aware of what could happen if I screw this up, Vanguard Grandmaster Jye even threatened to shoot me."

"I doubt Jye would shoot the most gifted Guild member in the city, without you we couldn't keep the city running."

"Knowing my luck, he would do it anyway, consequences be damned. By the way, you may want to go check on old Doc."

Taj groaned as a wave of fatigue suddenly hit him, Doc was a former Vanguard Grandmaster and current advisor to Jye, the man was also completely insane. He liked the crazy old goat, and had spent many hours with him, but their friendship could be trying at times.

"What happened this time?" he asked, rubbing his sore eyes and silently wishing he could go to sleep.

"The old fella set up an ambush in that little shack of his, scared his granddaughter half to death, the poor girl was crying for three hours from what I heard."

"Of course he did."

Taj bid his friend farewell and walked back towards the outer wall and Doc's shack. His new path took him past the great fenced agriculture pens where the Harvesters, groups of men and women who were responsible for growing all the food in Acropolis, toiled in the artificially grown fields, picking produce. They all wore brown jumpsuits and thick leather work boots, with a set of gloves and a cap to protect their hair from the dirt and grime.

All manner of livestock, cows, pigs, goats and chickens were housed in the same area, grazing between the thin, skeleton-like Harvesters. The animals varied in sizes and many were pale and sickly. In days past all their settlements had traded beasts to ensure the gene pool stayed diverse, but now Acropolis stood alone, and their animals were slowly dying out from the diseases caused by generations of inbreeding.

Taj stopped, observing the tired-looking men and women. Most were utterly focused on their work, only occasionally looking up to interact with each other. He had tried working in the fields when he was younger and immediately developed a distaste for it, the work was hard, thankless and often resulted in debilitating injuries; his back still twinged occasionally. The access to food also left much to be desired, despite being solely responsible for growing it, the Harvesters were often the last to eat; the Vanguards and other people vital to the defence of the city were always first.

With a heavy heart, he left the Harvesters to their work and continued to Doc's, navigating between several tightly packed buildings until he was in front of the former Vanguard Grandmaster's small one-room stone hut. The smell of a cooking fire seeped out through the cracks in the seams. He rapped on the thin sheet metal door with his knuckles, the resulting crash and cackle from inside let him know Doc was home.

"Who is it"? the elderly man cackled.

"Taj," he replied.

"I don't want any. Take your crazy concoctions somewhere else," Doc yelled.

"What are you on about, old man, I don't have any concoctions," Taj said, slapping his hand to his forehead.

The next thing he knew another crash came from within, and then the door screeched open revealing a thin elderly man wearing cloth brown pants and a white shirt with holes in it. His long grey hair had been dreadlocked and tied back.

"Ah Taj, what brings you by?" Doc asked. "I thought it was that damn witch Jil with more of her hooky potions."

Taj closed his eyes and took a deep breath before replying. "Doc, Jil is your granddaughter, and she probably brought you water again. Your family are worried about you in this old hut, I don't know why you moved here while the rest of your kin are in a bigger house near the centre of Acropolis with the other families."

"That's what they want you to think," Doc whispered looking around to make sure they weren't overheard. "The action's out here, I can't see everything that goes on inside that prison."

Taj sighed, often finding the old man's ramblings particularly taxing when he was tired. Doc motioned for him to come in, cackling like a maniac as he gestured with his long slender fingers.

The dwelling had no furniture, like most of the city's buildings, but its occupant had acquired a wide array of cast iron pots and pans that he kept stacked in the corner. A fire pit had been dug in the middle of the room, with a makeshift hole in the roof serving as a chimney.

Doc crouched by the fire pit and stirred a substance in the large cast iron pot that was sitting on the glowing coals. "Three clockwise, four counter-clockwise," he muttered to himself. "That's right, just keep stirring, it will all be worth it."

Taj took his usual seat on the dirt floor opposite Doc, stealing a look into the pot and immediately wishing he hadn't. The simmering green contents bubbled and emitted an aroma that reminded him of the dead Butcher.

"Hey," Doc growled. "Don't look in there, this is a secret recipe." The old man narrowed his eyes and pointed the wooden spoon he had been using at an angle.

"Wouldn't dream of it, Doc," Taj reassured him while stifling a chuckle.

"Why do you bother an old man while he tries to cook his

34

meagre meal, Kai?" Doc said without bothering to look up.

Taj stomach constricted at the mention of his father's name. Despite the passing of years, the loss of his parents still clawed at him like a monster that refused to die.

"I'm Taj," he corrected, his voice cracking a little.

"Ah yes," Doc cackled. "Of course, Taj. I swear you look just like him. Will you send him my regards? He doesn't visit anymore."

"He died, Doc. You were there. You brought us the news."

"Did I?" Doc looked up from the pot, his eyes becoming glassy. "It was at Agora, wasn't it? The last thing I ever did?" Doc dropped the spoon and stood straight, folding his arms behind his back. Talking strategy or fighting seemed to be the only times he had a semblance of sanity, which is why he still held an advisory position within the Vanguards ranks.

"It all happened so fast. They came out of nowhere, we tried to hold them on the walls, they were ready for that and countered our strategy. Then we lost more than half our number in a close quarter's nightmare, they boxed us in and took their time hunting. A small group managed to break away, but we left many to die that day." The old man returned to his crouching position by the fire, muttering to himself about flawed strategies and witches.

Taj remembered the event only too well. Doc had come to their house with the council and explained to his sister that their parents weren't coming home; they had visited many families that day. The veteran Vanguard later resigned from his position as grandmaster, a rank he had held for nearly fifty years.

Unwilling to dwell on the fate of his parents, Taj decided to change the subject.

"We saw a dead Butcher today with strange claw marks on it," he said, coughing to clear the catch in his throat. "It scared Tre enough to scrub our culling mission, I think he's planning to discuss it with Jye. Have you heard anything?"

Whenever Taj needed to find out information he wasn't supposed to, he went to Doc. The former grandmaster always seemed to know everything that was happening in the underground and wasn't shy about sharing it. The only problem was making sense of his answers, which varied from insightful, to downright insane, depending on the day.

"Tre is getting more cautious with age; did I ever tell you about the time he shot his captain in the foot?" Doc cackled.

Taj stifled a giggle, the thought of an adolescent Tre getting yelled at by a superior was the greatest thing he had heard all day. "No, I think Dal would love that story though. But what do you know about the dead Butcher? I have never heard of anything with five claws living in the underground."

"It was probably just a few Harpies, nasty things, creatures die all the time. They kill each other, we kill them, they kill us, the spiders, rats and bats feast on the remains, it's a never-ending cycle. Did I ever tell you about the time Jye mistook a Harpy for a lost girl?"

He knows something, and he's trying to deflect the conversation, Taj realised.

To most people, Doc seemed like a loon who had finally lost his mind, but hidden beneath his eccentric tics, he still had some wits and guile.

"There were two Butchers actually," Taj said. "Then a Lurker pack attacked, it was a very close call, luckily they were scared away by something far worse, if I'm any judge."

It was only a small movement, a break in Doc's stirring pattern, but it was enough to let him know the old man was close to breaking and revealing something.

"They always were sneaky things," Doc finally said after a brief silence. "Did I ever tell you about the time your mother fell into a Lurker's nest? Your father lost a finger trying to rescue her; it's actually how they met."

36

"Stop trying to change the subject," Taj snapped. "Enough games, you know I'm not going to drop it."

Doc stirred his dinner, his lined features betraying an uncharacteristic flash of fear. "There is nothing to know, boy, at least not yet, not until we flush them out and find proof, even then it will be a gamble, if we fail to stop them, it might be the end of us."

Taj began to fidget, anxious to hear more; the words were a confused jumble, however, the implication was clear, there was something else in the underground, and Doc feared it. He waited for the former grandmaster to say more, but as the minutes ticked by it became clear the old man was done talking.

"Is this why Jye has called a muster?" Taj asked, his impatience getting the better of him. Under normal circumstances he wouldn't keep pressuring Doc, but this time was different. "The last time there was a muster was fifteen years ago, right after Agora was destroyed and Acropolis became our last stronghold in the underground. Is the city under threat?"

Silence followed the questions, Doc kept stirring. "Musters are for times of great peril," he eventually muttered. "That should tell you everything you need to know."

Taj took a moment to ponder what was said, it wasn't a proper answer, but Doc rarely spoke directly.

"Leadership is hard Taj," Doc announced. "One day if you're lucky you will come to understand this burden. Our time down here is coming to an end, one way or another. We have lost all our other cities and settlements, our people die in their thousands every year from disease and creature attacks. The burden of finding a solution rests with the council and grandmasters, they contend with our inevitable extinction, while also trying to deal with the new and old enemies who are coming for us."

"What enemies are you talking about?" Taj questioned. "Do you mean the Surfacers? Or something else?"

Doc loudly exhaled before answering, "I do enjoy our talks, but I have said all I can on this subject. It's up to you to find meaning in what we have discussed."

Taj gritted his teeth, he wanted to push for more information, one thing stopped him. It had escaped his notice until that moment, Doc looked very frail, his back was bent, and his hands shook as he stirred his meagre meal.

Sometimes I forget how much he's suffered. I really should be kinder to him. The answers may not have been as clear as he wanted, it would be enough for now.

"So, tell me again about how Tre shot his captain?"

Chapter Four
Home

Three days Later...

Taj crouched on the battlements, watching as Acropolis burned. The faint sound of thousands crying out in terror and agony carried on the wind. Panic gripped him and he tried to run for help, his arms and legs refused to obey, two Vanguards ran past him, their faces masks of horror.

"Wait!" He tried to shout, but his lips only trembled in response. Then he heard it again, the heart stopping noise that had terrified the Lurkers enough to make them abandon three-man sized meals. It started as a deep rumbling, then rose to a thundering roar that sounded like laughter, followed quickly by the sound of something sharp dragging across concrete. Both Vanguards looked directly at him, their eyes were wide and unblinking. A shadowy five-clawed hand rested on his shoulder.

"The wall has fallen," a deep throaty voice whispered in his ear. The Vanguards suddenly disappeared and were replaced by torn up pieces of human flesh in a pool of blood.

"You're all going to die."

Taj woke with a start and automatically reached for the pistol he kept nearby. His hand closed over the cold steel and he raised the weapon, alert for any sign of enemies. As his mind began to recover from the initial shock, he realised there was no danger. Rather than being on the walls of the city, he was safe in the modest two-room hut he shared with his sister.

Beneath him was a sweat-soaked mattress, made from old clothes and other scrap material. Like his meagre bed, the rest of their home was in a severe state of disrepair, with several gaping holes in the main structure. The rest of the place was mostly empty; their possessions consisting of a few blankets, a comb, a handful of cooking utensils and two mattresses, one on each side of the first room. Like most homes in Acropolis, the main feature was the cooking pit in the centre of the house.

"Still having nightmares?" Sai, his sister, enquired. She sat next to his bed, dressed in her favourite plain cloth shirt that clung loosely to her slim frame, and denim pants that hung low on her narrow hips. She impatiently pushed back her shoulder length jet-black hair and bent over the pile of bullets she was loading into rifle clips.

Taj nodded, the images of his most recent nightmare were burned into his brain, tormenting him with visions of his home's demise.

"The wall has fallen," he repeated to himself, unsure of the meaning. *Is it a warning about the city walls falling?*

Sai offered him a ceramic cup without a handle, the only one they had. Draining the cooling, tasteless liquid it contained, he observed his sister's attempts to load bullets, her small porcelain face and dark eyes scrunched up in concentration as though the task took every ounce of her willpower to complete.

"What are doing that for?" he queried. "You're a Healer not a Vanguard."

"You fell asleep again, and I'm bored. I always wanted to learn how to do this anyway. Are you hungry?"

"Not really," he lied, stifling a laugh when his stomach let out an almighty groan.

"So am I," Sai giggled. "We really should have rationed our food better; we've gone through the whole week's supply in the three days since your return."

"Perhaps our mystery benefactor will pay us another visit soon. It's been a few weeks since the last drop."

In the years since the loss of their parents, food, clothing and other supplies would often appear in their house. At first, they had been suspicious and wary, but when the caches proved to be high quality, and their attempts to find out where it came from proved fruitless, they decided to just accept the gifts.

Taj quickly rolled out of bed, instantly regretting it when his back wound flared and sent shooting pains down to his legs. Upon his return from Doc's, his sister had spent an hour checking his cuts and applying more Gilo to stave off infection, it wasn't the first time she'd put him back together, and he doubted it would be the last.

"Careful," she snapped. "You'll hurt yourself, and then I'll have to pick up the pieces."

"I guess," Taj grunted. Sai was his elder by four years, and they had always been close, more so after the death of their parents, but she always seemed to baby him. It had caused many fights over the years. They were prone to fighting like any siblings, but this subject always seemed to create the most problems.

"I can't lose you too, little brother, as much as you annoy me to death, you're the only family I…" Sai trailed off, unable to finish her sentence. It had been fifteen years, but the loss of their parents still stung as though it were yesterday. For a moment they both sat in silence, trying to remember two people they had barely known and would never see again.

Sai returned to her work, while Taj went through the rickety door into the second room of the hut. It contained his armour and weapons, all stacked up in a corner with an old battered chest they used for storage. A cast iron shower head was set in the back wall, a sink and tap were fastened nearby.

Taj went straight to the sink and carefully turned the tap on, then quickly washed his face with the ice-cold liquid, taking care to use every drop. Acropolis only had a finite amount of water, most of it was drawn up from deep wells and springs. The Guild

41

also had moisture traps around the city that drew small amounts of water from the air, but they were always tinkering with new ways to get more water. With so many people in the settlement, the council was forced to enact strict rations of ten litres of water a week for each household, breaking the decree was strictly punished.

"All done," Sai announced upon his return to the other room. His sister proudly stacked half a dozen rifle clips next to the fire pit. "The next time you kill something, you can thank me. This is the last of your stash by the way, you might want to go to a Guild storehouse before you head out again."

"Is the sleeping prince finally awake?" Dal shouted from outside, interrupting their conversation. "Chop chop, we have a muster to get to."

Taj groaned and reluctantly went to the front door, pushing it outward, Dal knelt in front of their house cutting his long dirty blond hair with a knife. "Do you have to do that here?" he said, eyeing the chunks of hair on the ground with distaste.

"Someone's in a mood today." Dal laughed. "Yes, I do have to cut my hair here because then you can clean it up instead of me. Be careful though I've got bugs in my hair again."

"Hey, Dal," Sai exclaimed as she brushed past and embraced the half-shaven Vanguard, "I haven't seen you since Taj completed his training, how's your mother?"

"Still alive, so that's a good start."

Taj left the two to converse and went to retrieve his weapons and armour, he half considered a shower, then thought better of it. He was probably just going to get dirty again. He strapped on his armour and gingerly felt the areas where the Lurkers had dented it, luckily none of their attacks had left any serious damage, unlike the mysterious new creature which had left five gouges on his backplate.

Whatever you are, I hope we don't meet again, somehow, I

think we will cross paths again very soon though.

By the time he returned to the other room. Dal had finished his haircut and was seated with Sai.

"How are your little brothers, Dal?" she asked.

"Hungry, tired, the little blighters were pretty happy to see me when I got back, there are rumours going around about whole Vanguard Units are disappearing without a trace."

"That's a first," Taj quipped while he collected the last of his equipment. "Someone happy to see you."

Dal grimaced, but otherwise ignored the comment and continued his conversation with Sai. Taj didn't bother listening to the rest. It wasn't uncommon for people to disappear but considering the new threat that was stalking the Labyrinth, it was worrying to say the least.

I wonder why it let us go then, those Lurkers would have easily killed us if it didn't interfere.

When it was time to leave, Sai embraced them both. "Stay safe you two, a lot of the older Vanguards I've been patching up at the medical centre are saying the creatures are more vicious and unpredictable than they've ever seen."

"Don't worry, Sai, your little brother has me to watch out for him." Dal winked and swiftly punched Taj in the chest, then he ran towards the meeting amphitheatre in the middle of the city laughing manically.

Taj was stunned for a second from the force of the blow, he quickly waved goodbye to his sister who was shaking her head at the playful fighting, and chased after his friend, determined to get revenge for the cheap shot.

Chapter Five

Muster

Taj and Dal entered the courtyard in front of the colossal stone amphitheatre, thousands of Vanguards were already mulling around the vast open space. Next to it, sat a giant tower with a clock face; one of the few devices they had to help mark the passing of time, both were ancient relics of a period that had long since passed into history.

"Weapons shed," Dal said, pointing to the Guild storehouse on the other side of the courtyard. "We better hurry, before they are cleared out of gear."

Taj and Dal pushed their way through the rabble and heard snippets of a hundred different conversations; most concerned the purpose of the muster, the best ways to kill creatures or exaggerated stories of skirmishes in the Labyrinth. When they passed by the amphitheatre Taj couldn't help but pause for a moment and marvel at the circular six storey structure. No other buildings were within a hundred metres of it, as though the lesser architecture were afraid to get too close. *I wonder how the architects managed to build something so large.*

The Guild warehouse sat on the outskirts of the courtyard, nestled between the houses. Behind it loomed a three-storey factory where the Guild made most of the equipment, it was a common setup throughout Acropolis, with dozens of warehouses and factories situated amongst the sprawling metropolis.

"That little incident with those Lurkers cleaned me out," Dal said as they joined the line of Vanguards waiting to access the storage shed. "It's a shame we can't use grenades, just one would have blasted all those little buggers to bits."

"Yeah, and probably us with them," Taj said. "There is a reason they save them for emergencies only, I've heard plenty of stories about careless Vanguards nearly collapsing tunnels with explosives."

"As if, I think that's just an excuse, those old passages have stood for who knows how long, and I think they'll still be here long after we're gone."

The line moved slowly, and before long Taj had begun to people watch, one of his favourite pastimes. He saw plenty of interesting people, but his attention was drawn to a group nearby, standing around a table playing Knifepoint, a popular game in the underground. Players would take turns to stab a knife tip between their fingers in a display of dexterity and bravery. Failure would result in a knife wound that could cause irreparable damage or infection. Fortunes were won and lost betting on the outcome.

A boy around his own age held the knife and was nervously prodding the table. Taj smiled to himself, *I hope you do better than my first time kid, for your sake.*

Dal slapped him on the arm, bringing his attention back. Dal held a finger to his lips, and pointed to a Vanguard in front of them who had an unblinking eye tattoo on the back of his bald head.

"Creepy," Taj whispered.

"I think I want one."

Without warning the man turned around, his rail thin body swaying as though caught in a strong gale.

"Lies and slander," he slurred, nearly tipping over as he spoke. "It's all lies and slander." His mud brown bloodshot eyes glazed over them, a small smile coming to his thin cracked lips. Like everyone else in attendance, he was dressed in standard black Vanguard armour and had his rifle slung on his back.

"You boys young bloods?" the man asked, stopping and starting the sentence several times as though he kept forgetting

45

what he was saying. "I remember my first time out. Killed me a Berserker, lost three friends, I don't have to tell you that, get to your age you've definitely lost someone, it's inevitable, you know what I mean?"

Dal stifled a laugh and made a drinking motion to Taj with his hand, in full view of the man. Neither of them had ever had the chance to drink alcohol before, but they knew the signs, slurred words and being unsteady on your feet was a dead giveaway. The city had a thriving bootleg trade, and many denizens were known to indulge.

"Oh yeah," Taj agreed, doing his best not to laugh. "It's tough out there."

The man inched closer, flooding Taj with the smell of stale drink and an unwashed body; the drunk spent a few seconds staring intently before recognition lit up his tired features.

"Taj," the man boomed, launching forward and embracing him in a one-armed hug. "Haven't seen you since you was a young fella. I knew your father, saved me life more times than I can count, if I knew how to count of course. Wish I could have been there with him at Agora, we were sent out on a patrol just before the attack. That's when I first saw the demons, I'll never forget them, they led the assault."

Taj was ready to dismiss the rambling sot, but luckily, they had reached the front of the line and it wasn't necessary. The weapons shed had two windows cut into the front wall where Vanguards could ask the attendants inside to hand out whatever supplies they needed, one window was currently free.

"Name's Mal, by the way," the man slurred, releasing Taj from the smelly embrace, "Stay safe out there, boys, they are watching, always watching."

Mal stumbled up to the free window, retrieved some ammunition, and shambled off back into the crowd.

"Hey Dal, if I ever get like that, please shoot me," Taj said.

46

"If either of us end up like that fool, I'll kill us both," Dal replied.

Taj went to the right window of the storage shed and was greeted by an elderly man who was missing his left leg, right eye and had a pattern of scars on his face in the shape of a spiderweb. "Ex-Vanguard", he decided.

"What can I get for you, young fella," the attendant rasped.

"Four food packs and five hundred rounds of rifle ammunition, in clips if you have them, plus fifty for a pistol."

The old man grunted and collected the requested items from the various shelves that surrounded him. "Seems you are all getting ready for war, they might call me back up into the ranks before long. You could use some experienced hands at a time like this, too many young bloods and unproven fighters if you ask me. Used to be it was harder to join, now any idiot that can shoot a gun is accepted."

Taj nodded politely, unsure if the comments were serious or a joke. In his opinion, the old man would be dead in less than a day if he went out into the tunnels. He grabbed his supplies and tore the top off one of the food packs, inhaling the thick grey watery substance out of the square plastic package. It was made from distilling food scraps with other vitamins and minerals, it was supposed to have everything the body needed.

"I don't know how you eat that gunk," Dal muttered, eyeing the food pack with distaste. "To me, they always taste like old, burnt cabbage. I'd rather eat those weird coloured mushrooms that grow in the Labyrinth."

Taj shrugged, "It's better than nothing."

In the background, the courtyard began to empty, Taj and Dal thanked the attendants and joined the throng tramping inside the amphitheatre. Once over the threshold, they were met by the buzz of thousands of voices as Vanguards jostled for space and a seat on one of the six tiers of benches. Stern faced captains were positioned intermittently among the crowd and were fighting a losing battle to direct people.

I guess Tre wasn't lying last year when he told me that the Vanguards numbered over fifteen thousand strong.

Taj and Dal made their way to the second tier, which afforded them the best view of the raised platform in the middle. Despite their best efforts, it was nearly impossible to take a step without bumping into someone; by the time they found a place to sit at the end of a row, Taj was ready to hit the next person who touched him.

"There is no way Tre would even know if we were here," Dal remarked as they sat down on the cold hard stone bench. "We could have stayed at home and slept for a few more hours."

The rest of the theatre filled up quickly, and before long eight people appeared on the raised platform. One wore the garb of a Vanguard, the others were dressed in long, bright red robes covering everything except their faces.

"The council," Taj murmured. He had met them once before—the day his parents died at Agora they came to his house with Doc and offered their condolences. He remembered watching them leave, not fully understanding what had happened.

The members of the council consisted of four men and three women who were all well past their sixtieth year. Most of them looked like a stiff breeze would blow them over, but appearances could be deceiving, a fact which many of their political opponents had found out to their detriment over the years.

The Vanguard on the other hand was someone very familiar to Taj, he had seen him frequently during his training, even spoken to him a few times. Vanguard Grandmaster Jye stood just over six feet tall and had long, heavily muscled arms that were struggling to be contained by his armour. His short brown hair was cropped, and his beard was well groomed, but they were both prematurely greying. Most of his visible skin was covered in tattoos and markings that followed no discernible order or pattern.

Jye raised a hand and silence quickly followed as every Vanguard stopped talking.

"Thank you for heeding my call to muster," the grandmaster said, his deep voice echoing around the entire space. "Our second and final culling for the year has been postponed, as everyone is no doubt aware, things are different out in the Labyrinth. The creatures are not only more vicious but are roaming in far greater numbers. This matter needs to be addressed, especially if diplomacy with the surface is to continue, they expect us to contain the creatures and failure would see a swift end to peaceful negotiations."

A loud grumbling rippled through the gathering as the assembled men and women voiced their displeasure at working with the surface civilisation. It began with curses, then slowly escalated into shouting and threats of violence as the crowd began to work themselves up into a fever.

"Surfacer scum," someone screamed.

"Why should we risk our lives for them?"

"We should look to our own defences."

"If the creatures make it to the surface, let them all die."

"We should kill them."

Directly beneath Taj and Dal on the first tier, a short stocky man stood up and waved both arms signalling for quiet. After a few moments, the yelling died down enough for him to be heard.

"Captain Raf, Unit 237," the man said, identifying himself as was the custom in large gatherings.

"Jye, councillors, I think many of us are unable to understand your reasons for negotiating with the Surfacers. Their ancestors were responsible for the war that saw our forebears locked away in this underground prison. As we all know, they reopened the entrances to the surface, something that up until recently was thought to be impossible, we shouldn't be discussing ways to help them, rather we should be using this army to conquer."

A loud chorus of cheers and roars of agreement followed. Taj was one of the few who didn't join in.

I hope Jye and Tre haven't decided to go to war, there is something far worse coming for us, if I'm any judge. Even the creatures fear it.

Another captain on the third row stood up and signalled for everyone's attention. "Captain Tys, Unit 468," he said loudly. "Jye, Councillors, I agree with Raf, if we ever want to leave this rat-infested pit, we need to take the advantage and storm the surface. Our ancestors fought the Cannibal Warlords, the Chosen, the Rum Rebels, the Three Petty Kings along with dozens of other conflicts, and in the background, the creatures have always been hunting us. We deserve a safe place to live, where our children can grow and thrive. If they won't give it to us, we should take it."

Another wave of shouting began after Tys finished talking, and before long the muster descended into chaos again.

"Better to fight and die, then beg and scrape."

"Only traitors would want to talk with Surfacer scum."

"They don't deserve our protection."

"Kill them all."

Jye signalled for quiet with a flick of his hand, the move was subtle, but it held more power than any explosive display of shouting could ever hope to match. Despite only being in his early thirties, the man had amassed a fearsome reputation, everyone in the underground seemed to have a story about his fighting prowess.

"We have lost twenty-three units since calling the muster," the Vanguard Grandmaster announced. "Another fifteen have failed to return, and truthfully, at this point, I don't expect we will hear from them again. Enormous Lurker packs have come up from the sub-levels, Harpies have assaulted the wall of light and Berserkers have been gathering in large groups, the last time the Labyrinth was in this much turmoil, we lost Agora. Unless you want to see a repeat of that event, everyone here needs to put aside their desire for war. Negotiations with the surface may not be desirable, but we can't risk open conflict with them now, at least until the Labyrinth is under control, we don't have the numbers to fight on two fronts."

Silence followed Jye's statement, all that could be heard was the sound of thousands of men and women drawing breath. When nobody launched a fresh tirade, the grandmaster outlined the rest of his plan.

"After today, every Vanguard unit will be sent out at once, all four surface entrances will be reinforced with heavy weapons and have two units stationed there at all times. Everyone else will focus on clearing the tunnels of creatures, starting with those closest to the city, and moving outward. The vaults underneath the city were emptied of their wealth long ago, and now they are being re-opened and outfitted to house the city's population if Acropolis is threatened, Guild Grandmaster Tag assures me the work will be completed within a month. This will be our single largest undertaking in recent memory, everything in the Labyrinth will be driven back to the sub-levels or die. We begin in two days, captains report to the Vanguard compound for further orders, this muster is done."

At first nobody moved, the abrupt conclusion to the meeting seemingly catching everyone off guard. However, as the shock slowly wore off, a mass exodus began, and small pockets of fighting erupted as Vanguards vented their frustration in the only way they knew how. After witnessing a particularly violent argument between two burly, square-headed men who accidentally ran into each other, Taj and Dal decided to wait until the chaos died down before attempting to leave.

While Dal watched the unfolding drama with glee, Taj pondered all they had heard, and found he was troubled. Not just by the gravity of sending out every available fighter at once, but the fact that there was no mention of the new thing stalking the underground. He had spoken with Doc for many hours during his last visit, and one thing in particular had stuck with him..

"There is nothing to know boy, at least not yet, not until we flush them out and find proof," Doc had said.

Is this your plan to flush them out Jye? Whatever they are, why are you keeping it a secret?

Dal nudged Taj with his elbow, bringing his focus back to the present. His friend pointed to the extra person who had appeared on the stage with the Vanguard Grandmaster and the councillors. Tre and Jye appeared to be having a casual conversation, but Taj had seen the commander angry enough times to know when he was livid and close to violence. The councillors tried to give the appearance of everything being under control by wearing fake smiles, but it was obvious to everyone things were far from alright.

"Get ready," Dal whispered. "Looks like it could go off here." The remaining Vanguards in the theatre began to stop in the middle of whatever they were doing, at first it was only a few, then in a giant wave the entire crowd paused to watch the two most dangerous men in the underground argue. The room buzzed with anticipation of the coming conflict; but it was over before it began, Tre stormed off the stage. Despite the mass of people all trying to exit, nobody was willing to block the smouldering commander's exit, a path cleared in his wake and he was eventually lost to sight. Whispers of a challenge for leadership followed him out.

What has been started here? Taj wondered.

Maybe outside enemies are the least of our worries now.

"Surely Tre wouldn't be stupid enough to challenge Jye for leadership," Dal murmured. "Especially after what Jye did to ascend to the position."

The fight to the death between Jye and Doc's first successor Hal had been brief, and bloody. Even after the passing of years the story was often whispered about among the ranks. If they were pestered enough, the older Vanguards who claimed to have been there would even provide a detailed account, but the tales seemed to get grander with each re-telling.

"If anyone could beat Jye, it would be Tre," Taj said. "And from the looks of things, he wouldn't need to try too hard to get the votes of fifty captains to initiate the challenge."

Taj and Dal waited until the majority of the theatre had emptied, then joined the last few stragglers and made their way outside. Hundreds of their fellow Vanguards had remained in the area and continued to socialise around the courtyard. A group near the Guild storehouse was being given a wide berth, and Taj had a sneaking suspicion why.

The rest of their unit surrounded Tre, who was pacing back and forth, nobody else was willing to get anywhere near him. Taj pointed them out to Dal, and they joined their comrades.

"If you challenge him, Tre, you need to be sure," Ren counselled the still fuming commander. "Your disagreement with Jye has the potential to split the Vanguards and the city, we can't afford a civil war."

"He wants us to do nothing," Tre replied, his voice shaking with each word. "This plan of his will take months, maybe longer to bear fruit and while we waste our strength, the Surfacers watch on and laugh at us under the blanket of protection we provide."

Taj watched the unfolding spectacle with bated breath, he wanted to ask what Jye had done to anger Tre, and whether it had something to do with the thing that had killed the Butchers and scared away the Lurkers, but he held his tongue. Interrupting the two leaders to pester them with questions would likely result in a beating at the best of times, let alone when tensions were high.

"What are you going to do?" Ren demanded.

"I don't know yet, stay the course, for now," Tre growled through clenched teeth. "Get some rest, load up, I have a feeling it might be our last chance for a while."

Tre walked away without saying goodbye, his whole body shaking as his anger threatened to bubble over and explode.

"Righto, you heard the commander," Ren barked to the remaining members of Unit 17, "Stock up and get some rest, we leave again very soon."

Dal gave Ren a mock salute before departing and received a fresh lecture from the second captain. Taj ignored the exchange and wandered away in no particular direction, lost in thought about everything that had transpired.

Chapter Six

Grim Discoveries

Four Weeks Later...

Taj winced as the rough, gloved hand struck him in the face and woke him from his trance-like state.

"Oi, wake up," Dal bellowed slapping him again and lifting his hand for another assault. "You've been spacey since we split up from the others, I don't want to get caught unawares while you're daydreaming."

"I'm awake," Taj snarled, pausing in the middle of the straight tunnel section, it lacked side paths; and the rest of their unit was guarding the crossroads that led into the passage, all they had to do was watch the front.

"I've already been smacked once today," Dal whined. "I have no desire to repeat the experience."

Taj half-smiled at the memory, when they came to the crossroads, two Butchers had been waiting for them. The twins killed the first one, but the second had absorbed a lot of bullets before it finally fell. In its death throes, the distressed creature had charged into Dal, knocking him into a wall.

"All we have to do is get to the end of this tunnel, and mark it, then we can head back to the others and get our five hours rest." Taj yawned. *Or at least you can, I'll probably be kept awake by nightmares of five clawed monsters and have to go another two days without sleep.*

Dal muttered a curse. "Don't get overconfident, nothing in this place is ever straightforward, you saw what happened to unit 78, that's what happens when you don't pay attention."

"Not the best way to go," Taj agreed, shuddering slightly as the images of the previous day flashed through his mind. He wasn't overly bothered by the grisly remains of unit 78, it was just the eyes that stayed with him, the cold lifeless eyes of dead men. "We made it right though, that Harpy won't hurt anyone ever again."

They reached the end of the straight tunnel and found it converged into a T-intersection, prompting Dal to sigh. He flashed his rifle light down both paths, and grimaced.

"You take the right, I'll go left," he said breathlessly.

"Do you want to go exploring or something?" Taj asked. "If we go off mission, won't Tre be pissed off?"

"Do you know what the symbol to mark the extent a cleared perimeter is?"

"Two crossed rifles?"

"Exactly, it takes a few minutes to paint, and I want to make sure there is nothing nearby while I'm working, so just humour me, alright?"

Taj nodded. So far, the Vanguards had only managed to clear a five-kilometre radius around the ring of light, and they had paid for every metre with blood and lives. "I guess we can't be too careful."

He went down the right hand tunnel, moving his rifle torch back and forth, doing his best to scan for enemies. His beam crossed over the dripping algae covered walls and rested on the ropey tale of a plump rat, scurrying along with a black beetle in its mouth. The rodent looked back at him, its beady eyes narrowing in the light.

"Looks like you've been eating well," Taj said. "At least one of us has."

The rat twitched, and then recoiled as a fist sized brown spider pounced from out of a vent, landing on the screeching critter in a flurry. The spider's pincers quickly found their way to the rat's throat, and the struggle was over in an instant.

Taj spat in disgust, but found he couldn't look away.

The spider latched its long hairy legs onto its hard won prize, and dragged it out of the light and deeper into the Labyrinth.

"If there were creatures around, the spider wouldn't have risked attacking the rat," Taj decided. "All clear up here." He said loud enough for Dal to hear.

I don't fancy following the spider anyway. He had heard stories from some of the older Vanguards about spiders that grew bigger than men, but he had yet to see any evidence it was anything more than another ploy to scare youngbloods.

"Dal, you got anything?"

When there was no reply, his spine tingled instinctively, it was never a good sign when his friend was quiet. He turned around, and his blood turned to ice. Dal hadn't gone far, he was still in the mouth of the left tunnel, his torch fixed on a creature whose small brutish head was nearly touching the roof. They were rarely seen outside of the main tunnels, because their nearly fourteen foot frame was ill suited for the smaller passages.

"Slammer," Taj breathed. *Its eyesight sucks, if it doesn't hear our footsteps, we might be able to take it by surprise.* He slowly walked back to Dal, planting each foot and waiting a second to see if the Slammer heard before repeating the process with his other foot. His muscles twitched with each step, crying out to move faster, but he stayed the course, confident it was the right thing to do. *Lucky I didn't go very far away, or it would take hours to reach him.*

"If it's been separated from its pack, we should be able to kill it with just the two of us," Dal whispered when Taj finally joined him.

The Slammer lifted its small nose into the air, snorting and wheezing as though it were struggling to breath.

"Is it trying to catch our scent?" Taj muttered, his voice

trembling slightly.

The creature let out a deep throaty roar, spraying spittle everywhere and revealing square teeth and a long-barbed tongue.

Both Vanguards took a few involuntary steps backward.

The Slammers miniature eyes blinked and locked in on the noise, widening at the sight of fresh prey. The creature lifted its right calloused hand up, clenching its three fingers into a hammer like fist which it drove into the ground sending up a cloud of dust and chips of granite tile.

"Blast it," Dal yelled.

Taj quickly raised his rifle, everything seemed to be in slow motion as the behemoth roared and hurtled toward them. The first barrage smacked into the creature's broad muscled chest, and thick blood sprayed out, painting the ground and wall yellow.

Undeterred by the hail of bullets or its injuries, the Slammer closed the gap and raised its fists, ready to slam them down on the Vanguards. Dal swore and fell over his feet as he tried to retreat out of harm's way, his head narrowly missing the wall as he hit the ground.

Taj's stomach dropped, he tried to move, but his legs were frozen from fear and refused to obey. The hammer fists came crashing down and his legs crumpled, making him fall forward. He used the momentum to do a poorly executed roll that saw him evade the mass of bone and flesh by a hair as they came crashing down, sending stress fractures through the granite where they impacted.

He managed to complete the desperate manoeuvre and get back to his feet, just in time to see another body shattering strike come flying at him. He stepped to the side, and the fist connected with the wall behind him, barraging him with stinging chips of concrete and dust.

If that thing touches me, I'll be turned to mush, Taj automatically thought of the incident three weeks earlier when he had seen a Slammer shatter a two metre concrete barricade, and the resulting fight that saw two other units of Vanguards suffer heavy casualties to kill the creature. *We were insane to think we could do this on our own.*

"Over here, ugly," Dal thundered, his gunfire catching the creature in the neck and spraying the area with more yellow blood. The Slammer roared in pain and changed its attention to Dal.

Taj saw his chance and ran a few metres away, before resuming his assault.

Slammers will only die from a direct shot to the head, the rest of their body and vitals are protected by fat and tissue, the words echoed in his mind, as clear as the day they were first screamed at him. His eyes wandered to the creature's legs as a plan quickly formed. *It might not work, but it's better than nothing.*

Taj quickly readjusted his aim and blasted the Slammer's knees, emptying an entire clip into the flesh. The creature bellowed as its knees buckled under the attack, sending its massive body tumbling to the ground and exposing the vulnerable head to their weapons fire. The behemoth roared one final time and went limp.

Taj emptied the rest of his clip, and lowered his rifle, his hands trembling from the encounter.

That had been too close.

"That's how it's done," Dal cheered, pumping his fist in the air. "Those old goats back at the crossroads won't believe we did this on our own."

Taj scowled. *I doubt Tre will be happy with us, this was reckless and could have easily resulted in our deaths.*

Dal didn't share his friend's misgivings and walked laps around the corpse of their kill, his face alive with glee. "Lucky these ones aren't too bright, otherwise you'd probably be a stain on the pavement right now."

When Taj didn't reply, Dal stopped his pacing and stomped over to the Slammers brutish head, shooting it repeatedly.

Taj swore under his breath. *I know his father and uncles were killed by creatures, but his overzealous post kill rituals are getting ridiculous.* He watched his friend assault the corpse for a few more moments, delaying the task he both longed and dreaded to complete. In the weeks since the muster, he had checked every kill for evidence of the five clawed monster that haunted his nightmares.

Will I find something this time, I'm not sure if it's a good sign that we haven't seen it again. All his attempts to ask Tre about the subject had resulted in a swift smack to his head and an angry rebuke; it was clear the commander didn't want to talk about it. *I better check the creature before Dal gets too carried away and destroys it.*

Taj slowly walked over to the Slammer, a knot growing in the pit of his stomach with each step. *Why can't I shake this feeling of dread?*

He started with the back of the fallen creature, putting his light at an angle, he dragged the beam across the mottled grey flesh, searching for five distinct claw marks. The Slammers skin was already heavily scarred, the white marks haphazardly scattered around the body a record of its violent existence. *How many of these wounds were from Vanguards?* He silently asked the corpse. *Did you kill them all after they injured you?*

When he reached the base of the neck, he stopped, his eyes drawn to a rusted metal knife handle that was partially obscured by regrown flesh. *Who would be crazy enough to try and stab it in the neck? How did they even get close enough to do it?*

"Wake up," Dal insisted, slapping Taj's face.

Taj flinched; the hard-stinging sensation interrupting his thoughts. He lifted his clenched fist to retaliate, when a burst of gunfire sounded nearby, followed by a high-pitched scream.

"I think it came from that way," Dal murmured, indicating further down the left-hand tunnel of the T intersection where the

Slammer had appeared.

"Is anyone supposed to be in front of us?" Taj asked.

"No, this is the furthest point that has been cleared in this zone."

"What do you want to do then? If someone is in trouble, we should investigate, there might not be time to go back for Tre and the others."

"Agreed."

Dal and Taj followed the passage, walking shoulder to shoulder with their rifles aimed in front of them. A choking noise echoed down the tunnel, and both instantly knew what was waiting for them.

"Stalker," Dal said through gritted teeth. "Why did it have to be one of them? It's the only one of these damn things I can identify, and they are easily the creepiest."

Taj tightened his grip on his weapon, for once he was in complete agreement with Dal. Of all the things that roamed the underground, Stalkers were universally agreed to be the most unnerving. "Don't think it's far, sounds like it's nabbed some poor fool."

"If you see it, don't hesitate. Kill it on sight, and watch that damn stinger."

They kept following the path, and the choking sound got steadily louder until it was the only thing they could hear. Taj's heart started to hammer in his chest, his mind filling with visions of what they might find. *Maybe we should have gone for help after all.*

Eventually, the tunnel ended at an entrance to a small chamber. Their quarry, and the source of the noise, was crouched on the threshold. The Vanguards aimed their lights on the man-sized creature, the beams shined straight through its transparent skin and afforded them a view of its insides steadily filling up with liquid.

The Stalker sprang to its feet, green bulbous eyes alive with fury. The creature's two mouth mandibles extended, revealing a set of fangs dripping with blood and bile.

Taj fired first, his bullets ripping through the torso and knocking it to the ground. The Stalker hissed and flopped around, spurting blood like a fish out of water, so he kept firing until it lay still. He shuffled forward with Dal; and they took up positions either side of their downed foe, rifles at the ready.

"That was almost too easy," Dal said, firing an extra shot to the creature's head. "They're usually quicker. I remember one we tracked down a month or so after I joined was so fast, it dodged our bullets. By the time we took it down, I'd burnt through five whole clips."

"They are vulnerable when they feed," Taj stated. "They get so engrossed in draining their victims, it's easy to catch them by surprise." He passed his light over the Stalker's transparent skin, clicking his tongue when the beam settled on the organs, heavy with its last meal.

Dal shivered as he stared at the thick, sausage-like lumps of flesh in its chest cavity. "That's wrong in so many ways. Stop playing with it and let's go, we had better have a quick scout, make sure there are no more around, otherwise Tre will knock our heads."

"I don't think there will be anymore," Taj said. "Stalkers are mostly loners, they're too greedy to share food, there haven't been many recorded cases of them hunting with others of their kind." He prodded the dead creature's thin clawless hand with his boot, causing a long bone spike to spring out from underneath its wrist.

"Well, that's disturbing," Dal muttered nonchalantly as he circled around to the Stalkers kill. "Reckon this poor fella is still alive?"

Taj shook his head, "If the creature was feeding, its venom would have already liquefied this guy's insides. I'm no medic, but

I think that means he's probably dead."

The Stalker's victim was sprawled on the ground, his long black hair obscured his face, but his mouth was clearly visible, agape and frozen in what could have been a last scream. His armour was a similar design to the Vanguards, but Taj noted that there were subtle differences, especially in the thickness around the torso, with no gaps or exposed skin. It also had an unfamiliar red symbol printed on the front, two hands, one holding a sickle and the other a scythe in a cross pattern.

"Have you seen this rifle?" Dal lifted the nearby weapon. "Barrels longer and the clip size is halved, is it a new design?"

"I don't know. We should show this guy to Tre, something isn't quite right about him."

"You mean other than being dead?"

Taj opened his mouth to insult Dal, but the words died in his throat as two wiry arms
closed around his midriff, pushing the air from his lungs. He gasped and struggled against the iron grip, his body went limp as a sharp stabbing pain shot up his side. Another Stalker hissed in his ear, filling it with ice cold spittle.

A shot rang out, and the arms relaxed. Taj dropped to his knees, gulping in mouthfuls of air to his starved lungs.

Dal pushed past him and peppered the writhing Stalker until it stopped moving.

"Nice . . . shot," Taj panted while his fingers gingerly probed the hole in his side where the creature's stinger punctured his armour and flesh. At first each touch made his muscles retract as he cringed, then it began to feel warm. By the time Dal came back over, the feeling had spread to the rest of his body.

Taj tried to stand, but his limbs couldn't hold his weight and he stumbled back to his knees. *Paralysing venom*, he realised. *Soon I will be as helpless as a newborn.*

"Did it bite you?" Dal demanded, crouching in front of Taj, a rare look of concern plastered on his face. "I don't know what to do if you got a dose of poison from its fangs. Your insides will melt away like that poor fool over there."

"Pretty sure, it was just, the paralysing stinger . . . on its arm," Taj replied between ragged breaths. He planted his rifle on the ground and tried to use it as a crutch to rise, using his body weight to leverage himself. The whole endeavour proved to be a failure when his legs collapsed again. Three sets of green bulbous eyes appeared at the other end of the passage, a familiar hissing signalling their approach.

"Get out of here, Dal," Taj grated, "No point in both of us dying today."

Dal ignored him and started firing at the incoming Stalkers. The glowing eyes darted from one side of the tunnel to the next as they dodged Dals bullets with inhuman speed. He burned through three clips and still failed to stop even one of them, with every failed shot, they got steadily got closer to their prey.

While his fellow Vanguard tried in vain to kill the Stalkers, Taj crawled to the side of the passage, his movements slow and cumbersome as though he were stuck in a vat of honey.

We didn't even get a scratch killing that Slammer, how quickly things changed.

When he reached the wall, he rolled over onto his stomach and used the hard surface as a brace to hold his rifle steady. *At least I can shoot now.* His first shot missed, and the lightning fast Stalker was gone before he could pull the trigger again. Its eyes darted to the other side of the tunnel. Taj swore, and tried to move his weapon, but his weakened limbs were too slow, and his target was gone in a heartbeat.

Don't know if I'll be able to reload like this.

Dal's light flashed over a charging Stalker, the creature recoiled at the bright scrutiny, hissing and extending its mouth mandibles, spraying the ground with spittle. Dal didn't hesitate and mercilessly gunned down his stunned foe.

Taj caught the second Stalker a few metres in front of him, the creature had managed to sneak up on them by staying close to the wall. His light shone straight through its transparent skin, illuminating its thin empty organs. He pulled the trigger, and his bullets tore through its body, knocking it to the ground. The creature immediately sprang back to its feet, green bulbous eyes alive with fury as blue blood dripped from its many wounds. He fired again, but after two shots, his rifle clicked and went silent, signalling the clip was empty.

His heart skipped a beat, and his clumsy hands instinctively started to fumble for another clip, but it would take far too long to reload, and the Stalker knew it. The creature closed in, dragging its hand across the wall as it came forward, savouring the moment before it could gorge itself on his insides.

Taj managed to push the release on his rifle, ejecting the spent clip. He fumbled for a fresh one, but the creature was already close enough to bite him. It stood over him, fangs bared in a toothy grin as it prepared to feast. He reached for his knife, ready for one last act of defiance.

Only a second later, the Stalkers head exploded under a barrage of gunfire, covering Taj with its foul-smelling blood and chunks of skull. He loudly exhaled, relief washing over him, and resumed his attempts to reload his rifle as the headless body slid down the wall in front of him.

Surely that's enough close calls for one day.

"That's the second time I've saved you in less than a minute," Dal laughed. "That has to be some kind of record."

"Gloat later, there is still one more," Taj snapped.

Dal grunted and sprayed two quick bursts into the infinite blackness to attract their third enemy.

"I think the last one has run off," he said. "I can't see its eyes...."

The last Stalker suddenly leapt from out of the dark, knocking Dal's rifle from his hands and forcing the Vanguard back with a flurry of pinpoint strikes from the bone stingers in both its palms. He fumbled for his pistol, but the creature was too fast and slapped the weapon from his grasp before he could fire.

Dal retaliated with a quick left jab and a strong right cross, a combination that Taj had seen his friend knockdown ordinary men with, but the nimble creature was the farthest thing from ordinary. It dodged the strikes with lightning speed and countered with another flurry of its stingers.

Taj watched the two foes battle, swearing as he tried to redirect his weapon at the Stalker. No matter how much he willed his limbs to move, they were still slowed by the paralysing venom coursing through his veins.

I can't save him, he realised, the cold certainty dawning on him. *What do I do? It's only a matter of time before it catches him with one of those stingers, then we are both dead.*

A shot rang out and the Stalker stumbled, hissing and sputtering as a wound in the centre of its chest spurted blood like a broken pipe.

Dal took advantage of the lull in hostilities and drew his knife, descending on the wounded creature, stabbing it with unrelenting fury until it was reduced to an unrecognisable pile of mush.

Taj narrowed his eyes, searching the darkness for who had fired the life saving shot.

Maybe one of the others came to check on us, why haven't they revealed themselves?

"Nice shot," Dal complimented as he retrieved his weapons. "Looks like you saved me this time."

"Wasn't me," Taj rasped. "Dal, we need to go…"

"Poor Viscus," an unfamiliar voice interrupted.

Dal spun around, his rifle light illuminating a middle aged man with a hooked nose and long, black hair tied in a ponytail. The stranger squinted at the bright beam, but he otherwise ignored the Vanguards, his attention remained on the man killed by the Stalker's.

"Who are you? What are you doing sneaking around here?" Dal screamed. "You're lucky I didn't blow your head off."

"My name is Gaius," the man replied, swaying from side to side, revealing a stump with a loose tourniquet where his left arm should have been. His right hand clutched a long-barrelled rifle with a short clip.

"Where is the rest of your unit?" Taj demanded.

How did he make that shot with only one arm?

Gaius made a noise which may have been an attempt at a laugh. "No units, my squad are gone, Viscus was the last of the poor brave fools who followed me on this odyssey. We came for help, hoping that you could forgive us." He smiled, revealing bloodied and broken teeth. The newcomer's doe eyes glazed over, and he fainted.

Dal warily went over to the unconscious man and bent down to check his vitals. "He's got a pulse, but it's barley there. Something ripped this guy up, he's got—"

"What?" Taj roared "Dal? What—"

"You need to see this," Dal said as he walked over and pulled Taj to his feet. "You won't believe what I found."

What new hell have we uncovered now?

Taj put all his weight on Dal, and they shuffled over to Gaius. He didn't need his friend to point it out, he saw it immediately.

Gaius wore the same armour as his dead companion, but beneath the red symbol of two hands holding a sickle and a scythe, there were five deep gouges that were widening as an unseen force ate away the metal.

They're back.

Taj had been waiting for another encounter with the new

67

mysterious monster in the underground, and now he didn't know what to do.

If it's nearby, we are going to need help to kill it.

"Go get, Tre." Taj breathed, his voice growing unsteady. "Now."

Dal shook his head. "No way, I can't just leave you here. Lurkers will smell the dead before long and you can't even stand, let alone fight. There might be more Stalkers too, I know you said they don't hunt in packs, but it appears they do now."

"Then you better hurry, you can't carry both Gaius and me. You need to run for help, it's the only option Dal."

Dal groaned and started rubbing his bald head. "Alright," he relented. "Try not to die before I get back."

"Try not to die on the way there."

Dal let a bark-like laugh and carefully put Taj against the passage wall, avoiding the clusters of sickly yellow mushrooms and dripping brown algae. He then retrieved Taj's rifle and placed it in his stiff, useless hands.

"Be careful," Dal said, running back the way they had come and disappearing into the dark.

Gaius suddenly convulsed, and violently jerked awake.

"None of us is safe anymore, they will kill us all," he screamed. "The wall has fallen, we have failed, they are coming."

Taj's heart skipped a beat, he had heard the phrase many times in his nightmares. *Hurry up Dal.* "What does that mean? What wall?"

"You have to go find them, save my people, before it's too late, our sins were great, but we need your help."

"What? Find who?"

Gaius didn't respond, and Taj suspected he had lost consciousness again.

Hurry up, Dal.

Then it began, the noise which he had hoped never to hear

68

again. It started as a deep rumbling, then rose to a thundering roar that sounded like laughter, something sharp being dragged across the concrete quickly joined the discordant cacophony.

He had no chance now, the monster was coming.

Chapter Seven
Monsters in The Dark

Taj couldn't move, yet he could still see the shadowy shape out of the corner of his eye, gliding toward him, shimmering as it moved. Every fibre of his being was screaming to run, to hide, but paralysis had fully taken hold.

The shape floated past the comatose form of Gaius and came to a standstill just outside his rifle light. Two angular yellow eyes flashed, and he caught a glimpse of what lay beyond the light, a lean muscular body and a massive set of claws. The shape let out a thundering roar that sounded like laughter, and Taj tried in vain to grab his weapon. *Where are you Dal? You should be back already.*

The shape lowered itself and inched closer until it was right next to his face, sending his heart into overdrive as the small organ threatened to burst out of his chest. The yellow angular eyes narrowed, revealing double irises that reflected his visage back at him.

"Hurry up you bastard." He whispered. "Get it over with."

A set of claws came flying toward him, ramming into the wall above his head. The monster roared again and scratched downward, tearing through the concrete, showering him with chips and dust, obscuring his vision. *What's it doing, why hasn't it killed me yet?*

When the air cleared, he tensed, waiting for the next strike, but it never came, the monster was gone. *What was that? A waking nightmare? Hallucinations brought on by lack of sleep and paralysing venom?* Before he could ponder the matter further, rough hands fastened around his arm, and lifted him into the air.

"Are you alright?" Tre asked him.

"Yes," Taj replied, his words slightly slurred. "Tre, it's here, we need t.."

"Shut up boy," the commander growled. "We need to go, a pack of Lurkers is close, and we are in no position to deal with them right now."

Taj knew he couldn't stop them from leaving, and silently endured the indignity of being carried back to the crossroads on Tre's shoulder like a common backpack. The rest of the unit had been busy during his absence, four portable lights were set up in a square, illuminating the juncture. The two Butchers from earlier lay where they had fallen at the mouth of the entryway, the corpses had already begun to attract rats, several of the rodents squeaked from the dark corners, waiting for the chance to sneak a free meal.

Tre roughly threw him to the ground in the middle of the crossroads, sending shooting pains through his back and neck. *The paralysing venom does nothing for pain,* he realised. *That means Stalker victims feel everything as they are sucked dry.*

Wes dropped Gaius next to Taj and unstrapped his medical satchel of salves and tools off his belt, carefully laying it on the ground. He pulled a pair of long metal cauters out and started heating the ends with a lighter that spat out an intense blue flame. "I'll have to seal most of these wounds with heat, that's the only way to stop the bleeding." The medic mumbled. "The shock to his system could kill him, but I fear we have little choice."

"Do whatever you have to," Tre said. The commander then turned his attention to Dal. "Start talking, what the hell have you two fools been doing? I told you to mark the extent of our perimeter, not kill a Slammer, and definitely not get our youngblood paralysed."

Taj held his breath, anticipating the severe scolding they were about to receive. *Even if I survive the Stalker paralysis, he might flog me to death.*

71

"We did as you asked." Dal said, his voice full of apprehension, "When we reached the spot, I decided we should do a quick search, and make sure it was safe, a Slammer surprised us, we killed it, but we heard screaming, and went to investigate, that's when we were hit by the Stalker's."

Tre started pacing back and forth like a caged animal, his fists clenched. "Idiots, both of you, you're lucky I don't shoot you. Back when I was coming through the ranks, the elders weren't above clipping fools." The commander swore under his breath and drew his pistol, prompting everyone to take a few steps backward. "I know for a fact that I have taught you better than that." He exploded. "Always be aware of your surroundings, even the smallest sign could indicate great danger. Never assume there is only one creature, always expect more. If we weren't hard pressed for fighters at the moment, I would send both of you back to basic training so the lessons could be beaten into you."

For once, Dal wisely stayed silent, and Taj knew better than to talk back. Arguing with Tre was like banging your head against a wall; nothing was really achieved, and you nearly always ended up with a sore head. So, they waited for their leader to finish his tirade, but it appeared the commander was done yelling at them for the moment, instead he shifted the conversation to Gaius.

"What else do you know about this man?"

"His name is Gaius," Taj quickly answered in an attempt to stave off any violent intentions Tre still harboured. "His last companion was killed, it sounded like they had travelled a great distance looking for help." *Gaius has also been attacked by a shadow, a monster.* He wanted to say it but couldn't bring himself to utter the ludicrous sentence. *What if I only imagined it, they might think I've lost my mind and send me out into the tunnels to make The Sacrifice.*

Tre scowled. "He spoke to you? What exactly did he say? This could be very important, if there are more of his kind nearby, we need to know."

Taj took a moment to think about it before answering, *he didn't seem to care five minutes ago, what's changed?* "All Gaius managed to say before he passed out, was that his people needed help, and our forgiveness, then something about a wall falling. I think they have come from another city, one deep in the Labyrinth."

Tre didn't address the theory, and instead turned his focus to Ren. They didn't say a word out loud, but their silence and twitching facial features proved far more revealing.

I was right, Taj thought. *Tre knows where Gaius has come from, there must be another settlement in the Labyrinth after all, one that has remained a secret all these years.*

"There is something else, Tre," Taj began. *It's now or never, maybe if I tell him about the monster, I can get him to reveal what he knows.* "After Dal left, I saw something, I didn't get a great look at it, but it was big, and had glowing yellow, angular eyes. I think it attacked Gaius and killed those Butchers a few weeks ago."

"I agree Tre," the medic confirmed. "Whatever killed those creatures, attacked this poor fella too."

Tre remained impassive at the news, giving no indication of what he was thinking or if he believed the outlandish tale. Taj was half expecting a smack to the side of the head for being so impertinent.

"Ash, stay here and watch over the boy and Wes," Tre eventually said. "The rest of you, come with me, let's see if there is any trace of this thing."

Taj tried with every ounce of his willpower to move, but his body still refused to obey. "Wait for me," he beseeched. "I need to come as well."

"You can't stand, boy," Tre snapped. "If there is something out there, we need to be at our best, not carrying a cripple."

Taj felt like he had been struck, deep down, he knew what Tre said was true. Until he could move freely, he was beyond useless as a Vanguard. He watched the rest of the unit go with a heavy heart, a familiar feeling of dread welling up in his stomach.

I hope they are ready, whatever that thing is, even the creatures fear it.

Wes let out a deep sigh, "I hate this part," he lamented. "Burning flesh is always an unpleasant experience." The end of the cauters were bright red, and he lightly pressed them to the stump where Gaius's left arm used to be. The flesh sizzled under the heat, and a smell akin to burning pork wafted through the air.

Taj averted his gaze, his insides churning at the sight, and instead focussed on Ash who was walking around them. "You killed a few Stalkers and a Slammer, not bad for a youngblood," the twin declared. "I don't know many Vanguards your age who could replicate the feat."

Is he trying to make me feel better?

Taj didn't know how to respond, he had been with the twins nearly every day for the last few months, and they had never really spoken to him before. Initially, Dal had him convinced that their tongues were ripped out by a Harpy. A ruse that was quickly exposed when Ace heard the story and spent several days poking his tongue out every time they saw each other.

"Tre didn't seem to see it that way," he replied happy for the distraction from what Wes was doing. "I was surprised he didn't flog both of us for going off mission."

"Don't worry about Tre, that's how he is," Ash explained. "It's his job to ensure you make it back home, and he takes it very seriously. Every single one of us would have done the same thing in your position, the creatures are unpredictable, situations change, it's the ones who adapt and overcome who last out here."

"Are you saying Tre's orders are like guidelines, I can ignore them sometimes?"

"Yes, but not really. You'll understand soon enough, or you'll die, I hope it's the first one though. I'm getting tired of breaking in new recruits. The one we had before you was a clown."

Dal had told Taj in great detail about the previous member of Unit 17. Mot had tried to take charge from day one. He ordered around the more experienced members of the team and tried to make changes to their combat tactics.

On only his third mission, and after a particularly tiresome display of arrogance, Tre had relented and allowed the youngblood to lead. Mot walked straight into a Tickers' nest and had been torn in half by a horde of the winged creatures; they never did find all the pieces of his body.

"I've done all I can," Wes declared as he sat back from Gaius and used a bottle of water to clean his blood-soaked hands and face. "I've stopped the bleeding, and his skin doesn't appear to be dissolving anymore, he should live long enough to get him back to the Healers in Acropolis, beyond that, I don't know. Now what have you done to yourself, Taj?"

Taj smiled weakly. "A Stalker stung me, I'm fairly sure it didn't bite me."

Wes hummed to himself and picked up a plastic vial of purple liquid from among his many different coloured concoctions stored with his tools. "If you were bitten, you'd know, trust me." The medic crouched down beside him and unstopped the vial, an overwhelming vinegary smell wafted out causing everyone to cough.

"What is that?" Taj spluttered. "Do you expect me to drink that?"

"If you want to be able to move again, then you need to drink it, we will have to be careful though, too much and your heart might stop."

"You've got to be joking."

"Consider yourself lucky, it wasn't that long ago that the effects of a Stalker's jab were permanent. If the Healers hadn't invented this, you would be paralysed for life and probably be forced to undergo The Sacrifice."

Taj scowled, it was an unspoken law in the underground that anyone who couldn't contribute to their society was left to die in the Labyrinth, a process they called The Sacrifice. Sometimes the very old or sick, who knew death was imminent, left the safety of the city by their own accord, never to be seen again.

He sighed, and opened his mouth, *I guess it can't be any worse than dying alone in the dark.* Wes tipped five drops of the liquid on his tongue; the acrid taste instantly overwhelmed his senses. It burned like liquid fire all the way down his throat, until it came to rest in his stomach. The next thing he knew, burning pain shot out to every corner of his body and all his muscles constricted at once. He tried to scream, but when he opened his mouth, his stomach lurched, and the Stalker's venom was purged from his system.

Just when he thought he would die from the agony, the pain receded, leaving a deep aching in its place. Panting from the ordeal, Taj slowly moved his sweat-covered limbs, relief quickly replacing his pain.

At least it wasn't for nothing.

He sat up and wiped his mouth clean.

"That should do it," Wes said. "You should have full movement back, I wouldn't recommend running for a few hours, just to be safe."

"I feel like I have already run one hundred kilometres. Do I even want to know what was in that stuff you gave me?"

"No, you really don't. Let me check where the creature stabbed you, it would be a shame to die of an infection after surviving the Stalker antivenom."

Wes whistled merrily as he poked and prodded the wound, sending painful jolts through Taj's back.

"Punched right through the armour," the medic said. "You may want to get the Guild to fix this damage next time we are home. I'll put some Gilo on the wound now, but you should have your sister check it in a few days, for some reason, Stalker wounds seem to get infected frequently."

"We have company coming, lads," Ash interjected, pointing to the tunnel behind them. "I hear footsteps, that's the way back to Acropolis. Might be another unit, but we can't be sure a creature hasn't slipped through the lines."

Wes quickly finished applying the Gilo to Taj's wound, and they both retrieved their rifles, assuming flanking positions either side of Ash. Neither of them could hear the intruders yet, but the twin brothers' exceptional hearing had never led them astray.

"What is it?" Wes asked. "Lurkers? Berserkers?"

"Not sure," Ash admitted. "There is definitely more than one."

Taj squinted at the tunnel, trying to catch any sign of whatever was lurking just beyond in the dark. Seven people dressed in black burst across the threshold, a small bald woman was in the lead.

"Hold fire, it's the Harpies," Wes groaned, lowering his weapon. "This could mean trouble."

Despite Wes's misgivings, Taj couldn't help but feel a little excited as the group strolled over to them, he had heard more than a few stories about the fierce all-female Vanguard unit. Officially, they were called Unit 335; but the seven women preferred to be called the Harpies, after the creature of the same name.

Every member of the Harpies wore standard Vanguard armour without the arm coverings, which revealed a web of intricate flame tattoos snaking up their arms and disappearing to their backs where two bone-handled blades were sheathed in a cross pattern. All of them shared similar long brown hair, green eyes and delicate grimy features, leading Taj to conclude that some, or all of them might be related. The leader was the odd one out and had shaved all the hair off her head and face.

"Jaz," Wes addressed the bald woman and slightly inclined his head in a show of respect.

"Wes, Ash," Jaz replied, returning the gesture. "Good to see you."

Ash muttered something unintelligible and walked away without a backward glance, setting up a silent vigil in front of the tunnel where the rest of their unit had gone.

What was that about? Taj wondered. *I know he doesn't like talking to people, but that was really rude.*

"What are you doing skulking back there, Ash?" Jaz called after him. "Are you going to come and say hello? Or shall I come over there and give you a proper welcome."

The twin gave her a cursory glance, then returned to his vigil, his demeanour noticeably sullen.

"Where is the rest of your unit?" Jaz asked Wes, apparently abandoning her attempt to make small talk with Ash. "The Harpies have been assigned to check on the rest of the units in this area and make sure nobody has been overrun. There were several breaks in our lines recently, the creatures have been violently pushing back against our incursions, more so than usual."

"Tre took them out scouting," Wes said. "To investigate a pack of Stalkers, and a few other strange occurrences."

"Strange seems to be becoming quite common, we just found a lone Lurker hunting, never seen one without a pack behind it." Jaz laughed, but the sound was without mirth. "That's not even mentioning what's happening at home, I don't know if you've heard yet, but there has been quite a bit of fighting in the streets, anybody against war with the surface is being assaulted or accosted, the Watchers are struggling to keep order."

Wes shook his head. "Has it really got that bad? I knew people were angry with Jye and the council, I didn't think they would turn on each other so easily."

"I didn't think Jye and Tre would be ready to kill each other either, they were like brothers once, here we are though, on the verge of civil war."

"Nothing like political differences to drive everyone apart," Wes said with a pained smile on his face.

Jaz muttered several curses under her breath and turned to leave, when she noticed Gaius who was still unconscious and lying in the middle of the crossroads. "Who is that? One of ours?"

"His name is Gaius," Taj answered. "Found him with the Stalkers, we are not sure who he is, or where he came from."

Jaz looked right at him, but he got the very distinct impression she was only half-listening, a suspicion that was confirmed by her next question.

"You'd be Kai's boy then? You look just like him."

Taj nodded, unsure how to respond to the statement. It seems everyone knew his father, except him.

One of the Harpies stepped forward and stared at Gaius. "I don't recognise him," she said.

"Lex has a thing with faces," Jaz explained to Wes and Taj. "She has the unfortunate burden of remembering everyone she meets in vivid detail, she could describe to you in intricate detail the face of every kid we grew up with."

Lex gave them a blank stare. "I think we've spent enough time here captain, it appears they have everything under control, we should be moving on."

"That we should Lex, take care boys, make sure to tell Tre we were here."

The Harpies left the way they came and disappeared back into the Labyrinth, the dark swallowing them up like a great hungry beast.

"What is up with Ash?" Taj asked Wes when he was sure the Harpies weren't coming back.

The medic laughed, only stopping when Ash glared in their general direction. "Jaz can be quite forward sometimes," he explained. "A few years back, she tried to court Ash, as you know, the twins are a bit shy, it didn't end well, now they both avoid her at all costs."

The rest of Unit 17 returned a few moments later, none of them had any outward signs of injury, but all of them appeared to be unnerved by whatever they had found. Ren was glassy-eyed and somewhat jittery, while Dal and Ace kept nervously looking behind them as though they were being followed.

"Did you find anything?" Wes did his best to appear at ease, but the stalwart medic was wringing his hands.

Ren was the first to answer, he swallowed first and his voice was slightly uneven when he spoke. "They were gone, no Stalkers, no other body, no monster. We checked the area and found nothing."

Taj's stomach dropped, he had begun to hope that the monster he had seen was all in his head, now it seemed there was no denying it, there was a new predator in the Labyrinth. *Why would it steal all the bodies? Maybe it has a pack to feed.*

"We are heading back to Acropolis. Wes grab Gaius and get him ready to move," Tre ordered. "Ren go with Dal and the boy. You are on guard duty, watch the tunnels, make sure nothing unfriendly wanders in. Ace, Ash head to the next intersection and find Unit 45, they're led by captain Rax, we'll need him to send a few of his Vanguards to hold this position for us."

"The Harpies were just here," Wes said, a slight smirk on his face as he glanced at the twins. "They are patrolling, if we hurry, they might be able to cover here until we get back."

Ren let out one of his rare bark-like laughs, "That's a shame, aye Ace, you just missed her, bet your brother had a good time though."

Ace rolled his eyes and swiftly elbowed Ren in the stomach, which made the second captain cackle even more.

"Even better," Tre exclaimed. "Ace, Ash, track down Jaz and her sisters, and be quick about it, we move in five."

The twins both appeared crestfallen, but otherwise didn't

argue, they all knew how dangerous it was to leave an opening for creatures to reclaim territory. Everyone began to carry out their allotted tasks without further words, Taj lingered though, it was foolish to keep pressing Tre for information, but decided it was worth the risk.

"You know where Gaius came from, don't you?" Taj said to the commander. "You know what's out there?" It was a bold move on his part, not only was he questioning a superior officer, he was also implying Tre was holding back information from the rest of the unit.

Taj waited, his gambit was either about to pay off, or he was going to receive a beating, it wasn't the first time he'd played this game.

Tre glowered at him, the look alone could stagger grown men, "Very cheeky, boy. All I have at the moment are suspicions, if Gaius survives, perhaps we will know the truth of it, make of that what you will."

It was more information than Taj had been expecting, but it was still too vague to find any real meaning.

At least he didn't flog me.

Years later, whenever he looked back on this moment, he always remembered it as the time before everything began to change rapidly . . . and not for the better.

Chapter Eight

Unit 6

Ren and Wes held Gaius between them as they trekked back toward Acropolis, Tre had the lead, along with the twins, while Dal and Taj had the rear guard. Corpses paved the path, both creatures and the occasional fallen Vanguard, rats and spiders feasted on the abundant dead. Other units occasionally passed by, but none of them paid any undue attention, most were dead eyed, grim faced and completely focussed on getting to their destinations.

Before long they reached the ring of light, the first line of defence for Acropolis, which circled all the passages around the city, acting as a barrier between the creatures and the outer barricades. Blinding spotlights dotted nearly every inch of the ten foot tall continuous ring of steel and barb wire, giving the whole structure a glow rivalling the city it protected. The nearest gate screeched open, and Vanguards wearing thick black glasses to protect their eyes from the lights shuffled out to greet them.

"Tre," One of the men said, inclining his head in greeting. "Didn't expect to see you back so soon."

"Ran into trouble," the commander said cryptically. "Double your patrols along the ring of light, I have a feeling things are about to get a whole lot worse."

"Aye, sir."

A small village lay behind the fortifications, sprawling across the large open space. The buildings, like most of their structures, were simple one room huts where Vanguards could sleep for a few hours when they weren't patrolling along the ramparts inspecting for breaches. Dozens of people were sitting around on makeshift furniture, playing Knife Point and taking swigs from hip flasks that were being passed around. Taj recognised one of the revellers instantly, Mal was still upright and leaning on a table, but his eyes were closed, and from the slight movements of his chest, it appeared he had passed out. *How is it possible to fall asleep while standing?*

Before they could reach the tunnel back to Acropolis at the rear of the settlement, Gaius convulsed, shaking awake.

"You're all going to die," he screamed, fighting furiously against the firm grips of Wes and Ren. "Let me go, it's too late, you all need to flee."

The Vanguards on duty at the ring of light all stopped what they were doing and turned their attention the hysterically screaming man. Gaius' blood chilling screams reached a fever pitch before he went limp and lost consciousness again. Wes put a finger to his patient's throat and muttered a curse. "His pulse is getting weaker Tre, he needs a Healer, or he is dead."

"Understood, we are nearly home," Tre said, turning around to address the Vanguards protecting the ring of light, most of whom were still staring. "As you were," he shouted. "Get back to work, now."

After a few grumbles, normalcy slowly resumed, but everyone present had heard what was said, and it wouldn't be easily forgotten. They made it to the outer barricades without further incidents, but the curious glances of the Watchers on duty made it clear they had heard the screaming too. After safely passing through the main gates of the city, Tre and Ren whisked Gaius off to the nearest Medical Centre.

"Regroup here in 20 hours," Tre instructed as he replaced Wes holding up Gaius. "Go home, sleep, do whatever you need to."

Chances for rest were rare, even more so lately, and everyone quickly dispersed. Taj was about to start home when he realised Wes hadn't moved. The medic had been told many times he was always welcome at any of their houses, but the always polite and softly spoken man always felt the need to ask for permission.

"Would you like to stay at my house tonight?" Taj said. "There is plenty of room."

Wes nodded. "Thank you, Taj."

****

Taj strolled barefoot through the narrow streets of Acropolis, his movements slow and sluggish. The buildings around him were on fire and their doorways were choked with red hot ash that spilled out onto the street. The stench of burning filled his nostrils with each step, but it didn't bother him; instead, he felt a strange contentment.

"You took something from us," roared a deep unfamiliar voice.

A massive set of white claws closed around his throat and lifted him into the air, a pair of yellow angular eyes hung above him.

"Soon you will drown in a river of blood," the voice promised.

Taj woke with a start; his whole body dripping with sweat, his heart beating so fast it threatened to burst from his body. Wes's loud snoring filled the darkened room, the overpowering noise drowning out every other sound, but he found it somehow comforting, and his panic slowly receded. He sought the cup next to his bed, lifting it to his dry mouth with shaking hands and draining the liquid it contained in one frantic gulp. The vivid images of carnage were still burned into his brain, and he knew with a cold certainty sleep was going to elude him for another night.

The nightmares are getting worse, I wonder if they will send me mad one day? I need to get out of here.

Taj quietly got dressed in his civilian clothes—a plain black shirt Sai had knitted him and canvas blue pants. Wes lay in a corner, still fully dressed; Sai was curled up on her bed on the other side of the room. Unwilling to wake either of them, he gingerly tiptoed outside, stretching his weary body the second he was over the threshold.

I wonder if it means anything, repeatedly seeing the death in my nightmares.

He wandered to the end of the street, pondering where to go, when he saw a crowd of children sitting in front of a hut.

What are they doing?

"Gather round little ones," a familiar voice said.

Taj started, *I didn't even know old Ryn the storyteller was still alive, she was ancient when I was a kid, she would have to be over a hundred by now.*

Ryn sat on a crate, her back bent over as though she were in great pain. Her formerly blue eyes had turned a milky white, and her golden hair had faded to a dull grey, but the storytellers lined sharp face was the same as it had been when he was a boy.

"For today's story time, I have a cautionary tale for you," Ryn said to the assembled children. "Has anyone ever heard of Sif the Sorrowful?"

When none of the children were forthcoming, the old woman laughed to herself, waving her old gnarled hand and reaching for the wooden cane resting at her feet.

"Well it seems none of the parents have dropped off any little ones for story time today," she cackled. "I guess old Ryn will just go back inside and make herself a nice cup of tea, and perhaps find a biscuit."

Taj smiled to himself, it had been many years since he'd been to a story time, but he remembered the experience fondly. He could still recount many of the tales, and in his later years, Jun had told him the stories had elements of truth to them, a secret history that had been passed down orally for the past thousand years.

The children all giggled. "We are here," a girl in the front row said. "Don't go."

"Ah, there you all are," Ryn laughed, jumping slightly in her seat, pretending to be surprised by the sudden noise. She returned her hands to the folds of the deep black cloak she always wore and waited for the children's laughter to die down before starting the story.

"Now, our tale begins long ago, when our people had only just been banished from the surface. There were many great beauties in those days, but Sif was said to eclipse them all. Her golden hair was brighter than the sun, her eyes were bluer than the sky, and her face was so beautiful it was said that a thousand men had fought for the right to marry her. Young Sif was a free spirited girl though, and she left a trail of broken hearts in her wake. One day, Sif found a young man who she loved with all her heart, she forsook all others and asked for his hand in marriage. The fates are cruel though, and her chosen partner abandoned her on their wedding night. Heartbroken, Sif left the city, and her sorrow took her deep into the Labyrinth. Time passed, and the most beautiful women in the underground was forgotten, for like all things, beauty, and memories fade."

Ryn paused for a moment, and the children held their breath. Taj knew the routine well, the pause was both for dramatic effect and to stall for time while she tried to remember the final part of the story. *She's still got it.* The old storyteller hunched over and motioned for the children to slide forward.

"It wasn't until many years later that Sif returned home in search of her former betrothed," she whispered to her captive audience. "She scurried in like a great spider, evading the Watchers, and all who would try to stop. Sif quickly found her target, but as she stared through the window of the house they were supposed to share together, she saw him in the arms of another. Enraged, Sif stormed through the door, and as her victims begged for mercy, she tore their hearts from their bodies, for the Labyrinth had changed her into a creature of malicious rage and hate. When the deed was done, she left the city for the final time, and disappeared back into the Labyrinth. Sif hasn't been seen by the eyes of the living in hundreds of years, but remember these words boys, if you are unfaithful, old Sif might just return to steal your heart."

The group of children laughed and called out for more stories, but Taj couldn't help but shiver. As a child, the story of Sif the Sorrowful had been the one that had given him the most nightmares, closely followed by The Butcher of Agkai.

"Who knows what the lesson is here?" Ryn asked. "Stories are fun, but they can also have a message."

A brave boy stood up and wiped his nose on his hand before answering. "Nothing lasts forever?" he said.

Ryn made a show of considering the answer before replying, stroking her chin and humming to herself. "No young one, that is a good lesson, but not the one I'm trying to teach, try again."

Poor kids, they will spend years trying to guess the meaning behind her stories, then one day they will figure out that there isn't an answer that will ever placate her.

Taj turned around to leave, when he saw someone else he knew. The gangly man trudged past, his head down and back bowed, it was hard to see his face, but Taj would know the distinctive grey jacket and blue pants of a Guild member anywhere.

"Tig," he yelled. "Hey, Tig."

His boyhood friend didn't stop, and Taj had to run after him, shoving past the steady trickle of people heading toward the main gate. After repeated attempts to gain Tig's attention, he finally stopped, his sullen demeanour changing in an instant when he saw who was trying to hail him.

"Taj," he exclaimed. "When did you get back? I didn't think

there were any Vanguards left in the city."

Despite only being a little older than Taj, Tig's lined face made him look far older than his years; his brown mane and rough stubble were already developing patches of grey as well.

"We just got back," Taj said. "Ran into trouble, Dal and I found a stranger out in the Labyrinth, he'd been attacked."

Tig turned his head on its side and frowned. "What do you mean stranger? A Surfacer? What are they doing down here?"

"No, he wasn't a Surfacer," Taj was about to tell his friend everything, his suspicions, Gaius and the monster he saw, when something stopped him, a nagging thought at the back of his mind.

People are already scared, maybe I should wait until I know more before I start spreading panic.

"Who was he then?" Tig asked after Taj went silent for a few moments. "That's big news, the city seems to be awash with all sorts of gossip nowadays though, so it's hard to know what to trust."

"I'm not sure," Taj lied. "I think Tre took him to the Medical Centre, if he ever wakes up, I expect he will have quite a few questions to answer."

Tig nodded in response, a pained smile on his prematurely aged face. "Hope he pulls through, there is enough death in this place already."

He knows I'm lying; I just hope he doesn't take it personally.

"What are you doing out here anyway?" Taj asked in a clumsy attempt to change the subject.

"Just getting a last look at the old place, before I leave," Tig groaned. "I don't know if I will ever see it again."

Taj chuckled. "What happened? Didn't you get those generators working? Is Jye going to shoot you?"

"I wish it was that simple, I'm part of a group that's being traded, it was part of the latest deal the council cooked up with the surface leaders," Tig stated in a monotone, his displeasure at the assignment clear. "The Guild will help them maintain their technological marvels, in return, we get a chance to work with technology far beyond anything in the underground."

Taj clapped him on the shoulder. "Well that sounds like it could be a great adventure Tig, the surface gets the best of the Guild, and you get to play with some fancy new toys."

Tig's face lit up and he adopted a wide grin, exposing a complete set of yellowed teeth. "Oh, I would hardly call me the best," he said sheepishly. "I just wish my family could come, I've never been away from them before, my old mum hasn't stopped crying."

"When do you leave?"

"Soon, I'm on my way to a meeting with the Guild Grandmaster Tag, then we will depart with Unit 6, they are our escort."

Taj's eyes widened and his heart immediately quickened, there wasn't a boy in Acropolis that hadn't grown up hearing stories about Unit 6, the elite Vanguard kill squad. The special unit received their orders directly from the Vanguard Grandmaster and was made up of the seven deadliest fighters in Acropolis. All the previous members had been killed at the fall of Agora, and their replacements had spent the subsequent years carving out a reputation that had seen them credited with killing more creatures than every other Vanguard combined. They had been conspicuously absent during the muster, and many were speculating Jye was holding them back in case he needed to put down a revolt.

Tig was about to say something else, when he put a finger to his lips and nervously looked over his shoulder at two nearby Watchers. He stayed silent and motioned for Taj to follow him to one of the narrow side streets that snaked between the buildings around the city. They were forced to walk single file along the muddy track, and only when they reached a point where a large storehouse and factory loomed over them on either side of the trail, did the Guild member start talking again.

"I think Unit 6 might be using the escort mission as a cover," Tig said, raising his voice slightly over the sounds of the machinery in the nearby factory. "I saw them preparing earlier; it looked like they were getting ready for a long journey, judging from the number of provisions and ammo they were collecting. I think they intend to go somewhere else after they take us to the surface."

Taj swore. *Gaius must have told them something. Jye is sending out the best we have, they must be going after the monster. I should go see the old man, he might know more.*

"Perhaps it has something to do with your mystery man," Tig continued, "If the higher ups are sending the best Vanguards in the city, they must be expecting a fight."

"I'm going to see Doc," Taj announced awkwardly. "Stay safe, don't let those Surfacers boss you around too much."

Tig extended his hand in a gesture of farewell. "I guess, this is goodbye for now," he said sadly. "Stay safe."

Taj shook his friend's hand and quickly departed, guilt gnawing at his insides over the abrupt way he had dismissed the conversation.

Tig has enough on his mind. I don't need to burden him with conspiracy theories and stories of killer monsters.

He returned to the main street and started towards Doc's shack, but his progress was impeded almost immediately by two Watchers blocking his path. The older one, a man with no ears and a partially scarred scalp, ignored him. The other, a teenage boy with striking blue eyes and long blond hair tied back with a bit of cloth, was quick to embrace him.

"Pax," he grunted giving the Watcher a few seconds before assertively pushing him away. He had always found Dal's younger brother to be very polite, but the boy had a habit of hugging people as a greeting; an act that was annoying at the best of times.

"Taj," Pax squeaked, his voice exhibiting all the signs of a boy changing into a man. "I'm glad you are okay. Dal said you nearly died."

"Yeah it was close," Taj agreed while he extracted himself from the embrace. "You look more like your older brother every time I see you."

The boy stifled a giggle. "I wouldn't let Dal hear you say that, drives him mad every time he hears it."

"Is that right," he muttered, making a mental note to bring it up the next time he saw his friend. "How's your patrol going, has there been more violence?"

"Nothing yet," Pax whined. "I was hoping for some action, being a Watcher is so boring, I wish there wasn't an age restriction of eighteen years on joining the Vanguards."

The other Watcher curled his lip, his disgust evident. "Don't be too eager, young pup," he chastised in a harsh grating tone. "Every year thousands of young fools like you are sent out into those tunnels, most don't come back, and those that do are changed forever, both physically and mentally."

Taj watched the two argue, seeing echoes of himself at that age, he had also been eager for action and didn't fully understand what he was signing up for. What followed after starting his Vanguard training was two years of hell, beatings, injuries, and three deadly final tests administered at the conclusion. Many recruits dropped out, the toll on their bodies and minds too much to bear; the lucky ones joined the Watchers. Others would either escape with lifelong debilitating injuries or die horrible deaths in the tests, all this before stepping foot in the Labyrinth. He had been so proud to survive and join the Vanguard ranks, it had been his goal for so long, now he just wished he could make the bad dreams stop.

"I have to go, Pax," Taj said, cutting off the older Watcher mid-sentence which prompted the man to glower and swear under his breath. "There is someone I have to go see."

Dal's younger brother deflated, his enthusiasm faded. "Hopefully see you again soon," he squeaked.

Taj waved a quick farewell, dodged the hug goodbye and resumed his journey to Doc's house. *I hope the old man is awake and in a talkative mood.*

The former grandmaster rarely slept, but Taj had found out during one of his first visits, not long after his parents died, that Doc would often pretend if he didn't want to see someone. On that occasion, they had been talking for about an hour when Doc's son, Raz, knocked at the door, prompting the elderly man to drop to the floor and start snoring loudly. Raz eventually gave up and Doc ceased the ruse, returning to their conversation as though nothing had happened. The whole incident still brought a smile to his face.

He reached the old man's shack and lightly rapped on the door with his knuckles, as always, a loud crash and a mischievous cackle emanated from within.

"Who is it?" Doc shouted through the door. "Before you ask, I don't want any of what you are selling, go away."

This again.

Sometimes he thought Doc tried to further discourage visitors by being difficult whenever someone came over.

"I'm not selling anything, I just came to visit; I can't sleep, and there is something we need to talk about."

"I don't know you, and strangers are not allowed in my inner sanctum," came the reply. "How do I know you are not a Marauder, here to loot my valuables?"

"Because the Marauders are long dead, along with their masters, the Cannibal Warlords."

"That's just what they want you to think, they're still out there, lurking about. If you're not careful, the next thing you know they'll be picking out bits of your flesh from between their nasty

92

teeth."

"It's Kai and Jen's boy," Taj exclaimed, feeling the familiar twinge of sadness every time he mentioned his parents. "If I were a Marauder, I think you would know."

"Taj? Why didn't you say so, come on in."

He crossed the threshold and found Doc sitting at his usual spot near the fire, stirring a pot of green lush-looking stew. Since his last visit, the number of utensils stacked in the corner had increased by nearly half, and there also appeared to be several rocks of an unknown origin.

I hope he didn't buy those from that charlatan.

"Would you like some?" Doc said enthusiastically, pointing at his cooking pot. "It's fresh, probably my best recipe yet."

Taj pretended to consider the offer, before shaking his head and taking his seat on the other side of the fire. He had tried the old man's cooking only once and found it to be a wholly unpleasant experience. The soup had tasted heavily of garlic, onions and rotting fish, one bite had caused him to spend the better part of an hour bent over violently vomiting in the street. Upon his return to Doc, he received a lecture about how people used to have sturdier constitutions.

"Well what brings you here then?" Doc cackled. "Shouldn't you be sleeping? Girlfriend kick you out again? Maybe you should find another, come meet my granddaughter, maybe if she gets a hobby, she will forget about trying to poison me."

Taj sighed.

He really seems convinced she is trying to kill him. I might as well just ask him and be done with it, otherwise I might be here for days.

"Did you hear they're sending out Unit 6? I think it might have something to do with the strange man we brought back from the Labyrinth."

"Gaius," Doc said, his tone suddenly turning serious. "I was

93

there when Jye spoke with him, nasty business."

"What did he say? Where is he from?"

"He said many things and travelled a great distance, I would have liked to talk with him more, the wounds he sustained were fatal though, he died not long after arriving."

Taj hadn't known Gaius personally, but he felt a little sad at the news.

I wonder if the man had any family.

"I think I saw the thing that attacked him, it was unlike anything I've ever heard of. Gaius also mentioned something about a wall falling, maybe his settlement was destroyed by that monster?"

Doc exhaled loudly and stopped stirring his meal. "I am fond of you boy, your father was like a son to me, but this time, I can't give you the information you want."

"Why not? You have never kept secrets from me before."

"Some in Acropolis have always suspected they were out there; it needs to be investigated quickly and quietly. If word were to get out now it would cause a panic, and the already tense situation in the city would get far worse. If you seek answers, find them yourself, look to the main gate."

Taj balked at the cryptic response, it was nothing out of the ordinary when talking with the old Vanguard, but he still found it tiresome sometimes.

This is probably the best I'm going to get out of him, I guess I should head to the gate before I go home.

"Have you seen my new rocks, a nice young man gave them to me," Doc blurted out. "That fellow said they were special, personally, I just use them for squishing rats and other nasty crawlies."

Taj couldn't help but laugh. "I can't believe that charlatan sucked you in with that awful pitch," he teased. "You must be losing your wits, old fella."

The rest of their conversation was cut short when a man of middling years with greying blond hair and wearing tattered Watchers armour burst into the room. His lined face scrunched in a fierce scowl as he surveyed the hovel. Taj had only seen Doc's son, Raz, a handful of times in the last year, and each time he appeared to have aged significantly.

"Dad, this is ridiculous," Raz scolded as though they were mid-way through a conversation. "You need to leave this old broken-down wreck and come live with us. I don't like you out here all by yourself with nothing except rats to keep you company."

"You're not welcome here, boy," Doc breathed, his eyes returning to the cooking pot. "I will do what I please, you have no right to ask more of me."

Time to go.

Taj excused himself, he had learned the hard way that it was a mistake to interfere in other family's squabbles.

"Be careful my boy," Doc called to him as he exited. "There are dark times ahead."

After leaving Doc's, Taj decided to follow the old man's advice and go to the main gate. In truth, he didn't know what he would find at the cities entrance, the old grandmaster might simply be playing a joke on him or his addled brain might finally have broken completely.

Both options are possible.

To his surprise, upon reaching the main gate, he found a small congregation assembled. The red cloaks of the council were clearly visible amongst the throng of Watchers, Guild and Vanguards. He quickly ducked into a side street and ascended to a rooftop. Despite his best efforts to walk softly, the residents of the houses below heard his clumsy footsteps and hurled abuse and threats. Being careful to distribute his weight evenly to avoid falling through, he traversed over to the nearby roof of the Guild Factory that overlooked the main gate and dropped to his stomach, peeking over the side of the eaves.

The perch afforded him a perfect view of everything happening below, Tig was amongst the group; the gangly man stared into the distance, deep in thought while several of his Guild cohorts held animated conversations around him. Only a few feet away, a stout elderly man with a thick greying beard, short hair and dressed in the grey jacket and blue pants of the Guild spoke with the council, who all looked to him as he spoke with his hands, waving them in a peculiar fashion. Guild Grandmaster Tug was said to be one of the best minds in the entire underground, but he was also very eccentric, bordering on insane.

A lone figure stood statue-like apart from the rest of the group, dressed in the black armour of a Vanguard; his stern cold gaze averted to the western wall. Jye had his rifle slung on his back and appeared to be carrying two pistols and several home-made pipe bombs on his belt.

Why would Jye be so heavily armed? Surely, he isn't escorting the Guild to the surface as well. Maybe he is joining Unit 6 on their mission?

Taj observed the assembly for several minutes, trying to discern what they were all talking about. He tried his best to catch snippets of the various conversations by closing his eyes and trying to focus on the sound of the voices, however, the roar of the factory in full operation below made it a virtually impossible task, and he soon gave up.

Perhaps I should just go down there, pretend I'm out on a walk. What's the worst that could happen?

He slowly started to inch his way backward, when everyone below stopped talking at once.

Have they spotted me?

Then he saw them, seven hulking Vanguards joined the congregation. Jye greeted each member of Unit Six individually, while in the background, regular conversation slowly returned, but it seemed forced. Taj could practically taste the tension, the intimidating presence of the most dangerous fighters in the city was hard to ignore.

None of them was under six feet tall and they all had visible scarring that only added to their menacing aura. The largest had two long facial scars across his right, dead milky eye, the distinctive pattern identified him as Kel, the leader. It was said he lost his eye in an unarmed fight with a Slammer, a contest, if the rumours were to be believed, he won by beating the creature to death with his bare hands.

Taj found himself drawn forward, his curiosity getting the better of his caution, his gamble paid off, giving him a clear view, but the move had other unintended consequences. The roof creaked under his weight, catching the attention of Jye. He froze, unsure what the grandmaster would do. When no challenge was forthcoming, he moved back from the edge of the roof. *Why didn't Jye say anything? Perhaps he didn't see me.*

To be safe and avoid further discovery, he forced himself to count through three circuits of sixty seconds each before he returned to his perch. The bitter taste of disappointment flooded over him as he spied the last member of Unit 6 disappear through the main gate. The council and Jye were the only ones who remained, and after exchanging a few words, the red-cloaked leaders dispersed, leaving the Vanguard on his own. Then he was gone too, disappearing among the buildings.

Taj stayed for several more minutes, waiting to see if anybody would return.

I don't know if I got any answers here Doc, just more questions.

"You shouldn't have stayed in the same spot," A deep voice said. "If you had repositioned a few times, it might have been harder to notice you."

His stomach dropped.

Idiot, of course he saw me.

He slowly rolled over and found Jye crouched on the roof a few feet behind him.

How did he get up here so silently? A hundred excuses formed on his tongue, but they all died before he could voice them.

I might as well be honest; he probably already knows why I'm here.

"Where are Unit 6 going?" Taj asked. "Does it have anything to do with Gaius?"

"It has everything to do with Gaius," Jye stated. "He came here with two pieces of information, the first, he told us, the second were the wounds on his body. The thing that attacked him is clever, it knew exactly where to cut and ensure he died slowly, our Healers could only delay the inevitable."

"Will Unit 6 kill this thing? What did he tell you?"

Jye smiled. "Doc was right, you are a very curious young man. Unit 6 will do their best, but honestly, I'm not sure if they can stop this thing, especially if there is more than one out there, as for what Gaius said, you don't need to know, not yet anyway."

He felt the sting of disappointment for the second time. "What can you tell me then?"

"Nothing, but perhaps I can show you something, I'm heading to Agora, and I want you to come with me."

Taj frowned; to his knowledge nobody had been to the fallen city in years, it was considered too dangerous, even for Vanguards.

"Why risk a trip there, what do you hope to find?"

"Knowledge. Most of what we know of our past today comes from legends, tales of the countless wars we have fought. Even our oral histories only go back as far as the Cannibal Warlords, two and a half thousand years ago. We know nothing about our war with the Surfacers, where our people came from, or even why the Labyrinth was built."

"How will skulking around a creature infested city help with all

98

that?"

"The Grand Library at Agora held all our knowledge, if I'm going to decide what to do with our future, I need to know more about our past. So, what is your answer, are you coming with me?"

Chapter Nine

Agora

The moment they were past the ring of light, Jye set a blistering pace, and Taj struggled to keep up with the long, determined strides of the grandmaster. After he had retrieved his gear they had left from the rear gate and travelled for what felt like hours, the tunnel sections all passing by in a blur. Despite using a rarely travelled path, there were no creatures to contend with, aside from dead rotting ones being feasted on by the rats.

Occasionally they would come across Vanguard units, they exchanged brief greetings but otherwise kept to themselves. If any of them thought it strange the Vanguard Grandmaster was wandering the tunnels with a youngblood, nobody said it out loud.

They travelled in relative silence, which gave Taj time to ponder their destination and what they might find there. He had heard Agora was at least eighty kilometres away from Acropolis, and while he had never been to the vermin-infested ruin, the place had always held a latent fascination.

I wonder what we will find when we get there.

Jye paused at a fork in the tunnel and shined his light down both paths, whispering to himself as he darted his light back and forth.

Taj waited patiently, wiping the stinging sweat from his eyes, but as time went on, he began to suspect something had gone amiss.

"I haven't been this way in a while, but one of these paths leads to Agora, the other will take us to the city of Agkai," Jye said, confirming Taj's suspicion. "Unit 6 should have left a symbol for us to follow around here somewhere, where do you think it might be?"

Is this a test?

Taj aimed his rifle torch down the left path, dragging the beam across the concrete walls, methodically searching for the glowing symbol. His light reached an old alcove 50 metres away and glittered, reflecting off a polished surface. *What is that?*

Without consulting Jye, he went into the tunnel, his light trained on the strange object. When he was close enough, he crouched down and held the light aloft, revealing a skeleton. All the flesh had been picked clean long ago, and in its place were tangled webs and hundreds of spiders scurrying to find cover from the sudden flash of light. Rusted pieces of armour clung to the legs and arms, but some of the chest plate was still polished to a mirror like shine and held a faded red T.

"I know who this is, a Chosen Crusader Knight," he muttered, repeating a name Jun had told him many times, almost at nauseum. "This would have to be at least 1500 years old."

"You'd be surprised what you can find in forgotten corners," Jye said from behind him. "No doubt Jun bored you with the history of that damn crusade at tedium."

Taj smiled to himself, reliving a moment that felt like a lifetime ago. "Yes, the old goat loves demonstrating how Vanguard Grandmaster Tyr killed the Holy Emperor Vlad, usually with whatever props he can lay his hands on."

Jye snorted, and wandered past him, lighting up several more crusaders in similar condition to the first one Taj found. "This must be the road to Agkai, the Chosen dead still litter the path, all the way up to the city walls if the old tales are to be believed."

"Have you ever been there? To Agkai?"

"No, it had fallen into ruin long before I was born, and none dare tread there now, but I have been to the sanctum, the chamber where the last of the crusader knights committed ritual suicide with their families to be with their god."

Taj took one last look at the long dead men, trying to picture what they would have been like. The Chosen had been the last to believe in gods, some of the older people in Acropolis said a prayer before they went to bed or when they were afraid, but they were just words, a habit, nobody believed they held meaning anymore.

"Did they really all kill themselves after the Vanguards crushed their armies?"

"Who knows, when we still had control of our seven fortress cities, and the surrounding settlements, we still didn't travel to the furthest ends of the Labyrinth, the network is vast. The outer reaches, the sub-levels, any number of places could be hiding thousands of people, we would never know."

Taj immediately thought of Gaius, *I wonder how many more civilisations are out there.*

"Let's go," Jye said. "Agora awaits."

They returned to the fork and took the right hand tunnel, trudging along for over a kilometre before it opened up into a vast chamber holding forty round stone structures set out in a circle. On the other side of the chamber, a gateway loomed, the shattered remains of its great doors laying in the entranceway.

Jye took them past the structures, and Taj counted at least another twenty which had collapsed inward, their pointed roofs reduced to rubble. In the middle of the town, a pile of bones and twisted scrap metal were scattered on the ground, leaving no illusions about the fate of the last people to call the outlying settlement home.

Taj followed Jye through the gateway, taking care not to stand on the old doors. On the other side, the walls were glowing with yellow symbols depicting a CN that had a cross through the letters, he had never seen one in person before, but knew the meaning well: 'Dangerous Creature Nest, Stay Out'.

"Agora is at the end of this tunnel," Jye explained, his voice soft and full of reverence. "The way should be clear, stay alert.."

"I didn't think our culling missions came out this way," Taj said. "Aren't all the old fortress cities off limits."

"This opportunity only recently came up. With so many Vanguards in the underground the creature numbers in this area are the lowest they've been in years. I sent Unit 6 here weeks ago to search the city. They cleared the path, I had to recall them when you found Gaius, now it falls to us to complete their mission."

Taj scowled, his mind rife with suspicion.

Is this why you sent all the Vanguards out at once, so you could clear out enough creatures to come here and raid an old library?

He didn't say it out loud, there was no proof after all, and accusing the Vanguard Grandmaster of a scheme like that, was liable to get him a savage beating.

Unit 127 should be up ahead," Jye said, adopting a pained expression, "You should be careful, make sure you don't look the two captains in the eye; Jax is a dangerous man and his brother Taz is even worse."

"What do you mean? We are all on the same side, comrades."

"The Terror Twins don't see it that way, there are things they want to kill and things they don't, you should avoid their notice if you can help it."

In the distance, he could just make out bright lights flooding into the blackness. The source was four portable spotlights set up in the middle of the tunnel, two at each end, with a single Vanguard standing in the middle of them. Five others were asleep in an alcove off to the side, an old generator in a state of disrepair behind them.

"Jax," Jye inclined his head in greeting to the man in front of them.

Jax flicked his long brown fringe out of his face, revealing mismatched blue and green eyes that narrowed like a predator in the midst of hunting prey. His most striking feature though, were three bone white scars cutting diagonally across his gaunt, skull like face.

"Taz," Jye grunted as the second man on guard approached to meet the new arrivals.

Taz was identical to Jax in every way, except the entire right side of his face was a mess of scar tissue that made it look like he wore a leathery mask. The twins raised their rifles in challenge, revealing they had strapped knives to the barrels.

"About time you showed up," Jax growled in a soft husky tone. "We were getting bored."

"Who's the kid?" Taz added in a similar tone, showing the two men shared more than just a similar appearance.

"My names Taj," he stammered, doing his best to avoid looking either of the identical brothers in the eye. He would never admit it out aloud, but their appearance made him nervous. "Pleased to meet you."

Taz and Jax exchanged looks of amusement before they burst out laughing.

"Jye I know you're not so popular these days," Jax cackled, "But surely you could find someone better to watch your back, this kid is so green he's liable to shoot himself in the damn foot."

"Actually, I've found him to be quite capable," Jye said. "Anything to report?"

Jax's mismatched eyes narrowed, and his thin cruel lips twitched. "An overly curious Slammer and a few Harpies, nothing to worry about, should be all clear now."

Taj was doing his best to avoid looking directly at the demented pair, but something had caught his eye and his curiosity flared. Both brothers had contraptions attached to their wrists that were about a foot long and had a curved blade sticking out the end.

What is that?

"What are you staring at?" Taz thundered, abruptly springing forward and grabbing Taj by the throat.

"Your wrist," Taj choked as the crazed Vanguard backed him into the wall.

"You like it?" Taz whispered, a maniacal grin contorting his scarred features. "The whole thing is custom-made, based it on a Marauder design, they were savages, but they knew how to kill. Check it out." He held out his right arm and tensed, the blade sprang out with a snap and extended to over a metre long.

Taj swallowed. "Very impressive," he gasped while trying to extract himself from the lunatic's grasp. "I prefer to keep things at a distance."

Taz felt his struggles and tightened the grip, he then placed his mutilated face right next to Taj giving him a whiff of unwashed flesh and rotting meat.

"Shame," Taz hissed. "Nothing better than getting nice and close, so you can see the light fade from their eyes, the feeling is indescribable."

Taj gave up trying to get free and instead started reaching for one of his own blades he kept strapped to his belt.

"It's amazing how quickly something bleeds out when you open an artery," Taz continued. "Doesn't matter how big and strong you are, you get that artery right here in the neck, and you're done. If that fails, go for the eyes. Want me to show you?" he enquired, pressing his bladed contraption to Taj's neck.

Taj's fingers closed around the handle of his knife.

I'll show you something, lunatic.

"It's easy," Taz drawled. "Most of the time they don't even feel it."

Taj drew his blade with a whistle and pressed the weapon against the man's pale flesh, waiting for an excuse to slice open his neck.

"Like this?" he stuttered, trying his best to hold his voice and hand steady.

"Exactly," Taz trumpeted, a look of genuine mirth crossing his scarred face. "That spot is perfect, now just press it home."

Taj froze, racked with indecision.

Does he want me to end him? What if I don't, will he kill me?

His hand quivered, itching to drag the blade across the crazed man's throat.

I've never killed a person before, surely it can't be much different than stabbing a creature.

Before he could decide, Taz lowered his blade, then pushed Taj's away as though it were nothing but a bothersome fly.

"The boy seems alright," he reported to his twin brother. "Solid nerves, quick with a blade, maybe we misjudged him."

"If you're done playing knife games with my friend," Jye interrupted. "We are leaving for Agora."

"I don't understand what you want with that ruin," Jax whined. "Seems like a lot of effort for very little reward."

"Maybe we should come along," Taz suggested eagerly, "You could use the extra help, and we are bored senseless waiting around here."

"I need you two to watch our exit," Jye snapped back. "Stay here and keep alert." The grandmaster motioned for Taj to follow him, which he was more than willing to do. The Terror Twins watched them go but didn't offer any form of farewell.

When Taj was sure they were far enough down the tunnel to avoid being overheard, he breathed a loud sigh of relief and lightly massaged his throbbing throat.

"What is wrong with them?" he rasped. "They seem completely unhinged."

"They don't call them the Terror Twins for nothing," Jye replied, "To put it mildly, they are an acquired taste. I usually try and unleash them as far away from everyone else as possible, that's why their unit is strictly volunteers only."

"Would he have cut my throat?"

It felt like Taz wanted to.

"I doubt it," Jye told him. "If either of them was planning to kill you, they would have done it, there wouldn't be any discussion. Violence seems to be the only thing those two have any passion for. You handled yourself well though, they have gained some respect for you now it seems."

"They respect me for nearly stabbing one of them in the neck?"

"The Terror Twins have their own way of doing things, to them, it makes sense."

Taj shook his head in disbelief.

How could their way of thinking make sense? I hope I never see those two again. I wonder where they got those Marauder weapon designs though?

From what Doc had told him, the Marauders invented many deadly weapons while serving as the soldiers of the Cannibal Warlords. Each warlord had their own small city kingdom with a hereditary ruling caste. Rivers of blood flowed from all the territories in the underground as the warlords, and their Marauders treated the populace like livestock. Few people liked to talk about it, let alone use devices and weapons invented by the former tyrants.

"Where did they find Marauder weapons?" Taj said, voicing his thoughts aloud. "I was always told they were all destroyed after the end of the Cannibal Wars?"

"Some relics of that bygone era remain in the underground as well," Jye answered. "It may interest you to know that a handful of the Marauder armies survived the fall of their masters and lived on in makeshift settlements far from prying eyes for many years. Our patrols sometimes find the remnants of these survivors."

Taj winced as chills shot through his entire body, tales of the Marauders savagery often did the rounds among the younger denizens of Acropolis. Even considering the penchant for exaggeration when stories are re-told so many times, it painted a terrifying picture of the warlords and their soldiers.

The Chosen, Marauders, who knows what else is lurking out there.

The tunnel opened up into a colossal hollow with an air of familiarity to it. Agora was in the centre; bathed in shadow, but it was clear that it covered most of the vast expanse.

Jye produced several sun flares and threw the hissing devices in a wide arc all around them illuminating the area in a bright orange glow which gave them a glimpse of Agora's thick, concrete outer wall.

From what Taj could see, the entire defensive structure was riddled with breaches and stress fractures that snaked in every direction. Twisted piles of rusted metal the size of a grown man adorned the still standing sections, it appeared some vindictive creature had taken the time to rip apart every single big gun.

"What could break down the wall like that?" he said. "I have never heard of anything with the strength to shatter something so big."

"Slammers," Jye stated matter-of-factly. "Lots of Slammers, they gathered at key points and the combined assault collapsed the wall, then the smaller creatures flooded in, slaughtering all in their path."

"The creatures were working together; don't they usually just eat each other?"

"It is the only time in recent memory that we have seen a concentrated attack from them. Lurkers acted as cannon fodder, protecting the Slammers while they made the breaches, Harpies scaled the defences and tore apart anyone in their way. When the walls came down, Berserkers were the first through the breach, clearing out the majority of our defenders who sought to stem the tide."

"How is that possible? How did they organise such a coordinated attack?"

"Nobody knows, the creatures showed an intelligence far beyond anything we thought them capable of, and that ignorance cost us close to a million lives," Jye said, his voice carrying a bitter edge.

They crossed the expanse and entered through the main gate, their lights casting an eerie silhouette over the carpet of bones choking the paved streets. Most of the clothing had long since turned to dust, many of the weapons and armour still lay with their owners, rusted and useless.

Are they here? he silently wondered. *Are my parents hidden somewhere in this graveyard.*

"That's our destination, the Library," Jye informed him, pointing to the elevated apex of the city. "Stay close, Unit 6 were thorough when they cleaned this place out, but there could still be a few stray creatures lurking around."

The grandmaster continued to light sun flares at regular intervals as they ascended the winding streets. Ruined and crumbling buildings of various heights and sizes loomed all around them. The handful of intact structures, that had somehow survived the fall of the city and the subsequent occupation by the creatures, gave Taj the very distinct impression Agora and Acropolis were constructed by the same architects.

Is this our future? he mused while passing over a makeshift, waist-height granite barrier. *Will Acropolis one day be an abandoned ruin too?*

At the top of the city, the ground levelled out and revealed a flat courtyard with a set of stone stairs leading up to a large three-sided structure at the back, which Taj guessed was the Library. Many smaller buildings flanked either side and had freshly-killed creatures scattered amongst them. Swarms of rats feasted on the carcasses, occasionally letting out squeaks as they fought over the rotting meat. Spiders and other crawlies brave enough to fight the rodents for food darted amongst the larger scavengers.

"Unit 6 must have found a nest here," Jye decided striding through the dead and scattering all the vermin in his path. "This was once a booming hub of trade and learning, people would come from all corners of the city to exchange ideas and trinkets, it's a tragedy such a hallowed place has been besmirched."

Taj followed in the older Vanguard's wake, wincing each time he felt his boot touch a moving body. Every fibre of his being was telling him to run away from the rodents, but he held his nerve, fear of being thought a coward was more pressing than his distaste for the rats.

When they finally reached the stairs, Jye hesitated, his eyes alive with the memory of a place that would never exist again. He waited a few more seconds, before shaking off the nostalgia and climbed up the steps.

The main entrance to the Library had been wide enough for at least six people to walk abreast, but time, or a creature had collapsed most of it, forcing them to go in single file through the rubble. On the other side, Jye lit up several sun flares, scattering them around and revealing a cavernous room with the mangled remains of multi-storied shelves at regular intervals, a double set of stone stairs were either side and led to the darkened upper floors.

"This place is trashed, like everything else," Taj said bitterly. "Whatever you seek here is probably long gone."

"We are looking for a chest made of copper. It should be red," Jye explained, "The Librarians kept it locked in a glass case in the middle of the room where they could keep an eye on it. The old thing was sturdy, I expect it's buried around here somewhere."

The Vanguards searched in a parallel line to each other, stopping every few feet to rummage through the bigger piles of wreckage. Every so often, a rat would be uncovered as well and run screeching from the room making Taj jump and reach for his gun. By the time he reached the halfway point across the room, his scepticism of ever finding the mysterious red chest began to grow exponentially. The few books that were still whole and hadn't been gnawed on turned to dust at the slightest touch, giving him a sense of loss each time.

I wonder what knowledge they contained, what story they had that is gone forever now.

"You would have loved this place in its prime," Jye called from across the room. "Your curious mind could have been indulged in this place for hours, learning the many secrets of our world at your leisure. I'm sure the old Librarians would have been happy to welcome you, they were strict old goats, and quick with the cane, but good at heart."

"What happened to them?" Taj asked while lifting an old shelf and revealing several more piles of yellow paper.

"During the assault, the last grandmaster of the Librarians ordered all under his command to come here and protect the books, none were ever seen again, their bones are probably somewhere in this place."

Taj eventually reached the rear of the Library and found two sets of collapsed stairs that once led up to the second floor. He reluctantly turned around and started his search anew, double checking every spot for the chest.

This is going to take forever; it might not even still be here. He did two more laps of the ancient building and found nothing of value. Just when he was ready to give up, a whistle beckoned him back to the rear of the structure near the collapsed stairs.

"Taj," Jye exclaimed, his excitement bubbling over. "It's here, underneath the stairs, we need to dig it out."

Taj found the grandmaster pointing at a barely visible red speck amongst the cold grey stone.

How had he seen that? They cleared the debris, piece by piece, when the labour was finished, it revealed a copper chest roughly a metre long. The partial remains of a skeleton were draped over the container, whoever the person was, they had died shielding the contents.

Jye effortlessly lifted the chest with one hand and placed it on his shoulder. "Time to go," he said without any sign of strain in his tone. "Unless you want to explore some more?"

Taj shook his head, taking one last look at the sad remains of the Library.

****

"Rest here a minute," Jye said while carefully placing the chest down in front of Agora's main gate.

"What's in the chest that is so special?" Taj asked, suddenly realising the older Vanguard hadn't told him anything specific about what they were seeking. "Must be something important to come all the way out here for it."

Jye didn't answer at first, instead he pulled his knife out and started trying to force the chest open by sticking his knife in the seam underneath the lid, a task which he failed miserably.

"A complete record of our history," Jye eventually told him, "Inside this container is all the information we have about what year it is, why our ancestors were imprisoned, the wars we have fought, all our knowledge. Up until fifteen years ago, when Agora fell, the librarians kept meticulous records. There is nobody left alive who knows all the information contained in this chest. For years it has been collecting dust, I couldn't risk lives trying to recover it, until now."

"What's changed?"

"Everything."

Taj scoffed at the flippant response. "You aren't going to tell me what you find, are you, even after all this."

"Not right now," Jye admitted. "One day you will know, so will everyone in Acropolis, but not today."

Taj swallowed the rash words he was about to voice and instead confined himself to an annoyed grunt.

What I wouldn't give to see those records, to read our complete history.

Then it hit him, Jye's sudden urgency to find the chest was no coincidence.

"You are looking for information on Gaius, and whatever attacked him? The thing Unit 6 are hunting as we speak."

It was a complete stab in the dark and he didn't expect to get an answer. The Vanguard Grandmaster fixed him with a cold predatory stare. Taj's heart rate increased, and his legs involuntarily quaked, but he held firm, using every ounce of his courage and willpower to keep his body from trembling. They had been on friendly terms since their meeting, but Jye was still a very dangerous and violent man, not to be trifled with lightly. *Maybe I shouldn't have said that.*

Jye laughed, the deep booming sound resonating around Agora filling it with a sound it hadn't heard in over a decade.

"Doc was right about you," he said, returning to his struggle with the container of records. "You are far too clever for your own good."

Taj smiled. "That does sound like something the crazy old sot would say."

I didn't get a direct answer, but he did imply I was right, I suppose that's the best I'm going to get, at least for now. There was still one question that had been plaguing him since they arrived; he knew it was risky to pester the Jye again, but he had to know.

"Did you know my parents?" he asked, "They were killed here, I'm not sure where their final resting place is."

Jye's shoulders slumped, and he ceased his attempts to open the chest. "Yes, I knew them," he mumbled, pointing to a tattoo of the letter K and J clearly defined in black on his right hand. "My tattoos represent things from my life," he explained. "Events, friends, family, those I've lost. I mark them on my skin and armour, so I never forget them. Kai was like a father to me as well, and your mother, always made sure I was fed. In a way, we are like brothers."

"Then how come we have never talked about this before now, brother?" Taj said with more venom than he intended.

"Because it's an awful thing leaving those you love to die, and I have no desire to relive it," Jye said bitterly. "I knew the day would come when we would have this conversation, and I think now might be the right time. Honestly, it's half the reason I brought you."

Taj knew what he wanted to ask next, nobody had ever told him the exact details of how they died, and while he feared the answer, he knew it was a conversation that needed to happen. "Then tell me, how did they die?"

"Are you sure about this? it's not a pleasant story, there is a reason Doc refuses to talk about it."

This is it, no going back now.

Taj nodded, unable to form the words.

Jye took a deep breath as though he were about to physically exert himself, and began the tale that neither of them really wanted to hear.

"As you now know, after the walls fell, thousands of creatures poured into Agora, Clickers, Harpies, Stalkers, before long the city was awash in a sea of blood as they ate their fill of the inhabitants. The fighting was fierce and short, your parents and a few hundred of us managed to secure some buildings and rally survivors, ultimately we were fighting a losing battle."

The grandmaster stopped talking for a few moments, lost in his memories, when he started again, his voice had taken on a bitter edge. "When it became clear there was no stopping the creatures, Doc gave the order to abandon Agora and escort any survivors to

114

safety, it was a terrible choice, save a few hundred, or no one. The decision still haunts him. We fought our way through the chaos, each metre gained cost us lives, by the time we made it to this very gatehouse, less than half our original number remained. What we hadn't realised was that several of the slower families had fallen behind during the march, and rather than leave them to their fates, your parents went back to help."

Taj held his breath, he had never heard the full story before, but knew in his heart what was coming next.

"We waited for them to return," Jye said. "A Lurker pack was baring down on us, a dozen Vanguards had already been torn apart, the fight was hopeless, and we were forced to leave, your parents were left behind."

A single icy tear ran down Taj's cheek. *They were left to die, along with so many others.* He wanted to rage, to blame Jye, Doc or somebody, but he knew it wasn't their fault. Every Vanguard had been trained to prioritise the needs of the many over the needs of the few in a crisis. Several hundred civilians were always going to take precedent over the lives of two Vanguards, even if they were his parents. It was a hard truth, but life in the underground was full of them.

Jye continued his story, each passing moment seemed to make him stoop a little lower, as though the telling was weighing him down.

"What followed when our ragtag group from Agora returned to Acropolis, I'm sure you know? Doc called a Muster that same day and we went back with every fighter at his disposal. The battle lasted for weeks and many more died, the city was won and lost more times than I can count. In the end, despite untold acts of heroism, Agora couldn't be retaken, and Doc called a retreat and stood down as grandmaster."

Taj had heard many different accounts of the drama that followed Doc standing down. Hal succeeded him and spent months ordering failed missions to Agora that grew steadily more unpopular. By the time Jye challenged for leadership, Hal had lost all support due to his costly failures."

"Did you ever find out what happened to them?" he asked, a catch forming in the base of his throat.

"I never saw them again," Jye breathed. "However, during one of Hal's many missions to Agora, we found a band of survivors who had been living in the tunnels for weeks, they had news of a male and female Vanguard fitting the description of your parents. From what they told us, Kai and Jen saved them, but your mother took a hit from a Berserker, shattering her sternum, Kai refused to leave her. That was the last anyone saw of them; their ultimate fates are a mystery. I think it's safe to assume neither of them ever made it out of here alive. Hal was a fool to send us back here so many times, finding those people was probably the one good thing that came out of it."

"Is that why you challenged him? Killed him?"

Jye grimaced. "One of the reasons, Hal was a decent man, and a good fighter, Agora became his obsession though, it sent him mad. The creatures stayed here in their tens of thousands for years after the fall of the city, there was no way to reclaim it, Hal wouldn't let it go, I gave him a choice, face the challenge or step aside, he refused."

At least I finally know, I just hope that when they died, they were together.

It was a silly childish thought and he knew it, but it somehow made him feel a little better. The more realistic alternative was far too distressing to even contemplate.

"I think that's enough rest for now," Jye said. "This chest will need to be opened back at Acropolis, I don't think any keys remain, it will take quite a bit of effort to get inside. The old Librarians built this thing strong."

Taj was about agree that they should leave, when a loud

clicking interrupted him. Both Vanguards lifted their rifles in unison and the noise got steadily louder, until it was the only sound in the dead city.

"Clickers," he muttered, wildly swinging his rifle and light around as he tried to spot the gliding creatures. "Sounds like there is more than one, can you see them yet?"

When there was no answer, Taj turned around and found the Vanguard Grandmaster crouched, his weapon pointing in the air and moving slowly as it tracked a target.

Jye fired three shots, and three objects fell from the sky, hitting the ground around them with a heavy thuds. Another Clicker landed behind him, its muscular arms tipped with dual curved claws driving toward his head. Jye rolled underneath the attack, drew his knife and decapitated his foe with a backward swing.

The next Clicker landed on a nearby roof, digging its three clawed bony feet into the stone to steady itself while its useless grey eyes swivelled around. The creature bared its protruding fangs, driving them together and sending out a jarring clicking sound. Its pointed ears pricked up as the sound waves bounced off nearby objects, giving it a rough idea of the surroundings. Veiny, nearly transparent flaps of skin hanging from either side of its arms extended as it prepared to take flight, but Jye wasn't about to let that happen. His knife flew through the air like a bullet, driving into the Clicker's chest and sending it sprawling from the rooftop.

In all his years, Taj had never seen anyone move so fast or with such deadly accuracy, all five creatures were killed in a heartbeat. *Jye's reputation hasn't been exaggerated, if anything the tales of his deeds were understated.*

"We should go, they are coming to reclaim their territory," Jye said, effortlessly lifting the chest of records again.

"They are welcome to it," Taj spat. "I hope to never lay eyes on Agora again."

Taj went first, jogging through the ruined gate and past the sun flares from earlier, the devices were still shining, but had diminished significantly, allowing the shadows to creep back up.

The wind from a circling Clicker slapped into his face, and Taj slowed, searching for the culprit. Behind them, a Clicker landed on Agora's ruined gatehouse, while three more of its brethren glided over the top and toward the Vanguards.

"Those ones are yours Taj," Jye said. "Take them down."

I'm not sure if I can, he wanted to say, but it wasn't the time for self-doubt. He sprayed a hail of bullets in the air, sacrificing accuracy for the chance to try and hit all of them in a short span of time. His tactic saw two of them fall, their gliding patagium's riddled with holes. The last flew overhead, forcing him to duck the swipe of its claws. The creature gracefully landed a few metres away, blocking the way out.

"It's all yours Taj. Remember to breathe," Jye coached. "Aim carefully, don't rush the shot, you have a few seconds."

Taj took a deep breath, finding the sudden intake of air slightly soothing, all other sound was drowned out by his rapidly beating heart, then he took carful aim and fired. The first shot connected with its arm, failing to cause any serious damage. His second missed, and the Clicker leapt into striking distance. Before he could shoot again, the creature convulsed, and a metre-long curved knife emerged from its chest.

Jax grunted as he used his boot to push the corpse off his blade, spitting on the twitching body for good measure.

"We will handle this," he boasted. "Jye, take your youngblood back to Acropolis before he shoots someone."

"What's in the box?" Taz jeered, appearing out of the gloom with five other grim looking Vanguards. "Treasure?"

"Knowledge," Jye answered simply.

Both brothers scowled, an identical look of disgust on their faces.

"Old books you mean?" Jax mocked. "What a waste of time

and effort, surely you could have found something more valuable, I bet those old Librarians would have had some weapons from the old days hidden somewhere."

"Never mind," Taz growled, "Leave these two to their old bits of paper, let's go find something to kill, brother."

"Oh, I like the sound of that," Jax said happily. "Everyone spread out, one-metre intervals, let's go hunting."

"Will they be alright on their own?" Taj asked Jye once they reached the mouth of the passage that went back into the Labyrinth. "If the creatures really are returning now, the Terror Twins might need help."

"They've survived far worse," Jye replied. "I doubt there are many who would be willing to risk their lives to help those two anyway, many hate and fear them."

"Then who were those Vanguards in their unit? They didn't seem to care."

"Other like-minded individuals, there are plenty of other psychopaths among the Vanguards, people like that seem to be drawn together."

****

"Open up," Jye commanded to the Watchers on duty at the outer barricades. The city guardians didn't bother asking them to identify themselves, everyone knew Jye.

The return journey to Acropolis proved to be uneventful, with no more creatures crossing their path, for which Taj was grateful. *I've had enough of death for one day.* His eyes drifted to the red chest, still resting on Jye's shoulders.

"Do you think there will be anything about the monster in there, the one with the yellow eyes?" Taj asked, voicing a question he had been pondering for most of the trip.

Jye smiled, "You really don't give up do you? You're very

much like your mother."

Taj looked away, his face growing warm.

"To tell you the truth," Jye said. "I expect there will be more than a few accounts of these things, they've been out there for a while."

The gate screeched open, and Jye walked through, leaving Taj in stunned silence at the revelation. *What does he mean? If they've been out there for a while, how come I've never heard of them before.* He ran after the Grandmaster, eager to learn more. "Have you come across them before?" he asked.

"Only once, the day Agora fell, but this time I think there are more, a lot more."

Taj's blood went cold, and he immediately regretted asking the question.

Chapter Ten

From Bad To Worse

Two months later…

"You're doing it again," Dal complained, "Stop daydreaming and pay attention."

Taj rolled his eyes. Their unit had recently been assigned to relieve the guards protecting the surface entrance nearest to Acropolis, only a kilometre from the ring of light. The tunnel they were walking had been clear since the surface entrance had been re-opened over a year ago, nobody was expecting trouble. "There is no danger here," he grumbled. "We aren't on the front lines anymore, relax."

Dal immediately adopted an air of superiority. "Once you've been a Vanguard for a few years, you'll learn there is danger everywhere, especially now. You've seen all the bodies being carried back to Acropolis, people are dying every day, and even more are going missing, this isn't the time to relax, far from it."

Taj grunted, he couldn't fault the reasoning, despite the danger that they had always faced, it had somehow contrived to get worse. "What do you think those two are discussing," he said, nodding at Tre and Ren who had made sure to keep out of earshot since leaving Acropolis.

"I'd wager the same thing they've been talking about since the muster, ditching the plan to clear the tunnels and starting a war with the surface," Dal mumbled. "I hear they already have the support of two hundred and fifty captains, that's all they need to initiate a leadership challenge against Jye."

"This needs to end soon, one way or the other," Ace said. "When we got back to Acropolis yesterday, I spoke to a few Watchers, they have been struggling to keep the peace. Those against war, and those who are in favour of it have been steadily getting more violent, riots and fighting in the streets are becoming all too common."

Wes shook his head. "I heard something similar from the Healers, they were already getting run off their feet by all the Vanguard casualties, now they have a lot of civilians coming into the Medical Centres with broken bones and stab wounds as well."

I guess that's why Sai wasn't home yesterday, Taj thought. *I hope she is alright.* He hadn't seen his sister since they brought Gaius back to the city two months earlier. After returning from Agora, his unit had gone back into the Labyrinth almost immediately. What followed was a series of bloody battles that saw the outer perimeter shift more times than he could count, every time they gained ground, hundreds of creatures appeared and pushed them back. It was a constant and bloody tug of war with no end in sight.

"People are angry and scared," Ash muttered. "That's a dangerous combination, I'd say a civil war is more likely than anything else at this point."

"Do you think it will come to that?" Taj asked. "Are we really going to start killing each other just so we can go fight another war with the Surfacers?"

We should be out there fighting those yellow eyed monsters, not each other.

"Perhaps, especially with Jye's absence the last few weeks, "Ash replied. "I don't know what he is doing, but it can't be more important than preventing a civil war."

"I heard he is somewhere plotting with Unit 6," Dal said. "They are going to wipe out everyone who is a threat to Jye's leadership."

"I doubt it," Taj whispered. As far as he was aware, Jye was holed up somewhere poring over the records they had recovered from Agora, but it wasn't his place to tell the others what the grandmaster was doing. *I wonder if Jye has found anything of value yet.*

"Alright, cut the chatter," Ren barked, his discussion with Tre apparently over for the moment. "Surface entrance is up ahead, this is only a guard job, but we need to be alert for anything." His stern gaze landed on Dal and lingered. "Try to avoid pissing off the other Vanguards this time, we can't do this by ourselves."

Dal laughed, "Don't know what you're talking about old man. I'm a delight."

Everyone knew what Ren was referencing. A few days earlier they were in a cleared section with Unit 670, waiting for reinforcements so they could launch an assault and reclaim lost territory, Dal challenged some of them to a game of Knifepoint to pass the time. After a few rounds, he was accused of cheating and a brawl had erupted, three members of Unit 670 were sent back to the city with dislocated shoulders and ruptured eye sockets.

"Everyone quiet," Tre growled. "Why are there no guards on duty here?"

The tunnel was empty, and the chamber just beyond was eerily silent, which was never a good sign.

"I don't like it," Ren said. "Mac is in charge here, he is a bit crazy, but there is no way he would leave one of the tunnels leading into the entrance chamber undefended."

Tre swore under his breath, "Rifles ready, follow me," he said, storming off.

This can't be good, Taj thought. He followed the rest of his unit into the huge chamber and nearly vomited as his nostrils and mouth were filled with the strong pungent aroma of rotting flesh. Nobody else appeared bothered by the stench, so he swallowed the rising bile and kept moving.

Ten portable lights were set up around the area, revealing a main tunnel parallel to the Vanguards, and another off to the side. The surface entrance itself was at the top of a two-hundred-metre-high shaft carved into the roof. Previously inaccessible, the Guild had spent months building the complicated system of steps and ramps which spiralled upward allowing easy access to the surface. Surrounding the stairs was another recent addition, a waist-high barricade with four big guns in each corner.

"Spread out," Tre instructed, "Dal, Taj, go left, check that side tunnel for enemies, it goes deeper into the Labyrinth, so it's important you keep your eyes open. Ace, Ash check the one in front of us, it leads to another surface entrance, but be on guard anyway, the perimeter could have fallen again. Ren, Wes, with me."

Taj and Dal circled around to the tunnel, their rifles up and ready. When they reached the mouth of the passage, Dal went first, stepping across the threshold and shining his weapon light into the endless dark. Taj paused briefly, the smell of death grew stronger the closer he got, *there is something dead nearby.* He added his beam to the search effort, uncovering dozens of rats who squeaked and scurried away from the brightness.

"Can you see anything?" Dal whispered.

Taj shivered, *I hate rats.* "No, nothing but vermin," he said. *Maybe it will stay that way for once.*

"Everyone over here," Tre commanded, "Now."

I may have spoken too soon.

Everybody quickly converged near Tre, who had found the sole occupant of the chamber at the base of the stairs, lying in a pool of blood which had blemished his well-kept, short blonde hair and golden-brown skin. The man's mirror like white armour had a hole punctured straight through the chest, but the most unnerving thing about the find was his bright blue eyes, which were wide open and staring.

"Who is he?" Wes pondered.

"A Surfacer, known as a City Guard, similar to our Watchers," Tre murmured, his lip curling in disgust. "Looks like his heart is missing."

So that's what Surfacers look like, Taj thought, inspecting the body with renewed interest. *Why is his skin so brown?*

"I don't like this commander," Ren grumbled. "Where are the Vanguards who were stationed here? And how did this Surfacer get down here?"

"There was a fire fight," Ash reported, kicking a nearby spent bullet casing. "There is fresh blood in several spots around here, I don't think any of our people left this place alive."

"That doesn't make sense," Tre declared. "How did the creatures strike this deep inside our territory without anybody noticing, the front lines are several kilometres away." The commander paced back and forth, then looked up. The ramshackle stairway to the surface ended at a round hatchway big enough for five people to comfortably walk through at the same time. In times past, the doorway had been blocked with reinforced steel and surrounded by concrete so thick their best weapons couldn't even scratch it. Now only a metal portcullis covered the hole, giving a partially obscured view of the darkened night sky above.

"Whatever did this, didn't bother trying to get to the surface," he said. "Strange… Ace, Ash, get back to Acropolis…."

Ace held up his hand to signal for quiet, then turned his head on its side. If anybody else had been so rude, Tre would have struck them immediately, but they all knew the value of listening to the soft-spoken twins. "I hear something," he warned. "It's coming this way."

A moment later, a screech of rage echoed around the chamber, threatening to drain the courage of everybody who heard the sound. The Vanguards all turned in time to see an eight-legged creature leap out of the tunnel that went deeper into the Labyrinth.

Tre didn't need to give the order, they all knew what to do, all seven rifles blared to life, barraging the creature, it shrieked in pain and shock, before slipping back into the safety of the passage.

"Harpy," Ash said as the gunfire ceased. "Could be more."

"How'd she breach the perimeter?" Ren exclaimed.

"Why don't you go ask her, Ren?" Dal mocked. "I'm sure the old girl would be happy to tell you while she rips your face off."

"Shut it, Dal," Tre thundered. "Ash, you are the fastest, head back towards Acropolis, Jaz and her unit should be on their way here. Find her and get the word out, there are creatures inside the perimeter, we need immediate reinforcements."

Ash gave a pained smile and looked to his brother. They didn't usually baulk at Tre's orders, but anything to do with Jaz seemed to provoke disdain from the identical siblings.

"I don't want to hear it from either of you," Tre bellowed, his voice was gruff, but didn't contain its usual edge, "I know you aren't on the best of terms with her, she is the nearest help, get going, now."

Ash silently walked away; his shoulders bowed. He gave a final look of exasperation before breaking into a run.

"What I wouldn't give to be there when he finds Jaz," Dal said, provoking chuckles of amusement from everyone, including Ace.

Tre's eyes narrowed, and his brow furrowed as he grappled with indecision. "Alright, here is what we are doing," he said after a few more seconds of contemplation. "Ren, Ace, stay here and wait for Ash to get back with help. Get on two of those big guns and make sure nothing gets topside, the rest of you, come with me, we are going after that Harpy."

Ren shook his head. "Wait a moment. Is it wise to split up right now? Shouldn't we wait for help before we go hunting. Our ammunition stores are low, we have no sun flares, we are also out of grenades."

"We can't afford to let that thing escape and wander unchecked

126

behind our lines," Tre insisted. "She could flank our forces, and if we wait, comprise more of the perimeter. It will be tricky spotting her with only our rifle lights, but that's what we are trained for, to adapt and overcome."

"Aye, commander."

Taj, Dal and Wes followed Tre into the tunnel that went deeper into the Labyrinth, while Ace and Ren made ready the defences.

"Keep your eyes on the walls and the roof," Tre cautioned. "They are known to attack from above."

"Great," Taj muttered. He had not fought a Harpy properly yet, his only experiences had been with dead ones killed by others, but he had been told many times about their ferocity and lighting fast ambushes on unsuspecting prey. *This isn't going to end well.*

The end of the tunnel split into three, each passage branching off in a different direction, but it was clear which way they needed to go. A Vanguard was propped up against a wall in the middle path, a gaping hole in his chest.

"Who is it?" Tre asked. "Mac?"

Wes bent down and carefully moved the dead man's head, recoiling when he saw what had been done to the face. Whoever the dead man was, it was impossible to tell, the eyes had been gouged out, and the nose and lips had been gnawed off.

"I can't tell," Wes said, standing back and wiping his hands on his underclothes. "His face is missing, Tre, and I'd wager his heart as well."

"Found another," Dal announced, pointing to a body a few metres away. The man's armour had been torn up along with the rest of him, but there was still enough left to see it was the same design as the City Guard they'd found in the entrance chamber. A white rifle with two prongs at the end and no clip was clutched in what remained of his right hand. Further ahead were the remains of more victims in various states of dismemberment, leaving them a macabre trail to follow.

Wes checked the first two bodies, though it didn't take an expert to know that there was nothing that could be done for any of them. "These two have died recently," he reported, "Can't have been dead more than an hour or two, I'd say the same Harpy killed both."

"What the hell are Surfacers doing down here," Dal said as he shoved past Wes and began trying to wrest one of the two-pronged Surfacer rifles from its former owner. "I thought they hated the Labyrinth and everything in it with a passion."

"Something serious must have happened here to make them risk a trip underground," Tre said. "I just hope there are survivors, so we can ask them what happened. Let's keep moving. Dal, please leave the weapon," he added.

For once, Dal did precisely as he was told, taking his boot off the dead man's face and letting the arm clutching the gun fall back to the ground. Tre had never said 'please' to them before, especially not to Dal.

Something is wrong.

They followed the trail of dead for another hundred metres, until the distinct sound of flesh being torn off bone made Tre signal a stop by holding up a closed fist. "I think it's coming from there, an old storage hall," he whispered, indicating a wide-open doorway cut into the wall with machine precision.

"Do you think there is more than one?" Wes asked. "I seriously doubt a lone Harpy has caused all this carnage."

"Only one way to find out," Tre replied. "Go quietly, wait for my word, then kill anything with more than two legs."

Taj slowly moved toward the door, each step making his muscles twitch in anticipation of the coming battle. Eventually, Wes and Taj waited on one side of the door, while Tre and Dal were on the other. *This is it*, he decided. *That thing isn't getting away again.*

"Now," Tre roared. "Take it down."

The Vanguards burst into the hall, finding a creature the size of a man with eight legs on each side of its fat stocky body crouched in front of them, gorging on a fresh kill. The Harpy's small flat ears pricked up, then it sprang into the air, latching onto the roof with the bone hooks at the end of its long gangly limbs. The creature's black sunken eyes darted between each of the Vanguards as they opened fire, then it shrieked and scurried away, disappearing somewhere in the dark, trailing yellow blood in its wake.

"Cease fire," Tre ordered. "We will need to lure it out of hiding."

Wes took the lull in hostilities to quickly check on the Harpy's victim, his grave demeanour betraying the unfortunate man's fate.

"Dead, only recently though, hearts gone too, like the others," the medic said, wringing his gore covered hands.

"They eat hearts?" Dal said, his voice cracking to a slightly higher pitch. "What for?"

"Harpy's love hearts, they will keep eating them until they are sick, then go back for more," Wes explained. "Nobody knows why, I guess it's a delicacy for them."

"Remember Old Ryn's story about Sif the Sorrowful?" Taj teased. "Maybe she was actually telling the truth."

"Enough chatter," Tre interrupted. "We need to find that thing and kill it, Wes, you and the boy head right, I'll take Dal left, keep to the edges, it is most likely hanging off a wall, waiting to strike."

Wes nodded and walked away. Taj smiled weakly at Dal, and quickly ran to catch up. *I don't like this, we shouldn't be splitting up.* It became clear after starting their search, that the storage hall was far grander than any of them realised, even with their weapon lights working in unison, they couldn't see everything in their field of vision, and the end still wasn't in sight.

What I would give for a sun flare.

The flickering light beams to their left signalled Tre and Dal's progress; the duo following a parallel path on the other side of the hall.

"It might already be gone," Wes mumbled. "These buggers will generally only attack if they have the advantage."

Is that why Tre told us to split up, to lure it out? Taj pondered. *Is he using us as bait?*

He didn't have long to consider the idea, his light passed over an arm on the ground in front of them, the hand clutched a knife and dried blood trailed off into the dark.

"You see that, Wes?" he said, holding his light on the severed limb.

"Careful," the medic cautioned. "This creature is clever."

Before Taj could reply, a Harpy sprang out of the dark, bowling Wes to the ground and shrieking as it's two front legs raised, preparing to maul the helpless man with the vicious hooks on the end of its limbs.

Taj reacted without thinking, blasting the creature with three of the most accurate and deadly shots he had ever fired in his life. The first two struck it in the chest, and a third hit it right between its cold, dark sunken eyes. It fell without a sound, crumpling in a heap next to the visibly relieved Wes.

He wasted no time in checking the kill, pressing the warm barrel of his rifle into the Harpy's face and waiting patiently for a reaction. The many-legged creatures were known to play dead, and there were more than a few Vanguards who bore scars from being drawn in by the deception.

Taj lightly caressed his trigger, wincing as the Harpy's grey clammy skin sizzled under the heat from his weapon. When it didn't stir, he was confident that it wouldn't be getting back up, and wandered over to Wes, grunting as he helped lift him back to his feet.

"Looks like I owe you one, Taj," Wes muttered. "That thing came out of nowhere."

The medic bent down, his face suddenly becoming grave. "How many times did you shoot it?" he asked.

"Three, two in the chest, one in the head," Taj replied, his voice betraying a touch of pride at the feat.

"This isn't the one we were hunting, it's only been shot three times," Wes stammered, indicating the three holes on its body. "We clipped the other one several times, it was trailing blood. There is at least one more Harpy here, maybe more."

They both tensed as gunfire exploded on the other side of the chamber, followed by the shriek of another creature being gunned down by their comrades.

"Got it," Dal called out, his calm indifferent voice trailing across the vast expanse between them.

"We killed one too," Taj shouted back.

"Keep searching the area then," Tre ordered. "We need to make sure there aren't more, they might be trying to make a nest here, we can't allow that."

If there is another one, I bet I know where it is. Taj found the severed arm and followed the trail of dried blood. He found the rest of the body only forty metres away, and the sight almost made him vomit.

So that's where the smell is coming from.

Wes saw what Taj had uncovered and swore loudly, his voice wavering.

"Tre, Dal get over here, you need to see this."

Chapter Eleven

The Creatures' Snare

The four Vanguards stood around the giant pile of flesh and bone, transfixed by the grisly sight. Every corpse had been mauled beyond all recognition, the only indication of who lay amongst the dead was the twisted scraps of City Guard and Vanguard armour that clung to the larger pieces of flesh.

"It's a killing field," Taj said, breaking the silence that had reigned since the gruesome discovery.

"Looks like we won't be finding any survivors," Tre mused, his voice betraying a deep sadness.

"Did you know someone here?" Wes asked.

"My sister's boy," Tre lamented, "It was his first time out, he was so proud to be going on his first mission, even if it was only guard duty."

No one said a word, they had all lost family before, either to disease, infection or creature attack; death was the only constant in the underground.

"No point in dwelling, his death can't be stopped now," Tre continued. "I'm not sure what did this, but if it can kill this many armed men, we will need help to take it down."

Taj's mind immediately drifted to his growing obsession, there hadn't been any sign of the yellow eyed monster in weeks, now he wagered, it was back.

Unit 6 must have failed, or maybe there really is more than one of these things.

"It looks like these bodies have been placed here from somewhere else," Wes said, pointing to the bloody drag marks that came from all different directions and converged where the pile sat. "I don't know anything that groups its food in once place like this."

The shriek of more Harpies ended the rest of the conversation, and a collective shiver went down each of their spines. *Sounds like a whole pack.*

"Call out when you spot one," Tre commanded. "We can't let them get close or they will tear us apart."

Taj's hands jittered, so he tightened his grip on his rifle to keep them steady. *We need to get out of here.* He nervously flashed his light upward, catching two Harpies scurrying across the roof in front of him.

"Two," he shouted, opening fire a second later. He sprayed bullets in an arc, fear giving way to precision in a stark contrast to his earlier encounter, but his foes were ready for him and evaded the attack by darting aside and hiding in the shadows.

"I see four more," Dal reported.

"Three," Wes added.

The creature's circled the Vanguards with dizzying speed, Taj fired until his rifle was empty, but despite his best efforts, he failed to hit a single target. *How do they move so fast?* Just as his gun clicked, signalling the last bullet had left the chamber, a lone Harpy broke off from the pack and charged, its two front legs slashing the air, seeking warm flesh to dig into.

He cursed and reloaded, the voice of the Vanguard Grandmaster repeating in his head. *Remember to breathe, aim carefully, don't rush the shot, you have a few seconds,* Jye had told him at Agora.

Taj took a deep breath and aimed down the sight, his hammering heart blocking out all other noise. He lightly squeezed the trigger, and to his surprise, the shot went through the creature's head, exploding the back of its skull and spraying the roof with blood and brains. The remaining Harpies quickly dispersed, their shrieking getting steadily further away until all was quiet.

"What happened?" Dal demanded, "Did they just run away?"

"I think this may have been a trap," Tre guessed, ignoring Dal's questions. "And we fell for the snare, they are getting smarter."

If this was a trick to get us here, then why did they leave before killing us? Taj wondered. Then it started, the sound he hoped to never hear again. It began with a deep rumbling, just like always, then rose to a thundering roar that sounded like laughter. Tre and the others started yelling something, but he couldn't hear them over the din.

A shimmering dark spot moved in front of him, and he blinked, unsure if his eyes were playing tricks. When he looked back, a big pair of yellow angular eyes attached to a nightmarish grey monster materialized out of thin air. Unlike his previous encounter, he could see it perfectly. The monster stood over seven feet tall, and had dark veins snaking around its thick muscular body. Its smooth hairless face was contorted into a hideous mockery of a grin, revealing black gums and a double set of pointed triangle teeth that it caressed with a red forked tongue.

Taj's whole body went numb, and he lost all perception of what was happening around him. He wanted to shoot, but his hands refused to move, all he could do was stare into the bright yellow eyes of death. His comrades didn't hesitate, and the next thing he knew, Tre, Dal and Wes were either side of him, weapons firing. Their bullets tore through the monster's flesh, spraying black blood in an arc, but it didn't fall. The two slits above the monster's mouth flared, and five knife-like claws extended on each hand.

It's not going down; they need my help.

Taj shook his head, breaking the transfixing gaze. The monster roared and vanished in a flash.

"Where did it go?" Dal exclaimed. "How did it do that?"

"It can camouflage itself somehow, hide in plain sight," Tre said. "We need reinforcements, the four of us won't be able to kill this thing by ourselves."

Not even Dal felt the need to argue, and they ran from the storage hall. For once Taj and Dal were in the lead, while Tre and Wes hung back a little, the experienced veterans watching for pursuers.

"What the hell was that thing? Our bullets didn't seem to bother it," Dal babbled.

"That's an understatement, it hardly even flinched when you shot it," Taj replied while nervously looking around. *If it can go invisible like that, it can move around virtually unnoticed, this thing is more dangerous than I thought.*

Dal stopped, his brow creased as though he were pondering something of great importance.

Taj slowed, "What are you doing?"

Dal muttered something under his breath, and then he was in the air, launched into the wall with such force it shattered his rifle, littering the ground with the debris.

Without thinking, Taj started toward Dal's motionless form, swearing in annoyance as rough hands held him back.

"Let me go," he screamed, thrashing with all his strength against the firm grip.

"Wait, Taj," Tre whispered. "Look at Dal, tell me what you see."

Taj gritted his teeth, *this isn't time for a lesson,* he wanted to yell, but the voice of reason came swift and loud. *Tre wouldn't be doing this unless it was important.*

He ceased his struggles, and looked down at his fallen friend, squinting in the gloom. The air above Dal shimmered, as though smoke were billowing out from a nearby fire, and in that moment, he knew with a cold certainty that Tre had just saved his life, again.

It's there, waiting for us to try and save Dal. Idiot.

The grey monster reappeared, letting out one of its deep laugh-like roars, almost like it was trying to provoke them. *Is it toying with us?*

When nobody took the bait, the monster vanished.

"I think it's gone this time," Tre said as he released Taj and cautiously shuffled toward Dal, his rifle aimed where the monster had been.

Taj held his breath, *if that thing is still there, Tre is dead.*

The commander paused every two metres, and fired one shot, waiting for a reaction before he continued. When he finally made it to Dal, he sprayed one final burst, before signalling for Wes. "I think we are clear, Wes, grab your kit, Taj, watch our backs."

Taj turned, unable to look at his fallen friend anymore, but his gun barrel brushed up against something solid. The grey monster appeared in front of him.

"You are all going to die," hummed a growling, breathless voice.

Chapter Twelve
Berserkers

"Dal, can you hear me?" Wes shouted as he held a cloth to an angry red wound on Dal's head, blood gushed around the makeshift bandage and refused to stop. The rest of Unit 17, along with Jaz and her Harpies watched in silence as the medic tried to stop the bleeding.

Taj stood in front of everyone else, lightly banging his head with a closed fist, making promises to gods he didn't believe existed to spare his friend from death. *Whatever is up there, whoever is listening, please don't let him die.*

Dal hadn't moved since they brought him out of the tunnels and back to the surface entrance, and none of them had spoken about what had happened with the monster.

"I sent Captain Rax and his unit to gather more Vanguards," Jaz said to Tre, her voice low and serious. "He shouldn't be much longer." Tre nodded. "The Terror Twins are on their way too," she added. "Unfortunately, they were nearby when Ash found us, soon those two lunatics will be on the hunt."

Everyone shifted uncomfortably at the news.

"What happened to Dal?" Jaz asked, "And to the guards who were stationed here? I had a look at these big guns, and they haven't fired a shot," she said, pointing at the four cannons that were positioned in the corners of the fortifications beneath the stairs.

Tre shook his head. "Another time Jaz, honestly, I'm not even sure where to begin."

Jaz raised the muscles where her eyebrows should have been, it was a subtle movement, but it was more telling than any words could be.

"I've stemmed the bleeding," Wes announced, lifting the cloth slightly off Dal's head, and showing that the flow of blood had finally stopped. "Miss Ava, could you please use your staple gun to seal the wound."

Ava, the Harpies medic scowled and started fumbling in the tool pouch at her belt, "Sure, but make sure you hold him, if he starts thrashing about, he's liable to take one in the eye."

Like the rest of her sisters, Ava had long brown hair and green eyes, but her slight frame and thin physique were a stark contrast to rest of the heavily muscled and athletic looking members of her unit. She removed the staple gun from her pouch and crouched down, waiting for Wes to hold Dal's head steady before she pressed the device to the wound.

The click of the medical gun was relatively quiet, but Taj couldn't help but wince. *I always hate this part.* The sound flooded him with memories of pain, and a reminder of the many times Sai had to seal his wounds with the small devices.

"Was it the thing Jye warned the Vanguard leadership about? Did a Husker attack you?" Jaz asked Tre, restarting her previous conversation with the commander. "He said they were on the move."

Taj's ears pricked up.

Did she just say Husker? Perhaps Jye found information on them in the chest of records after all.

Tre sighed, "I think so," he conceded. "I have never seen anything like it in all my years, the speed, power, endurance, we hit it with enough fire power to kill a Slammer and it barely even flinched."

"What do you want to do then? If this Husker, or whatever it is, can't be injured by our weapons, should we really go after it?

"Give me another go at it," a weak voice chimed in. "I'm going to need a new rifle though."

Everyone turned to Dal, who was fighting to sit up despite

Wes's best attempts to hold him down.

"Stay still, otherwise Ava said she'd take your eye out," Wes said with a grin. "You're bloody lucky to get away with only a bump to the head."

Dal swore under his breath, "Hurry up then, this is already embarrassing enough, I should have seen it, how the hell did it appear like that?"

Taj's eyes darted between his friend and Tre, waiting to see if the commander divulged anything else about their new foe, but it appeared he was done revealing secrets for one day. *At least Dal is alright.* He would never admit it out loud but losing his best friend would crush him.

Ava sat back, taking a second to admire her handy work before re-joining her sisters. "Perfect," she said. "Some of my best art to date."

Dal slowly got back to his feet, swaying slightly as he poked at the fresh metal staples in his head.

"Looks like your thick skull saved you this time, Dal," Taj teased. "I feel sorry for the wall though, probably didn't know what hit it."

"What happened to the monster?" Dal hissed, his words slightly slurred. "Did it run away?"

"Not sure," Taj admitted. "After it knocked you, the damn thin vanished into thin air." "*But not before it threatened us*", he wanted to say, but he held his tongue. *How do I tell them that without sounding like I've lost my mind?*

"Maybe it let you go," Jaz suggested. "I've seen Butchers on the hunt injure scouting Lurkers and follow the blood trail back to the rest of the pack. Perhaps this Husker is attempting a similar tactic."

It wasn't a pleasant thought, but nobody was able to dwell for long, the thunder of heavy footsteps caught all their attention. A moment later, over twenty reddish creatures burst into the chamber from the same tunnel the Harpies had retreated down earlier.

"Berserkers," Ren barked. "A whole pack."

None of the creatures was under six foot, and their grotesquely muscled bodies rippled as they growled and howled at the Vanguards. The Alpha Berserker, which was a full head taller than the others, pushed its way to the front of the pack, ramming its brethren with the bone appendage on its forehead, snorting a fine mist out of the small holes it had for nostrils.

"Everyone to the barricades," Tre ordered. "Ash, Ace, get on the left big gun, fire on my command. Taj, help Dal."

"Jen, Liv, you have the right big gun," Jaz said to her Harpies.

The others sprang into action, taking up positions along the barricades, their rifles aimed at the interlopers. Taj grabbed Dal by the shoulder and led him back to the defences. The injured Vanguards eyes were glassy, and after he tried to wander in the wrong direction twice, Taj began to realise his friend was far from alright. *It's like he's drunk.*

No sooner had they reached the barricade, the Alpha howled, and the pack charged, thundering toward the entrenched Vanguards.

"Open fire," Jaz and Tre shouted in unison.

Three creatures fell under the first barrage and were trampled underfoot by the rest of their pack, another two were killed in front of the barricades. The rest lowered their heads as they reached the fortifications, using the bone appendage on their heads to crash through, sending stinging chunks of stone and metal flying.

The Vanguards scattered, forcing Taj to grab Dal by the arm and drag him away from the path of the rampaging Berserkers. Dal tried to draw his pistol, but his clumsy hands struggled to find the holster at his side.

"Dal can't fight like this," Taj realised. *Need to get him somewhere safe.* He glanced around, but Berserkers blocked every escape route. Jaz and her Harpies unsheathed their blades, falling on the closest enemies with savage strikes, cutting through flesh and muscle with alarming efficiency. Tre, Ren and Wes quickly entered the fray as well, blasting anything that came too close, while the twins darted around displaying dizzying acrobatics as they fired their weapons.

Taj looked past the unfolding battle to the stairs and a memory stirred in him of an early morning training session with Doc. "If in doubt, take the high ground," he had cackled. "You'd be surprised how being slightly higher than your opponent can change things."

They look pretty high. He grabbed Dal by the collar of his undershirt and lead the unsteady Vanguard through the chaos. Ava and Jaz ran past, locked in vicious close quarters combat with a Berserker. The sisters worked as a team, Ava acting as a distraction while Jaz lunged underneath and stabbed at the creature's vitals. Despite the blood pouring down its sides, the cumbersome creature still fought on.

Taj navigated around the fight, passing Ace and Ash who were shooting a downed foe at point blank range in the back of the head. He passed a decapitated Berserker, and finally reached the stairs, pushing Dal up the first flight.

Dal stumbled but managed to steady himself by holding his arms out. "Where are we Taj?" he slurred.

I think Wes will need to have another look at him. "Stay there, if anything gets past me, jump off the stairs."

Taj didn't wait to see if Dal understood and retuned his focus to the battle. A Berserker, uninterested in the melee, circled around, and lowered its head, lining him up with the bone on its forehead. *I don't know if I can get a headshot.* His eyes wandered to its stubby legs. *Shooting out the Slammers legs worked, I don't see why the tactic shouldn't work again.*

The Berserker howled, stomping past its dying brethren. Taj fired his rifle until it was empty. Some of his shots bounced harmlessly off the bone appendage, but many found their way to the creature's knees, shattering them and forcing the Berserker to fall. It thrashed and spluttered but couldn't stand back up.

An abnormally large Berserker stormed past, two of its fellows in hot pursuit.

The Alpha. Time to go.

"Dal, jump," Taj yelled as he leapt off the side of the steps, rolling to absorb the impact. Dal landed next to him, groaning as he collapsed. Taj spun around, ready to shoot the advancing Berserkers as they tried to follow, but they had no interest in him anymore. The ramshackle stairs groaned and creaked under the weight but otherwise held as the enraged creatures' ran toward the surface.

He cursed, realising his mistake too late. *They weren't after me, I shouldn't have moved, idiot.* The Alpha reached the portcullis and rammed into the metal with a full head of steam. The barrier proved no match for the attack and bent outward, with nothing else barring their way, the creatures went through the entrance, disappearing from sight.

Taj bent down and helped Dal back to his feet. *This could start a war.*

Wes and Ace waded through the carnage and attempted to pursue the escaped Berserkers, but the two men stopped dead on the bottom step, as though they were frozen in place by some invisible force. The rest of the creatures were dead or dying, and the Vanguards assembled for new orders. Taj let Dal lean on him, and the two hobbled over to listen to what Tre had planned next.

"Jaz, keep your unit here, make sure nothing else gets through," Tre ordered. "Everyone else, we are going up there and hunting those things down."

"I don't know if that is wise, Tre," Jaz said. "The surface leaders, the Directors, have forbidden our people from leaving the underground without permission, this could start a war."

A flash of anger crossed Tre's face, he hated being questioned

142

by subordinates at the best of times, but in a combat situation he was likely to turn violent. Only a month prior, Taj had seen him break a man's arm, the fool was from another unit and had argued with Tre about the best way to clear a creature nest, needless to say, the attack went ahead with one man less that day.

The Harpy leader wasn't intimidated in the slightest and defiantly stared down the simmering commander. She clicked her tongue in annoyance, waiting for a response that was slow in coming. "Glower all you want, you know I'm right," she said.

"I know, Jaz," Tre eventually growled. "But the City Guard have never faced a Berserker before, let alone an Alpha, if we do nothing, many Surfacers will die and that will cause far more problems than us going topside."

Jaz rubbed her shaven head, "I know, but I still think it's a mistake to do this," she said through a pained smile. "Just remember, if the Directors catch you up there, they'll kill you."

Chapter Thirteen

The Surface

Taj shielded his eyes from the sudden influx of stinging light as he took his first step into the surface city, Alexandria. After a few seconds of blinking and watery eyes, he caught a blurred glimpse of what lay in front of him, his jaw dropped. The surface entrance exited into a well-lit courtyard made of white marble, surrounded by massive multi-storey buildings disappearing into an eerily orange sky. Five streets branched out of the courtyard, leading deeper into Alexandria.

The mangled remains of at least a dozen City Guard were laid out across the area, but Taj only had eyes for the structures which were made from a reflective material that glowed with the light of a thousand torches. "How did they build something so large? They are even bigger than the Amphitheatre in Acropolis," he said to himself.

The rest of his companions were similarly captivated by the size and scope of the city, even the always ill-tempered Tre managed a sly smile as they all cried out in wonder. Taj laughed, but the sudden intake of air made his throat tickle, and he coughed.

Even the air smells different up here.

"All right enough gawking," Tre said breaking the spell they were all under. "We have a job to do. Wes, you stay here with Dal and protect the surface entrance, the rest of us will follow one of these streets out of here and try to find the creatures. It's currently night, so most of the city's population will be asleep, the streets should be clear."

144

A flying vehicle screeched overhead, making more noise than a hundred Harpies combined, and leaving a trail of white smoke. It was so fast that Taj didn't get a good look, but he had heard the stories of the technological marvels the Surfacers possessed, he hadn't truly believed them though.

How is that possible, for something to fly like that?

"Watch your shots up here," Ren cautioned. "Clipping someone will likely start a whole mess of trouble, and none of us need that headache to deal with. If you find the Berserkers, do what you can, kill them, or make enough noise to attract attention."

When the old Vanguard had finished speaking, he began to cough and splutter. "Damn tickle in my throat," he wheezed. "The air up here doesn't smell right, there is something about it."

"The Surfacers purify the air in their city with devices scattered around their city, similar to the air vents in the Labyrinth, but obviously far more advanced," Tre explained. "Without them, the pollution would make it too toxic to breath, our people aren't used to it, the Healers have been trying to find a solution for the last few months. Just try to ignore it, there hasn't been any ill effects reported from breathing it."

So that's why my throat itches.

Taj took a deep breath, trying to discern the difference. *It doesn't smell like death and decay up here,* he realised. *I've lived with the smell for so long, I didn't even know I'd gotten used to it.*

"Move out," Tre instructed. "We need to be gone before first light to avoid catching the sun sickness."

The Vanguards all shuddered at the name. They had all seen the vicious red burns and chronic vomiting that came along with the newly discovered ailment. Many traders at the Boondocks had already sickened, and in some extreme cases, died. A lifetime of living underground had left them ill suited to dealing with real sunlight.

Dal and Wes stayed by the entrance that went back into the

underground, a gaping hole in the courtyard that looked out of place in the clinically clean and bright city. Taj waited for the rest of the unit to pick a path, before he ran over to the remaining one on the other side of the courtyard. He glanced back and saw Wes holding up three fingers in front of Dal, it was clear from the shake of his head that the medic had discovered how severely injured the younger Vanguard was.

I hope Wes can help him, in his current state, he won't last long in a fight.

Taj ran down the street, doing his best to scan everywhere before moving on, but after a few metres, he quickly realised the folly of his search. The street was ten metres wide, and despite his best efforts the end was nowhere in sight. Either side buildings of various sizes loomed, some were of similar size and scope as the ones at the surface entrance, while others were only a few storeys high, but every single one of them provided a hundred possible hiding spots for the creatures.

We will never find them in this place.

Every so often, another street branched off, leading in a different direction, but he decided against getting off his current path.

Otherwise I might get lost, I'm not even sure if I can find my way back from here.

The street eventually opened into a park that rolled across the wide-open space and stopped just short of the buildings, which circled the space like great unmoving guardians. Taj's jaw dropped, impossibly green grass made up most of the park, along with flowers of every colour he could think of, and a few he didn't know existed, set out in square grids surrounded by waist height hedges. A large lake with a thin curved structure arching over it lay in the centre.

This is a paradise, if you put all of Acropolis's food and other vegetation together, it might equal half of this.

He carefully walked out onto the lush grass, stopping to touch it every couple of steps. He couldn't see anyone else around but kept scanning the surroundings.

I can't see any Berserker tracks, but that doesn't mean they aren't here.

The closer he got to the lake though, the more his thoughts shifted away from his mission, and focused on the plant life. He picked up a nearby bright red flower and instantly regretted it, recoiling as his fingers touched the jagged spines on the thin green stem. "Is this some sort of defence system?" he pondered. "They should grow the spines bigger then, it will barely break the skin as it is."

He left the rest of the flowers alone and continued to the lake, gazing around in wonder at the great body of water. When he looked back, his face went warm as he saw the path of destruction he had carved. Deep boot prints dotted the landscape, exposing the dirt beneath, he'd also managed to crush nearly every flower on the way, his clumsy feet apparently drawn to the delicate plants.

"Idiot," he muttered. "I've only been up here for an hour, and I've already destroyed something, if Tre finds out, he'll kill me."

He sighed in annoyance, and crouched down on the grassy bank, running his coarse grimy hands through the fresh, soothing water.

I wonder if I can drink this, I bet it doesn't have that stiff metallic pump taste our water has, it's probably fresh.

He briefly considered filling up his water bottle, but a man and woman strolled into view, appearing from behind some shrubbery a few metres away from the lake. Their arms were linked, and they were chatting merrily.

Taj eagerly got back to his feet and waited to greet them. Like the dead City Guard, the newcomers both had golden brown skin, blond hair, and blue eyes. However, neither of them were wearing armour, instead the man was dressed in loose fitting black clothing.

While his female companion wore a figure-hugging red dress that showed her taut frame in vivid detail.

Taj raised a hand in greeting. "Hello," he said awkwardly. "Can you help me? I'm looking for something."

The Surfacers froze, their faces masks of pure terror, the man raised his right fist threateningly, and nervously twirled his pencil thin moustache with his left hand.

"What is that thing," he shouted as the pair began to back away.

"Call the City Guard," his female companion shrieked. "Kill it, before it eats us."

The two Surfacers ran away at full pelt, flicking mud and foliage as they retreated back into the city.

The Berserkers are here, Taj decided, raising his rifle and looking around the park for the hulking red brutes. Nothing was in sight, and he frowned, unsure what had happened.

What did they run away for? His eyes drifted over the water and he caught sight of a shape, it all became very clear.

His reflection showed a pale muscled youth dressed all in black and covered in fresh blood. *I look like a monster*, he realised. *No wonder they ran.* All his happiness was sucked away in an instant, along with any delusions of exploring the garden. The only thing that remained was one cold hard fact: *I don't belong here.*

Taj left the park with a heavy heart; *I will probably never see anything like this again. I almost wish I hadn't found it, now I know what I'm missing.*

He had one last look at the paradise, taking in every detail of the serene image. When he couldn't bear to see it anymore, he trudged back into Alexandria's streets, returning to the hunt.

His next encounter with a Surfacer ended like the first, the woman strolled down the street, singing to herself. He was about to offer a greeting when she screamed and ran back the way she had come.

I hope the others are having better luck.

A short time later, he came across another marble courtyard similar to the one that contained the entrance back into the underground, except for one key difference, an elaborate twenty-foot-tall statue shaped like a man took up most of the space. In its prime, Taj guessed it would have been quite a sight to behold, but neglect had left the face chipped, and the body wrapped in red vines which snaked around like ropes.

Why would they bother to build something like this and not maintain it, seems like a waste.

He approached the effigy, but stopped in his tracks when he saw something he was all too familiar with. The corpse lay across the footpath next to the statue, the Berserker had mangled all their identifying features beyond recognition, and blood flowed freely from many wounds to the chest and legs, pooling on the marble,

Looks fresh, it's probably still nearby. "Where are their City Guard?" he muttered.
"If this were Acropolis, there would be at least ten units of Watchers converging on this spot right now."

We could have marched an army up here and conquered their city, an unhelpful voice hissed maliciously in the back of his mind.

"Death doesn't pay for life," he argued out loud. "We can't kill them and destroy their homes, it wouldn't be right."

Why not? If you believe your histories, they took everything from your ancestors, you would just be returning the favour.

"What's the meaning of this?" someone commanded, thankfully interrupting his internal argument.

The speaker was of a similar age to Doc, her lined face and measured gait betraying many years of life. Like the former Vanguard Grandmaster, the Surfacer had a wily twinkle in her green eyes that bespoke of a sharp mind. She slowly strolled over to him, her blue dress reflecting the light as she observed the scene with a hawk like gaze.

Three men that looked a little older than Taj followed behind her in matching black suits. Their appearance was the same as all the other Surfacers he had encountered so far—light fair hair and golden-brown skin. None appeared to be armed, although he was standing near a corpse, so he still had his rifle ready, just in case the need to defend himself arose.

"I didn't kill him," Taj insisted, pointing at the dead Surfacer to illustrate the fact.

"Well, that's painfully apparent," the elderly woman snapped. "Do all the people from the underground feel the need to point out the obvious, or just you?"

Taj snorted, trying and failing to hide a laugh. *It seems she is armed after all, her quick wits have probably felled many foes over the years.*

"And what may I ask is so funny," she demanded as though talking to a disobedient child. "If you're not going to fire that thing, put the gun away, boy, before someone gets hurt." Her tone was scathing, but polite.

I don't think they mean me any harm, better not cause any more trouble.

Taj slung his rifle, which prompted the woman to nod in satisfaction, making her greying heart shaped hairstyle bob up and down in slow precise movements.

"Now what is the meaning of all this?" She said, pointing to the body on the footpath. "Have your lot finally gotten the nerve to invade? About time if you ask me, you should have done it sooner; we've needed a bit of excitement around here. It's been far too boring for too long."

"Don't bother with him, grandmother," one of the young men chimed in. "He is nothing, a Subrat and probably a liar, like the rest of his ilk."

The woman swiftly backhanded her grandson, betraying a speed and dexterity of someone half her age. "If I wanted your

150

opinion, Valmus, I would tell it to you," she chided, glaring at all three of her grandchildren. "I never want to hear any of you use that vile slur in my presence again. Just because they had the misfortune to be born into poverty does not mean they are lesser beings. Perhaps I should send you home with this Vanguard, you can get a taste of what life is like outside of my walls."

Taj watched in stunned silence, he had never expected a Surfacer to defend him, let alone against her own family. *If there are more like her, willing to stand up for what is right, maybe there is hope for peace after all.*

The woman touched her hair, checking it was still in place before returning her attention to Taj.

"Now, what do you have to say for yourself?" she asked, her tone was softer, but still had a sharpness to it that made Taj feel like he was a child being chastised.

He shifted uncomfortably on the balls of his feet, eager to be away. "Three Berserkers have invaded," he explained. "Where are your soldiers? There are too few of us to check the whole city, we need help."

The woman cackled. "Our soldiers are all gone, we are left with nothing but City Guard, and you'll be lucky to find any of those useless sacks tonight, they'll be somewhere parading around in their polished white armour like they own the place."

She produced a small square device from the folds of her dress and began tapping it, the contraption lit up at her touch.

"Seems they might already know about you," she said to him. "There is a report of a disturbance in one of the first district's gardens, and all available squads are being called in. They are advising everyone in the first district to stay indoors, not that it matters at this hour. No mention of your beasts, perhaps they are in another district."

"How many districts are there?" he asked. *If we knew how big the search area was, it would make finding those creatures much easier.*

"Four," she replied curtly. "You have just entered the second district, make sure—" The rest of her reply was drowned out by a loud chorus of screams from nearby, the three young Surfacers shrunk in fear at the unfamiliar sound, but their grandmother didn't even flinch.

"I'm no expert, but I'd check over there," she suggested. "It sounds like your beasts have crashed the banquet for that self-important fool, Tarnas. What kind of idiot throws an all-night party for getting a medal he awarded himself? He is nearly as bad as that one." She pointed at the dilapidated statue. "Evander the Great, founder of Alexandria, and a self-important windbag from what I hear."

Taj smiled politely, unsure when social convention would allow him to excuse himself. *I don't want to offend her, but I really need to go.*

"Don't just stand there gawking like a fool," she eventually thundered. "Stop lazing about and go do what you are here for, the Banquet Pyramid is the next street over."

He nodded, and exited the courtyard, grateful to be gone from the women's presence.

She reminds me of Tre, but somehow more intimidating.

He ran along the street, frantically looking for a way through the impenetrable wall of buildings as the screams in the distance increased in pitch and frequency. Every door he went to was bolted shut, and when he pressed his face up against the glass to look inside, all he could see was darkness.

Where is everyone? I probably should have asked that woman for directions.

Cursing under his breath, he continued down the street, searching for a gap he could squeeze through.

This place is like our city, the buildings are built up on each other, taking up every spare space.

Just when he considered going back to find the old women and ask for her help, he spied an opening nestled between two towering structures. The darkened alley wasn't much wider than the dirt tracks that weaved through Acropolis, and like many of those paths, the stench of fresh urine wafted out.

Taj took a breath and went into the alley, splashing through what he hoped was water. The buildings blocked out all other light, and he nervously looked around, the darkened passage giving him the uncomfortable sensation of being back underground.

Not ideal, this is a perfect spot for an ambush, but who knows how long it will take me to find another way round.

He flicked his rifle torch on and kept a steady pace, only stopping to jump over discarded junk. The screaming steadily grew louder, and he knew with a cold certainty that at least one of the Berserkers was waiting for him up ahead. When he reached the end of the alley, he paused, checking his gun was still loaded, then leapt out, ready for a fight.

He rotated his weapon around, waiting for a roar or a snarl that would let him know where the creature was, but the Berserker wasn't nearby. What lay in front of him still provoked some stuttered swearing though.

All the streets angled upward to an enormous pyramid which glowed gold, lighting up the entire area in blinding light. The tip of the pyramid was still dwarfed by some of the large buildings around it, but it was still one of the largest things Taj had ever seen. A hysterical crowd of Surfacers were streaming out the front and running off into the city, while a roar and the sound of furniture being broken came from within.

Must be inside.

He sprinted up the incline, pushing through the throng of people. Some politely moved out of his way, while others just stared, or muttered insults. He tried to smile and appear at ease, but every survival instinct he had was yelling at him to get away.

I can handle one, maybe two by myself, but definitely not three. I hope the others are close, otherwise this could go very badly for me.

He passed through the open entranceway, entering a cavernous round room. Thousands of small lights adorned the walls, and dozens of mirror-like tables decorated with food and drink were placed strategically around the space, with the grandest being on the raised centre stage. Either side of the raised platform, slabs of meat roasted over glowing rods spreading the sweet scent of cooking meat.

Only a handful of Surfacers remained, scurrying away from the Alpha Berserker which had broken through a wall and was lumbering around. It snorted and sprayed a fine mist as its double clawed hands grasped around for a victim.

Why did it have to be the Alpha?

"Run," Taj shouted at the nearest Surfacers, who hadn't moved and were instead standing in a huddled group. "Don't just stand there, you useless fools."

What the hell is wrong with them?

The Alpha snarled and closed in a young couple, the man yelled and threw nearby cutlery, but the creature wasn't bothered by the feeble attack. The Berserker slowed, a flood of drool cascading out if its mouth, savouring the terror of its prey before the kill.

Taj let out a slow breath and closed his left eye while looking down the sight and lining up Berserker with his right. *I better not miss this time.* He lightly squeezed the trigger, and a lone bullet launched into the creatures heavily muscled back, it howled, abandoning the young couple and turning to see who had shot it.

Need to get it away from them, then I can hit it with everything I've got.

"Over here, you ugly bastard," he yelled, peppering it with a few more precise shots. "Dinner time, right here, come and get it."

His ploy worked, and the Berserker stomped toward him, lowering its head for a bone shattering charge. Taj threw caution to the wind and emptied his entire hundred bullet clip, spraying his enraged foe until it stumbled and slid the last metre, landing at his feet.

Another close call, I don't even know where I hit it.

He reloaded his weapon and circled his defeated enemy. Despite the danger, several people still lingered, eyeing him and the creature with equal looks of disgust and fear. He wanted to shout at them again, but thought better of it.

Stay focused, don't get distracted. Check the kill and get out of here.

One Surfacer was apart from the rest, her elfin features relaxed and emotionless. Like most of her people, she had golden brown skin but her blazing green eyes and jet black hair made her instantly stand out in a crowd. Taj tried and failed to avert his gaze; he knew it was rude to stare, but his interest was piqued. Her figure hugging blue dress revealed the slim and toned physique of an athlete, but it was her complete disinterest in the Berserker that fascinated him the most. Everyone else was fixated on the creature, but her attention was on the gaping hole left where it had burst inside.

What a strange girl, she doesn't seem afraid at all.

Her eyes abruptly darted over, and he felt his face grow warm. He involuntarily raised his hand in a clumsy greeting, she scowled and crossed her toned arms. *Maybe I should go say hello, it couldn't hurt to explain the situation, maybe she can help me find the other two?*

Taj took one step, and the next thing he knew, his legs were swept out from underneath him. After a few seconds of dizzying vertigo, his body slammed into the ground, dislodging his rifle. The bloodied Alpha Berserker leered over him, gums drawn back in a snarl, and he heard the words that had been drummed into him a hundred times. *Never take your eyes off the target until you've confirmed the kill.*

The Alpha lunged, its dual claws aiming straight for his stomach. He arched his back and drove both his feet into its jaw, wincing as his knees jarred from the impact with the dense bones. The creature recoiled from the blow, giving Taj enough time to roll back into a prone position and grab his pistol. He pulled it from the holster and fired one shot before the Berserker slammed its forehead into his sternum, sending him flying into a nearby table.

The furniture shattered under his weight, sending fist sized pieces whistling in all directions like shrapnel. He gingerly crawled off the remains of the table, his body aching with the promise of more pain to come.

Why aren't I dead, a hit like that should have crushed my chest. His pistol now lost as well, he pulled out his twin curved knives and waited for the next assault. The Berserker kneeled a few metres away, growling and trying to charge at him, but its bullet riddled legs failed to hold the bulky frame and collapsed.

"It's legs buckled, must not have hit me properly, still packs a hell of a punch," he mumbled, grimacing with each breath as his tender chest throbbed and ached. "That thing can't attack me again, but how the hell am I going to kill it without a gun."

I can't afford to take my eyes off it and search for my guns, that's what got me in this mess in the first place.

Racking his brain for a solution to the puzzle, the words of a lunatic came to him: *it's amazing how quickly something bleeds out when you open an artery*, Taz had boasted. *Doesn't matter how big and strong you are, you get that artery right here in the neck, you're done.*

"Might as well give it a try," he muttered.

Taj walked over to the disabled Berserker, darted to the left and leapt forward aiming his blades at its thick neck. The creature roared and started slashing its claws in the space between them, forcing him to step back.

Maybe I can distract it by attacking another body part first, then go after the artery.

Undaunted, he ducked under the next swipe and jabbed at the face, but the Alpha was ready for him, and he was met by a muscular arm to chest, followed by a heavy clubbing blow to his legs that sent him sprawling backward.

"I expected more from a Vanguard," a sharp voice quipped.

Taj groaned and got back to his feet. The girl with the green eyes stood over him, her arms crossed and a sly smile adorning her features.

"The stories about Vanguards' fighting prowess have obviously been exaggerated, I was hoping to see firsthand what all the fuss was about; it seems I'm to go home disappointed."

Taj opened his mouth to respond; nothing came out. He was at a loss. He had been insulted, threatened and called every name imaginable, but her cutting remark somehow felt worse than all those combined.

"Are you going to say something, or just keep staring at me like a slack jawed halfwit?"

"What?" he managed to stutter.

He was saved from having to say anything else by the sudden influx of six men dressed in black, who charged through the hole in the wall, and made a beeline for the injured Berserker.

The Vanguards wasted little time and opened fire at all at once. With a final anguished whine, the creature fell under the stream of bullets, writhing in a mess of blood and bile. Once the spasms had ceased, the tallest of the men fired an extra shot into its skull.

Tre mumbled a few words to the other members of Unit 17, and they dispersed. Wes and the twins started rifling through the food, eating anything that was untainted by the Berserker. Tre and Ren went over to the remaining Surfacers and were immediately met with insults and threats of violent retribution.

"Get out of here you filthy brutes, you are not welcome," a man wearing all red clothing screeched while his friends nodded in approval. "Do you know what you have done? I could have you shot for this."

"You need to clear out," Tre growled. "It's not safe here anymore."

If they knew how easily Tre could kill them, they wouldn't be so rude to him, Taj thought. *I'll never understand why these people think they have the right to talk down to us, from what I've seen they aren't particularly good fighters.*

Dal was the only one who stayed with the dead creature, he had managed to find another rifle since Taj last saw him, he was still unsteady on his feet, but a slight spark had returned to his glassy eyes.

Taj awkwardly waved goodbye to the young woman and joined Dal.

"What happened to you? looks like you got your ass kicked again," Dal teased.

"I'd like to see you fight an Alpha Berserker and come out looking better," Taj countered. "Did you find the other two?"

"Yes, Jye had already killed them. It was crazy, he hunted them down by himself, we found him right after he took out the second one. He told us where you were."

Taj started. "What's he doing up here? I thought we were the only Vanguards in the city."

"Jye came with the council, when word got to Acropolis about the Berserkers breaking containment, they reached out to the Directors. There are emergency peace talks taking place right now," Dal bent down on one knee, his breathing heavy, the recent exertion sapping him of what little strength he had recovered.

"What are they angry about? Without us, those creatures would have torn through half the city."

Dal laughed, "Apparently, the Surfacer leaders aren't happy

158

about us 'invading their sovereignty', whatever that means. Tre thinks we could be at war before morning."

Would it really come to war? We only came up here to help and they will kill us for it.

Taj's thoughts drifted back to the Husker, and what it had said to him: *You are all going to die.* In his heart, he knew it wasn't an idle threat, those monsters were the real enemy, but he couldn't prove it, and even if he could, nobody seemed to care.

"You might want to get your weapons, I expect we will be needing them very soon," Dal rasped, pointing to the Surfacer in red who was still screaming at Tre. "If the rest of them decide to have a crack at us, we might have to shoot our way out."

"We should go home now, before this escalates," Taj said. *And before somebody loses their temper*, he added silently.

"Jye told us to wait for him here," Dal said. "I overheard Tre saying the Directors want to talk with us."

What do they want with us I wonder? He hadn't forgotten Jaz's warning. "Just remember, if the Directors catch you up there, they'll kill you," she had told them. *Would they really kill us? We saved the city.*

After a quick search of the surrounding area, he found his rifle among the splintered remains of a table. The weapon had acquired a few more scratches and dings to the frame, but otherwise still appeared to work. His pistol was a few feet away, near the twins, who were gleefully helping themselves to a cake that was twice the size of them. He retrieved the gun, taking care to avoid the chunks of food the twins were inadvertently splattering around the place.

"Why did your leader shoot that thing again after it was dead?" A voice asked him.

Taj's heart skipped a beat. *I thought she had already gone.* The green-eyed young woman had followed him.

"Is that part of your creed?"

Like the last time they had spoken, Taj wasn't quite sure how to respond. "You wouldn't get it," he eventually said. "You can't be too careful, we have all lost family to these things."

"I see," she said. "I guess I can understand that, I've lost people too."

"I doubt it's the same thing," Taj murmured. "You have no idea what's it like to live in constant fear, knowing that every time you go outside you could be torn apart. From what I've seen of your city, the only thing people here you need to worry about is too much good food."

His mind drifted back to the garden and lake, and he had to clench his jaw to stop a tirade of nasty words spilling out.

"Alexandria isn't everything it appears, we may not have beasts like yours around every corner, but we have our own monsters, at least yours are easy to spot. Monsters up here can hide in plain sight, they come with smiles and kind words, but they are just as deadly."

Is she seriously complaining about living in this paradise?

"I would take that over the squalor I live in. You have no idea about anything beyond your perfect little bubble, do you?"

Her blazing green eyes narrowed.

"I don't know why I even bothered," She said under her breath. "Your unfortunate predicament doesn't give you the right to be a jerk."

Without another word, she stormed out, leaving through the entranceway.

Taj cursed, guilt gnawing at his insides like a hungry animal. *Idiot, she was only trying to be nice.*

Two burley young men dressed in matching blue suits had seen the exchange, and after the woman was gone, they approached Taj. Both had the golden skin and fair hair he had begun to associate with most people from the surface.

"Don't hassle our women, cretin." The larger of the two

threatened.

Despite their evident hostility, Taj found he didn't fear them.

I've fought far worse than these two fools.

"Oh, and what are you going to do about it," Dal shouted, suddenly appearing at Taj's side. "You two were cowering like frightened children no more than five minutes ago." Ever the antagonist, Dal then raised his middle finger and waved it in their faces.

Taj sighed, *even in his weakened condition he can't resist trying to start something, one of these days he's going to start a brawl with someone who can fight better than him.*

"Careful, Subrat," the smaller one said, his voice thick with self-righteousness, "Last time our two civilisations fought, your treacherous kind were slaughtered and locked away. Our ancestors were kind, we won't be."

Dal let out a loud fake laugh and moved closer to the two clueless men "If you two are the best that your people have to offer, I could conquer your whole city without even trying."

Taj knew Dal would wait until he got close enough to strike before he started throwing punches. He had seen it many times; Dal would distract his opponent by hurling insults, then get into a perfect position to knock them out, most of the time they didn't even know what hit them.

"Let's go," he said, putting a restraining hand on Dal's shoulder. "This isn't worth our time."

If he was honest, he wanted nothing more than to join his friend and give the two loud mouths a beating, but the nights events had already used up the last of his patience.

I need to get out of here before I hurt one of these idiots and give them another reason to start a war.

Dal resisted for a moment, his blue eyes alive with hatred and a thirst for a fight, but he eventually relented, and the two Vanguards started walking away from the looming conflict.

"Where are you going, Subrats?" the smaller one teased. "Wait until I tell my friends about how I made two fearsome Vanguards tuck tail and run."

"Maybe we won't kill you all," his larger friend added. "I'm sure your mother would make a nice serving girl."

The next thing Taj knew his fist was colliding with the bigger man's face, sending him to the floor. Deep down he knew his actions would have serious consequences, but in that moment his body was pumping with adrenalin and he felt nothing. He followed up the first hit with a barrage of punches to his downed opponents head. All his training was forgotten in a red haze of clumsy relentless strikes.

Two sets of strong hands closed around him, and before he could start smashing his foe's head against the ground, he was dragged away kicking and snarling like a cornered animal.

"Let me go," he thundered, struggling in vain against the iron grips of Ren and Dal. "I'm going to tear his head off."

The man Taj had assaulted slowly got back to his feet with the assistance of his smaller companion, the ruined remains of his nose spread across his face. The assault had left him unsteady and sporting several dark bruises on his neck and forehead, but he still managed to give off an air of smug superiority.

"You will pay for that, Subrat," he spluttered through blood-drenched hands. "You will be in a cage before the night is finished, you mark my words."

Dal laughed, this time with genuine mirth rather than sarcasm. "Have you ever been in the underground? It's a rat-infested hellhole with very little water, scarce food and death around every corner, is your prison worse than that?"

The injured Surfacer glowered, and his smaller friend lunged at Dal.

"This is done," Ren barked. A command from the grizzled veteran was enough to give most people pause, and these two were no different.

The big Surfacer's glassy eyes raked over the three Vanguards, his mangled features a mix of disgust and anger. He appeared ready to continue the fight regardless.

"Come on Nathaniel, let's get your injuries looked at," The smaller Surfacer whined, his wide fearful eyes locked on the other members of Unit 17 as they came over to see what the fight was about. "We will settle this another time."

Nathaniel swore and wiped some of the blood from his face. "I'll be seeing you again," he snarled at Taj. "Next time your friends won't be here to save you."

"Looking forward to it," Taj said, his voice full of menacing promise; it was clear he had made an enemy.

Nathaniel and his friend stalked away, joining the last of their people who were finally leaving the pyramid.

"Cowards," Dal called after them. "Happy to fight when you have the advantage of numbers."

"That was reckless," Ren scolded. "Taj, what were you thinking, I expect stupidity from Dal, but not from you."

"They started it, Ren," Dal argued. "He deserved it, if Taj hadn't hit him, I would have."

"He wanted you to attack, idiot," Tre interrupted. "They are probably reporting this to the City Guard right now, they are looking for a reason to shoot us, and you've just given it to them. Don't ever let yourself get manipulated like that again, Taj, you are better than that."

Chapter Fourteen
Prelude to War

Taj shook off the restraining hands. He was still fired up, and unwise words were forming on his tongue. He didn't get a chance to voice any of them though because dozens of men in white armour and gold trimmed red capes flooded into the room. They were all armed with rifles that had two prongs instead of a barrel, similar to the one Dal had tried to steal from the dead City Guard in the Labyrinth.

"To the stage," Tre yelled above the rising cacophony.

The Vanguards all reacted on instinct and quickly ran to the raised platform, placing the grand tables on the stage around them in a defensive barrier; the whole action was completed in a few seconds. By the time all the City Guard had filed in and surrounded them, the Vanguards were ready to fight. Taj and Dal stayed with Tre, crouched behind a table, while Ren and the others positioned themselves around the stage, so they couldn't be taken unawares from different directions.

"Hold fire, we don't want to get caught in a shootout," Tre commanded, "Wait for my word, if they attack first, drop them."

Taj looked around the room and started counting the number of City Guard they faced, losing count somewhere past sixty.

Bad odds, even for us. They can hit us from every angle, I've never seen what fires out of those prongs on the end of their weapons, but I doubt these tables will be much help, I guess it's better than nothing.

The Surfacers were so close he could see their facial expressions, and they all looked incredibly confident and at ease.

Nearly all of them had a small orange screen over one eye.

Is that like a scope, to help them aim? he pondered.

A tall middle-aged man with greying blond cropped hair strode out from amongst the mob. He was dressed in the same white armour as the rest of the City Guard, but his armaments were also decorated with gold and silver script, and four blue triangular insignias that stuck out proudly on his broad muscular chest.

"Drop your weapons, and come with us," the man ordered in a polite cultured voice. "You've unlawfully entered our city, as Field Marshal of the City Guard, I order you to disarm immediately."

Taj looked to Tre, trying to glean what he would do; the commander was utterly still and betrayed nothing, *I can probably guess what he is thinking.*

Surrender was not an option for them, it was one of the fundamental lessons they were taught during the fourth and final trial to become a Vanguard. It involved fighting three seasoned veterans. Recruits were told failure to defeat them all would result in instant dismissal. The task was virtually impossible and nearly always resulted in the recruit being soundly beaten. Only after the fight was over would the ruse be revealed. Losing didn't matter, the only way to truly fail the trial was to give up and stop fighting.

"We decline your offer," Tre announced to the surprise of no one except maybe the field marshal. "Our presence here was solely to hunt down the escapees from the underground. Now our duty is completed, we are waiting for word from our leaders, try to detain us, and we will defend ourselves by any means necessary."

The field marshal listened intently, his face impassive. When Tre had finished speaking several of the City Guard nervously looked over at the dead Berserker, which everyone was giving a wide berth.

"I can't allow that," the field marshal replied. "Aside from the invasion of our sovereignty, one of your number is responsible for an assault, he will need to be segregated and appropriate charges might be laid. The rest of you may be released at a later date."

This is my fault. Taj realised. His anger had begun to subside as the adrenalin wore off, and in its place, a great pit of shame welled up inside him.

I've put everyone else in danger because I couldn't control my temper.

"It was a disagreement between boys, nothing more," Tre said. "This is your last chance to leave and save your men from dying pointlessly."

I won't be the cause of war. If they want me, they can have me.

"Tre let them have me in exchange for releasing the rest of you," Taj said. "I'll be alright, as Dal said, their prison can't be worse than living with creatures and rats."

"Shut up, boy," Tre muttered. "The field marshal is only using you as an excuse, if we hand you over, it will change nothing, and they will have a hostage to use against us."

"Don't be daft, Taj," Dal added. "We are not leaving you here with them."

"Regardless of the intention behind the attack," the field marshal continued. "It was still an assault, and as the guardians of this city and her laws, we can't let it go unanswered, relinquish your weapons, now."

"If you want our weapons, come and get them," Tre shouted. "Either get out of our way, or kill us, we will not surrender to you."

"Throw down your weapons, now," the field marshal bellowed, his composure evaporating. "I will not be spoken to in such a disrespectful manner, especially not by a filthy Subrat. The Mech and Sky Corps are on the way, you have until they arrive to come to your senses, otherwise you won't be leaving here alive."

Tre didn't respond, and the field marshal went silent. No more threats were exchanged, and the minutes ticked by without a shot being fired. The Vanguards knew that's all it was going to take—

one shot— and the situation would explode. None of them were afraid of death, it had been their constant companion since birth, it was a predator that would eventually claim them all.

As the standoff dragged on, Taj began to fidget, and his eyes wandered from the City Guard to his comrades. They were all tense, waiting for a battle that seemed inevitable; Tre on the other hand appeared completely calm, almost suspiciously so.

What does he know that he isn't telling us? Perhaps there is help on the way.

"Are we expecting reinforcements soon commander?" he whispered when the curious voice in his head became too loud to ignore. "I don't fancy our chances otherwise, especially against Mechs and Sky Corps, whatever they are."

The commander subtly inclined his head. "Mechs are giant machines with the strength and fire power of thirty men. The Sky Corps are a fleet of flying vehicles, rest assured, you don't want to fight against either of them. I wouldn't worry though, because here she comes."

Taj didn't have to wait long to discover whom Tre was talking about. A bald woman appeared at the hole in the wall made by the Berserker, her face was glistening with sweat, and her bone-handled knives were drawn. Her sisters came in behind her, along with at least four more units of Vanguards.

Two men he had hoped never to see again led several more units through the entranceway. Jax and Taz already had their arm blades extended; it was clear they were expecting to use them. The army from Acropolis promptly circled the startled City Guard who were still greater in number, but had failed to stop the Vanguards from boxing them in.

Many of the City Guard, either through nerves or lack of training swivelled on the spot, unsure of which direction to face. The field marshal quickly recovered from the shock and screamed out orders to ensure half the Surfacers were now facing their new enemies, but the damage was already done, and he knew it.

"Everybody hold fire until I give the order," the field marshal said, his voice cracking slightly as he turned to address Jaz and the terror twins. "Who has authorised you to be in Alexandria? Your presence here could be construed as an act of war, throw down your weapons now, all of you."

"We are ambassadors," Jaz shouted for all to hear. "The council has sent us to retrieve our lost unit while they negotiate with your Directors, there will be no fighting here today."

The field marshal bared his teeth in a humourless smile. "Do you seriously expect me to believe this rabble are ambassadors?" he drawled. "Most look barely capable of coherent speech, let alone diplomatic negotiations, none of you are leaving until I hear word from the Directors."

"There is no avoiding battle now, when it starts, watch your shots and hold the stage until it's over," Tre said so everyone in their unit could hear. "I don't want any of you idiots dying here today, so watch your backs."

Taj exhaled, suddenly realising he had been holding his breath. *The waiting is worse than the fighting.*

Despite his earlier outburst, his anger and desire to hurt the Surfacers had disappeared, now he just wanted to go home.

Then it happened. A single shot rang out from amongst the mass of bodies, and the room instantly erupted in chaos as every weapon came to life. A hail of bullets tore through the City Guard ranks, killing and maiming indiscriminately. The Surfacers returned fire, the prongs on their guns glowed green and launched glowing projectiles that melted whatever they touched.

Taj hesitated for only a second before he sprayed a barrage at the City Guard in his line of sight. Only one fell, clutching at a badly bleeding wound in his side, his heart wrenching cry of pain quickly lost amongst the din. None of the Vanguards had been hurt so far, and it quickly became clear that the City Guard were either

168

terrible shots or inexperienced.

If these are the best fighters they have, the war will be over very quickly.

The vibrations of Taj's rifle mirrored his beating of his heart, steady and constant, several of his targets fell, clutching non-fatal wounds, but he couldn't bring himself to kill any of them. His wild imagination showed him images of every one of them as a father, a brother, all with someone waiting for them to come home.

Killing other people is harder than I thought, leaves a strange feeling, having someone's life in your hands.

The other members of his unit didn't suffer any misgivings, and he saw more than one Surfacer lose their head to a precise sniper shot. Through the haze of battle, he occasionally caught glimpses of the others; Jaz locked in a violent melee with two City Guard, Taz slicing a someone across the face while Jax impaled the man who tried to shoot his brother. After a time, he lost himself, forgetting everything and putting all his focus on emptying each clip and reloading. It became almost like a ritual, one that seemed like it would go on forever.

It wasn't until a man crashed through the table barrier and landed on him that he woke from his trance-like state. The startled City Guard stared at him with wide terrified eyes and held up both his empty hands. His cries were lost among the sounds of battle, but Taj knew a plea for mercy when he saw it. He stared at the terrified man in front of him, and he still couldn't bring himself to take the life of another person, especially one who was unarmed.

Someone slammed into him from behind and he fell from the stage, landing on the ground below with enough force to send his rifle flying from his hands. He instinctively brought his arms near his face and was just in time to block two bone-shattering hits that left the coppery taste of blood in his mouth.

Taj waited for the next flurry of strikes, peeking through his raised fists just in time to see his attackers head explode in a mist of red. He shook off his surprise and got back to his feet. He was met by the rock hard end of a rifle, and his vision clouded with pinpoints of light. He kept enough of his senses to duck under the next strike and tackle the culprit to the ground, latching onto the City Guard's rifle with both hands as he tried to wrestle it from his foes vice like grip.

A massive explosion rocked the area, sending Taj backwards in a cloud of debris; he covered his head and braced, knowing there would be more. He had only seen Vanguard grenades used a few times, but the powerful devices left a distinctive impression. A second explosion rang out, then a third and fourth, followed by a deathly silence, which was broken by the cries of the wounded and dying.

Who is crazy enough to throw a grenade in here?

With everyone scattered all over the place, there would be no way to guarantee it wouldn't kill Vanguards as well. He didn't have to wait long to get the answer to his question.

"Enough," roared a loud voice with the unmistakable echo of command to it. "This battle is over. Vanguards cease fire."

Taj used the lull in fighting to quickly jump back on the stage, giving him an uninterrupted view of the entire room. Dal and Tre were the only ones still on the raised platform, along with a half dozen dead City Guard. The rest of the area was chaos, a light haze hung over the tattered remains of the food and furniture from the party. The Alpha Berserker still lay where it had fallen, the formerly menacing creature just another corpse among the field of white armoured bodies blanketing the ground.

Vanguard Grandmaster Jye stood at the pyramid entrance, another grenade in hand, four craters surrounding him. His usual calm demeanour was gone, replaced by a sinister glowering that made all who saw him feel unsafe. "Vanguards gather our fallen, and get back to Acropolis," he roared. "Leave no one behind."

The room instantly erupted into a hive of activity as the

Vanguards carried out the command without question. Some were bloodied beyond all recognition and wandering around in a haze, but the majority were unscathed. Jaz quickly made herself known, her voice loud and booming as she ordered those around her. None of the remaining City Guard attempted to resume hostilities, most of the survivors sat down and silently sobbed.

"That got out of hand very quickly," Dal declared as he swayed and nearly fell over. "I can't believe they tried to rush us like that, all they achieved was a higher body count, it's like these fools haven't been trained properly."

"Something tells me these people don't see much real fighting," Tre agreed. "They had us at close range with superior numbers and nearly every shot missed."

"I think their real soldiers are gone," Taj informed them. "A lady I met said something about it."

"That would explain a lot," Tre muttered, waving at the multitude of dead and dying City Guard strewn around the Banquet Pyramid. "They would be fools to start a war now, it's clear they can't field a real army, it would be a massacre."

"All the more reason we should strike now," Dal said. "This lot are already beaten, I doubt they would be able to stop us."

"What is going to happen, commander?" Taj asked. "Will we be killing Surfacers instead of creatures from now on? And what about the Husker, are we going after it?"

"Don't worry about any of that," Tre said, after a moment's contemplation. "Go find the others, and be quick about it, meet me back here."

"Why are you hiding here," Dal sniggered. "Are you avoiding Jye?"

"None of your damn business, Dal," Tre snapped. "Now go before I give you a clap over the ear."

Taj grabbed Dal by the shoulder and dragged his friend away before Tre lost his temper and flogged them both. They jumped down off the stage and entered the crowd, searching for the rest of their unit. The ground was slippery with blood, and the air was thick with the smell of recent defecation, but the worst thing was the sounds, all they could hear was dying men crying out for aid.

What have we done? he pondered as they passed a man not much older than him. The young City Guard's arm was severed below the elbow, and he had two large gashes out of his stomach. Whatever had slashed him had cut straight through his armour. *This isn't right, we shouldn't be killing people, we should be saving them.*

"Over there," Dal shouted, nodding his head at Ren, who had made his way to the centre of the room during the battle.

Taj didn't bother replying and started following Dal. He stopped after nearly standing on a Surfacer bleeding from a deep neck wound. The man spluttered and coughed, each breath draining his life away.

I should do something.

Taj dropped to a knee and grabbed the man's cold clammy hand. It was a silly gesture, and he knew it, but in that moment, letting the dying man know he wasn't alone was more important than anything else. The Surfacer smiled and blood poured out of his mouth, then his struggles ceased forever.

Taj let the dead man's hand fall to the ground and slowly stood back up.

"Get away from him, monster," a voice cried out.

The speaker was another City Guard laying nearby, his left leg had been severed below the knee, however, he still had enough strength to haul threats and insults.

Taj recoiled at the words, but didn't retaliate, his desire for violence had long since faded.

He trudged over to Dal, who was watching Ren argue with another Vanguard, a man with slicked brown hair and a knife tattoo on his forehead. Wes was crouched nearby, stitching up one of the few casualties from Acropolis, an older woman with a wound in her side. Ace and Ash were assisting him by handing over tools when prompted.

"Gather your men and get ready to go Cal," Ren grumbled. "I'm not going to tell you again."

Cal grimaced, exposing his chipped yellow teeth. "Ren, we can't leave now, these weaklings are on the run, there may not be another chance like this."

"You heard Jye, now go."

"We both know Jye might not be in charge for long, if Tre would hurry up and…"

Ren was surprisingly fast for an older man, and Cal was too slow to stop the swift backhand.

"Careful what you say," Ren growled. "Jye is still the grandmaster, and until that is no longer the case, you will show him the respect he is due. You are a captain, an example to those under your command, act like it."

Cal spat blood and glowered at Ren, his fists clenched. Very few men could get away with striking someone above their rank, but Ren's age and experience gave him a lot of leeway.

"Aye sir," Cal said as he skulked away.

"Trouble Ren?" Taj asked.

"It's nothing, don't worry about it boy."

"Maybe we should be worried," Wes said. "Cal isn't the only one who will be reluctant to leave, we got a taste of victory here, it will be a tall order to persuade everyone to back down."

"I'm with Cal, we should deal with these cowards before they can regroup," Dal said. "Our casualties would be minimal, they can't even shoot straight."

"Lucky for us," Wes muttered. "The bullets from their guns leave wounds like nothing I've ever seen before, the flesh is cauterised around the impact site, I just had .."

Wes trailed off as Jye passed, flanked either side by the Terror

Twins who were covered in blood, none of it their own. The grandmaster's destination was clear, Tre waited in a statue-like vigil on the raised platform in the middle of the room.

"Nobody move," a loud cultured voice screamed. The field marshal stormed out of the throng and deposited himself in Jye's path. The City Guard leader didn't have a scratch on him.

He is either very skilled, or hid during the battle, Taj thought, he had a sneaking suspicion it was the latter.

"Field Marshal Reinhart," Jye lamented, curling his lip as each syllable came out. "To what do I owe the pleasure of your company?"

"I hope you aren't suffering from the delusion that you are leaving here," Reinhart shouted a few centimetres from Jye's face. "You're all under arrest, for crimes against the people of our fair city, Alexandria."

"What the Vanguards do now is none of your concern," Jye said, his tone wavering as he tried to stay calm. "Your Directors have made a deal with the council to ensure the events of tonight go no further, now get out of my way."

Reinhart's face went bright red, and he puffed his chest out. "How dare you speak to me in such a manner. If you're not careful, I will detain you along with your men, regardless of your rank."

Jye had no weapons other than the grenade he still clutched in his hand, but the man oozed a dangerous energy which made his next words even more threatening. "Get out of my way, or I will kill you."

In a great wave, every Vanguard and City Guard still alive lifted their weapons, waiting with bated breath for the battle to resume.

"Hasn't there been enough killing for one day?" Taj groaned. He was one of the few who hadn't raised his gun.

You were the cause of this, an unhelpful voice whispered in the back of his mind. *They are fighting because of you.* The guilt gnawed at his insides like a hungry creature, and he knew the feeling wouldn't abate for some time.

An unarmed City Guard sheepishly approached Reinhart, neither side paid him any attention due to his lack of armaments. The man smartly saluted, and when the field marshal ignored him, he started talking anyway.

"Sir, the Directors have sent word, they've been trying to get in touch with you, your radio appears to be off," the messenger stammered. "You are to cease hostilities immediately; all the Vanguards are free to go."

Reinhart went deathly still, and the messenger slowly inched away.

"Goodbye, field marshal," Jye said as he pushed past the seething man.

"Someone needs to answer for the lives of my men that were stolen tonight," Reinhart called out to the grandmaster. "Regardless of whatever deal was struck, they deserve justice."

"Take that up with your Directors," Jye replied without turning around. "Tonight has cost both of us more than we would like."

Reinhart spat in disgust and aggressively screamed orders at the harried-looking messenger. The field marshal had lost, and there was nothing he could do about it, for now.

The Vanguards returned to helping their wounded, but nearly all of them kept an eye on Tre and Jye as they met on the stage and began talking in low voices. Jax and Taz took up guard positions on either side, the demented twins still hadn't bothered to clean the blood off themselves yet.

"What do you think they are talking about?" Taj wondered out loud. "Surely Tre isn't still advocating for war, not after what we've seen in the Labyrinth."

"I expect we will know soon enough," Ren said, the older man gazed out at the carnage, a look of deep sadness on his grizzled features. "One way or another, tonight will change everything. When the first casualties of this fight make it home, Acropolis will ignite with renewed calls for war. Jye will be hard pressed to ignore them. I'd say the Surfacers will be the same, Reinhart doesn't strike me as the forgiving sort."

To the surprise of everyone, Jye and Tre finished talking a moment later and shook hands, the two seemingly coming to an agreement. Tre walked down off the stage and re-joined Unit 17, Jye came with him.

"We are required at the Director's Tower," Tre announced. "It seems we have no choice. I don't want to hear any whining, I'm in no mood to hear it."

Tre motioned for everyone to follow him through the battlefield. More Surfacers had shown up to help their casualties, but it had done little to alleviate Field Marshal Reinhart's mood, his loud obnoxious ranting could still be heard above everything else. When they reached the exit, Jye instructed the Terror Twins to stay and help with the evacuation, much to their disgust.

"Who is going to watch your back up here?" Jax argued. "The kid and these pretenders? You'll be dead in five minutes."

"We are just going to talk, Jax," Jye said sternly. "Your particular skills won't be needed for this."

"If they try anything," Jax snarled. "Rest assured, Taz and I will avenge you."

The Terror Twins departed, and the Vanguards of Unit 17 breathed a collective sigh of relief.

"I will never understand why you keep those two lunatics around Jye," Tre remarked. "They are no better than rabid animals, someone should have done the world a favour and put them down a long time ago."

"They serve a purpose," Jye said. "I think we will all be glad to have them before long."

Jye took them outside where a row of stern-faced City Guard

waited; behind them were giant bipedal machines a little over five metres tall. Each of the machines had two arms attached to multi-barrelled guns and a rounded enclosed cockpit at its heart. Above them several aircraft with twin engines and triangular bodies hovered, their wings heavy with cannons and other weapons.

"Mechs and Sky Corps", Taj guessed. *There is no way we could have won this fight if those machines were involved.*

A Surfacer with jet black hair and slight elfin features approached and greeted the Vanguards with an air of forced joviality, his blazing green eyes trailed over them until he found Jye.

"I am General Valens," he said to the Grandmaster. "My men and I will escort you to the Director's Tower."

Like Field Marshal Reinhart, General Valens's armour had gold and silver script, and several blue triangles, only three, which Taj assumed meant he was the rank beneath Reinhart.

"Stay close to us," the general advised. "Otherwise you may not make it home again."

General Valens didn't wait for a response and wandered deeper into the city. Most of his men followed, but a handful waited for the Vanguards.

Tre went first, then the rest of Unit 17 followed after a brief moment of hesitation. Valens took them on a path that seemed too have no clear direction, then turned around and went down an alley, before returning to a main street.

Do they not know where we are going? Taj wondered. *How can they be lost in their own city?*

After three more detours, Taj began to suspect Valens was deliberately leading them astray. *Is he trying to confuse us? So we don't know a direct path to their leaders.*

More City Guard followed in their wake, he counted at least twenty, but it was impossible for him to get a full account of their numbers because they were keeping their distance. Other than their escorts, he couldn't see any other Surfacers.

Everyone is hiding, they fear you now, a voice whispered in the back of his mind. *And who can blame them, dozens were slaughtered, all because you couldn't handle some childish taunting.*

His guilt returned with a vengeance, and the voices of doubt multiplied until his head throbbed and ached. When it finally became too much, he went to Jye, who was a few paces behind the rest of them.

"I'm sorry," he said to the stoic grandmaster. "This my fault, I shouldn't have lost my temper like that."

Jye smiled and lightly clapped him on the shoulder. "Relax Taj, this isn't your fault, a battle was inevitable. For now, we must endure whatever the results of tonight are, and look to the bigger problems we face."

"Did Tre tell you about our encounter with a Husker?"

"Yes, fortunately, the knowledge has made your commander see sense, Tre knows now the Surfacers are the least of our worries."

Taj couldn't help but feel a little better at the news, the two greatest warriors in the underground were on the same side again. "What about Unit 6? Have they failed in their mission?" Like most of his conversations with Jye, he didn't expect to get an answer, especially considering he was asking about something that only the top tier of leadership was privy to.

"There is no point hiding it anymore, soon everyone will know," Jye said after considering the question for a moment. "After Tre reported what happened on your first mission, I knew the monsters were back, the things that had destroyed Agora. I sent all the Vanguards into the Labyrinth to flush them out, once they were revealed, the plan was to have Unit 6 eliminate them. Our best fighters failed to kill any during their skirmishes with the Huskers, and there are far more than we realised."

178

Taj tried his best stay silent, but his mind burned with a thousand more questions. He had been obsessing over the Huskers for weeks, and now the long-awaited knowledge was within his grasp.

"I have read through the records we brought back from Agora," Jye explained. "Our ancestors named them Demons, and not long after our people were banished from the surface, they fought an unending war against these Demons. This conflict saw the Cannibal Warlords and their Marauders come into power, and while it wasn't clear how they managed it, the savages defeated the Huskers. That's where Unit 6 are going now, to look for any surviving Marauders and hopefully find the key to beating the monsters for a second time."

"Do you really think the Marauders might have survived all this time?" Taj asked. "Surely they are all long dead by now."

"Perhaps, but there are plenty of places to hide in the Labyrinth, especially in the outer reaches, far beyond the eyes of our patrols," Jye said. "Before he died, Gaius gave us the location of his city, his people might know where to find them, or at the very least provide us with more allies to fight the coming war."

Taj hummed to himself, pondering what he had learned.

How could they keep this from us, our people have been risking their lives this whole time based on a lie.

The rest of their talk was cut short when the top of a great spire appeared on the horizon, towering high above every other nearby structure.

"Is that where we are going? What kind of leaders would choose to rule from such a high place, so far removed from their people," Taj asked.

"The worst kind," Jye muttered. "Those who think themselves far above the people they claim to represent."

Valens took them down a street leading to a vast open plaza that afforded them a full view of the building that housed the

Directors. The spire was constructed on an elevated platform in the middle of another lake and surrounded by vividly green plant life. A double set of metallic doors were built into the base, which could only be accessed by using a long flat bridge erected over the water. Two guards were stationed either side of the doors, both wore the same black armour that left no visible skin, and had a vividly painted red skull symbol on the chest plate.

General Valens paused at the bridge, fidgeting on the spot as his eyes rapidly darted from the two men in black and back to the city as though he were contemplating a hasty retreat at the first opportunity.

"Everyone waits here," he said, his voice wavering. "I'll get them to open the doors. No matter what happens, nobody shoots unless I give the command."

He seems afraid, why? Taj wanted to ask Jye what was happening but stifled his innate curiosity, there wasn't time to pester the grandmaster with more questions.

Valens cautiously walked across the bridge, his shaking hands in the air. When he was halfway, the two guards came alive, pointing their two-pronged rifles at the general.

"Should we be worried here," Tre asked Jye. If they start shooting each other, what are we supposed to do?"

"Nothing," Jye replied. "If it comes to that, get out of the way and let them kill each other, this isn't our fight."

Valens started speaking, but what he said was lost in the wind as a cold chill descended on the area. Eventually the big double doors hissed and opened revealing a glass elevator. The general kept his hands raised and backed away.

"It's safe to enter now," he said to Jye. "You need to be quick though, don't dawdle."

Jye waved for Unit 17 to follow him. The City Guard remained where they were, while Valens reluctantly accompanied the Vanguards to the spire.

Like his fellows, Taj found he couldn't stop staring at the two guards. *What the hell are they? Even the other Surfacers seem to fear them.*

Dal was the only one who didn't seem to have a wary respect for the men in black, and he illustrated this point by pulling a bullet out of his pocket, and before anyone could stop him, threw it at them. The projectile missed the left one's head by a hair and clattered harmlessly to the ground. The reaction was instantaneous, the men in black raised their weapons and pointed them at Dal, who sniggered and extended his middle finger. The Vanguards were quick to react, and another standoff ensured as both sides waited for the other to shoot.

"Enough," Valens screamed as he ran between the two groups. "Haven't we had enough killing for one day? Enforcers, stand down, the Directors have called for an end to the fighting."

"Put your weapons away," Jye said, waving his hand. "We are here to talk, for now."

Everyone slowly lowered their rifles, and Tre clapped Dal over the back of the head with his closed fist.

"Idiot," he growled. "Do that again, and I will shoot you myself."

"What?" Dal whined. "I wanted to see what would happen, weren't you curious?"

Chapter Fifteen

The Directors

"What were you thinking?" Director Barons shouted. "You're lucky your indirection wasn't more costly." He had been lecturing the Vanguards since they had entered the sparkling oval office he shared with the other two Directors. Taj stood with his comrades in a line, listening to the tirade with little interest, it didn't take long for his mind to wander back to the breathtaking ascent in the elevator, which had afforded a birds eye view of Alexandria and the red-orange glow of a rising sun.

When they reached the top of the spire, they had exited into a windowless room where the leadership council from Acropolis were waiting. Seven more Enforcers, dressed in the same black armour as the two at the base of the tower, waited in front of a double set of shiny wooden doors that led into the Directors office.

One of the Enforcers didn't have a face covering, revealing grey cropped hair, and smooth unmarked features that were slack and completely emotionless. The only sign that the man lived was when his cold blue eyes tracked over each of them, and rested on Jye, expertly finding the biggest threat in the room.

Barons suddenly started heaving, bringing Taj back to the present. Like the other two surface leaders, he wore smart blue clothing trimmed in gold, but the effort of his rant had caused the heavyset balding man to sweat profusely, drenching his garments. Taj couldn't help but stare, there were no fat people in the underground, with strict rations in place at all times, it was impossible to reach an unhealthy size.

I wonder how much he eats during a normal day.

Despite the sizeable glass panel office housing the full council from Acropolis, Jye, Unit 17 and the other Directors, Barons had not yet let anyone else say a word. The portly man leaned on his marble desk at the back of the room, while his two colleagues waited for a chance to give their input at their desks either side of him.

"It was irresponsible of you to let your people loose in the city without first telling me, Jye," Barons said between breaths. "With things as they are, you should have sent word via the proper diplomatic channels and awaited my response before ascending to my city."

Director Myrans loudly cleared her throat, forcing Barons to cease and pivot his flabby neck to the right. The woman's face was heavily lined, her fading blonde hair was tied up in a smart bun and her frail frame was bent over, but she spoke with a strength that made it very clear why she had been elected to her position.

"Our response," the matron corrected, tapping her long slender fingers against her table. "They should have awaited our response, or did the people vote to have you cede authority from Director Tiberius and I without our knowledge?"

Barons casually waved one of his heavily adorned hands. "Of course. I am simply caught up in the moment. It was an honest mistake, my apologies," he grovelled.

"In future, you should be careful to avoid such mistakes," Myrans replied coldly.

"Yes, of course," Barons murmured. "Now, where was I?"

Taj fought the urge to swear, suddenly realising why Jye had been so angry earlier. *This man is an arrogant blowhard, if the other two are anything like him, the council have done well to negotiate thus far.*

"Ah yes," Barons announced after a prolonged silence. "I have called you all here to discover why you thought it prudent to invade our city. I have provided food, medicines, a trading quarter and training for some of the gifted craftsmen among you, and this is how you repay that generosity. With violence?"

When nobody from Acropolis's delegation responded, Barons took the time to wipe the sweat from his brow and flop into his chair. The council had warned the Vanguards to be careful about revealing information while in the spire, during the last few meetings, the Surfacers had displayed an uncanny ability to know the Councillors' thoughts beforehand and outmanoeuvre them in negotiations.

"Now, who is the one among you that led this incursion?" Barons wheezed, even after sitting down, the large man was still out of breath. "I believe you owe an explanation."

Tre looked to Jye, who gave him a slight nod of consent.

"I did," the commander confirmed, stepping forward so he could be seen by everyone. "The creatures were forced above ground; we pursued them in the hopes of containing the threat, it was my choice. My men are not to blame."

"Honourable, to try and protect your people," Barons said while mockingly clapping his hands together. "However, this whole affair was due to your incompetence, and don't even get me started on the good honest citizens you and your ilk murdered in cold blood. I have been in contact with Field Marshal Reinhart, and he paints an alarming picture of the events that transpired."

Jye forcefully grabbed Tre's shoulders, while Ren and Wes drifted in front of him, pre-empting the commander's violent response to the accusation.

"You are a fat fool," Tre growled, "Speak to me like that again, and you won't leave this room alive."

Baron's face reddened, and a thick vein on his forehead pulsed as he tried and failed to retort. The man choked on his own anger and white-knuckled the side of his desk for support.

"How dare you," he finally stuttered. "Our new peace agreement is barely hours old, and you are already looking to provoke further conflict."

The Director gathered himself and got back to his feet, due to his bulk it took several attempts, which severely lessened the impact of his next threat.

"You are just like the beasts you hunt in that subterranean prison you call home," he bellowed. "If I were not so committed to peace, you would be executed on the spot for your transgression. Rest assured, if you speak to me in such a manner again, I will have ten thousand of our best City Guard march on Acropolis and wipe you from existence."

"That's quite enough of that, Barons," Acropolis Councillor Ira snapped. "We have already settled this matter. You all voted to maintain the peace agreement, and Tre's Vanguards were only brought here to talk as a courtesy, there was to be no more fighting."

Barons glanced at the only way out.

"Perhaps, I should invite the Enforcers in to help settle our dispute," he drawled.

"Enough of this," Tiberius boomed, the impossibly tall and skinny Director hadn't spoken yet, instead he sat quietly watching the exchanges and fiddling with his long blond dreadlocked hair. "The Enforcers impose our will and protect us from threats, they are not your personal vendetta squad."

"You overstep again, Barons," Myrans agreed. "Any action undertaken by the Enforcers needs to be voted on, by all of us, not just you."

"We are committed to peace," Tiberius assured the delegation from Acropolis. "Any further acts of violence would not help either of our civilizations at this point. Especially considering your tales about this new monster."

Taj had been adrift, his tired mind wandering to places far away, but his ears pricked up at the mention of the Husker and he started to listen with keen interest to the unfolding conversation.

How does everyone seem to know about these things except us? Who knows how many have died because of this secret?

"Have you made a decision on whether you will help us deal with this," Ira inquired. "This monster is far beyond anything we have ever seen before; it has upset the natural order and we face greater dangers every day. We can't hope to stand against the coming tide alone, we need to unite our efforts."

Myrans and Tiberius exchanged a strange look which appeared equal parts fear and excitement, it was over in an instant, but something passed between them.

"Unfortunately, as we have said previously, we can't just trust your word," Myrans declared. "There needs to be an investigation, we have lost people, there is no proof at this point that it was anything other than the regular beasts from the Labyrinth."

Not wanting to be left out, Barons blundered his way out from behind his desk. "There will be a thorough investigation," he repeated as though he had come up with the idea. "I have yet to see proof that anything out of the ordinary is happening, and I refuse to cause a panic over nothing."

"An investigation? Surely more is warranted," Ira exclaimed, to the murmured agreements of the rest of the councillors. "We have reason to believe these monsters were directly responsible for the Berserkers invading your city tonight."

Myrans sighed. "Let us be frank, we can't send our forces to fight an enemy that hasn't been proven to exist. As per our agreement, the Vanguards are tasked with fighting those beasts below and keeping them contained, until we decide otherwise, they are your problem, not ours."

"It is clear this is nothing but a ploy, you want us to do your jobs for you," Barons said triumphantly as though he had discovered some great secret that nobody else could see. "Huskers are nothing, a legend, I fail to see the threat posed by an old story concocted by dead men."

186

The room went silent, and Barons skulked back to his chair. The other Directors stared incredulously at the heavyset man who sat back down with a smug smile on his face, Ira and Jye were also visibly shocked.

Why though? Taj wondered. He went through several possibilities, then it hit him. Nobody had called it a Husker since they got here. *Barons shouldn't know that name, unless the Directors already had knowledge of them and they were trying to keep it a secret from us, surely he isn't that stupid.*

"I never mentioned Huskers," Jye said, confirming Taj's suspicion. "In fact, nobody has told you the name of these monster yet, how is it you know what they are called?"

Barons sprang to his feet faster than a man of his size should have been able to move. "Ah, you did," he stammered as he began to fan himself, "I remember it specifically, during our previous negotiations. Enough of this, let's return to the matter at hand."

"Everyone in this room knows that you are lying," Jye accused. "You haven't shut up since we got here, and when you finally say something interesting, you suddenly don't want to talk about it. I just can't work out why you'd be stupid enough to ignore this."

The blustering Director shrank like an old piece of fruit left in the sun. He opened and shut his mouth, failing to bring forth words each time. When he finally managed to say something, it was full of rage.

"I do not have to answer to Subrats."

"Enough of this foolishness," Myrans interrupted, shooting Barons a look of pure contempt. "We had hoped to investigate further before broaching this matter with you, it appears there is little choice now. We have been going through our repositories where our histories are recorded, there have been some references to Huskers around the time of the Great War with your ancestors. Truthfully, there needs to be more research before a decision is made."

"They are very real," Jye cautioned. "When they are done with us, you will be next, this is a fact."

"That remains to be seen," Myrans countered. "In time, perhaps a joint taskforce can be created to address the situation, for now, the Vanguards will remain the sole military force fighting in the underground."

Barons walked out into the middle of the room with his hands behind his back. He appeared to be getting ready to voice his own refusal for aid when he was pre-emptively cut off by Tiberius.

"These people are quite energetic, aren't they?" he exclaimed. "If they feel so strongly about this, perhaps we should entertain the idea of sending some of our forces down below."

"You can't be serious," Barons chortled.

"This is not what we discussed," Myrans said. "We agreed that the people of Alexandria should not have to expend lives and resources for a problem that is not our own. There are far greater concerns than these animals, as you very well know."

"This sounds like a problem that will affect us all," Tiberius retorted. "Even if these Huskers are not real, the situation in the underground has become far worse than we've anticipated. If the people of Acropolis are destroyed, we will have lost our only ally and have a flood of beasts overrunning Alexandria. We have not heard from any other continents in centuries; we should act now while we have the help."

"The City Guard is primarily for our defence," Barons whined. "They will have no air support underground, and who knows if the Mechs will be able to operate in an enclosed space."

"What about Vincent and his Enforcers then?" Tiberius proposed. "They are few in number, but very deadly, they could help tip the balance back in the Vanguards favour."

"That will leave us unprotected," Myrans argued. "Out of the question, it will not happen."

"Shall we vote then?" Tiberius said breathlessly. "Seems to be the only way to settle this, I call a vote for action, to send military aid to the underground."

"No," Myrans hissed coldly.

Barons made a show of his decision, waiting several minutes to ponder the question loudly and go through what, in his opinion, were the positives and the negatives. To the surprise of no one, he eventually voted with Myrans against sending aid.

"Two to one," Myrans announced. "This meeting is concluded." The debate between leaders apparently over, she spoke directly to Tre. "In recognition of your efforts to contain the threat this evening, and the interests of maintaining good relations, we will allow your men to enjoy some refreshments in our private courtyard while we confer with the council on another matter. Upon the conclusion of our business, you will be escorted home.

The rest of the council appeared indifferent, but Ira was shaking with rage.

"Jye, Tre, please go downstairs and wait for us," he said through clenched teeth. "When we are done here, you can escort us home, we have much to discuss."

The Vanguards left the office, and found the Enforcers waiting just outside, the man without a helmet went straight for Tre.

"Next time you threaten one of our leaders, I will kill you," he rasped. "I've been wanting to test myself against one of your kind ever since we found you rock-dwelling worms, your skills are said to be exceptional."

Tre reached for his knife, but Jye was quick to grab the commander's arm and stop him from assaulting the confident Enforcer.

"Careful Vincent," Jye cautioned. "One day soon, you might get your wish, and I doubt it will end the way you want."

****

"Re-call all the Vanguards as soon as we get back to Acropolis," Tre demanded as they descended in the elevator. "With no one guarding the surface entrances, they will be overrun within a week. When the Surfacers are choking on their own blood, then start negotiating again."

The tense standoff between Tre and Vincent had been brief, the Enforcer refused to move and it took a command from Barons, albeit with some reluctance to de-escalate the situation.

"We need to be cautious; the Huskers are on the move," Jye muttered. "We can't afford to cede territory now, our movements have drawn them out, we need to find a way to kill them, before they wipe us out."

The elevator doors opened halfway down the spire to a courtyard bathed in the orange glow of a recent sunrise. The Vanguards piled out of the elevator and were shocked into silence. On top of a long flat piece of marble fixed into the ground, were a dozen wooden tables groaning under the weight of fish, vegetables, meat, and a dozen other things none of them could name. Either side of the display was fresh green vegetation and smiling marble statues of men and women.

"This is a trap," Tre mumbled. "They know they can't keep us with force, so they bribe us with food."

"Eat your fill, and steal what you can," Jye told them. "If they wish to occupy us with food, I see no reason not to eat everything in sight."

Dal didn't need to be told twice and was the first to grab something, a slab of steaming meat, he tore the flesh right off the bone and loudly chewed the tender meal. Taj went straight to the end of the nearest table and grabbed a chunk of something brown and cold. He poked it with his tongue, and an influx of tastes flooded his senses. He swallowed the whole thing and started working his way down the table, trying one of everything.

The drinks turned out to be just as good, and before long they stopped using cups and were drinking out of the jugs. Anxious Surfacers in white uniforms darted around them replacing plates as they were finished. Not long after they started feasting, Dal tackled one who took a plate to early, provoking terrified shrieks from the attendant, and loud cackles from Wes and Ren. Taj ate until he felt ill, the first time in his life he had ever managed it, and still he kept eating.

No wonder Barons is so fat.

He grabbed another herb bread, and several other things he couldn't identify and shovelled them all down.

"Maybe they are trying to feed us to death," he laughed to Dal who hadn't stopped wolfing down food either."

"If that's their plan; I'm all for it," Dal said through a mouthful of bread, spraying spittle, and chunks of food in front of him. "Gunna be hard to go back and eat food packs after this."

Taj was about to agree, when his stomach churned and the food in his mouth came flying out, along with a stream of chunk filled vomit. He dropped what he was holding and brought his hands up to try and block the torrent spewing forth, when that failed, he ran over to the statues, emptying the rest of his stomach contents at their feet while his comrades laughed and jeered insults through mouthfuls of food. When the stream finally stopped, he used the nearest statue to pull himself back up and caught a close-up glimpse of the monument for the first time.

"Barons," he spat, fighting back a fresh wave of nausea.

Beside him were effigy's of Myrans and Tiberius that looked so real, he half expected them to come alive. *The rest must be past Directors*, he mused, gazing at the hundred or so other statues that dotted the courtyard.

Taj retuned to the tables and grabbed a piece of meat, tearing a steaming chunk off with his teeth, but unlike before, the food no longer gave him enjoyment. The acrid taste of vomit was still fresh in his mouth, and his stomach groaned a warning with each bite.

I might have overdone it.

He abandoned his half-finished meal and decided to explore, suddenly noticing another had already left the feast. Jye had only eaten a little and with the enthusiasm of someone who took in food to sustain themselves and nothing else, now he stood alone on the retaining wall on the outskirts of the courtyard, his perch offering a clear view of the city below.

As the others became steadily rowdier and started throwing food and drink, provoking looks of barely contained disgust from the Surfacer attendants, Taj wandered over to the grandmaster, taking up a silent vigil next to him. He still had many questions but didn't have the energy to ask them, the nights events had drained him of everything except the desire to curl up and go to sleep. Below them, Alexandria began to awake after the night cycle, its inhabitants blissfully unaware they were being watched from above as they went about the business of the day.

"We nearly started a war," Jye said after a time. "The Directors were ready to wipe us out, nobody would have been spared."

"Many of our people would welcome a war," Taj said. "There were plenty of Vanguards who were ready to keep fighting tonight. I don't know if you can stop this, eventually someone will take matters into their own hands, whether it be someone from our side, or theirs."

Jye sighed, and his shoulders drooped. "I know, but if we go to war with Alexandria, we will all die. Those Mechs you saw at the Banquet Pyramid are nothing compared to some of the weapons they have in their arsenal. The Directors could destroy Acropolis with the push of a button."

Taj frowned, unable to fathom the level of destruction. *How is that even possible?*

"What are you going to do then?"

Jye didn't answer, and the conversation died, leaving Taj to ponder what kind of weapons could destroy an entire city with the push of a button. It didn't take long for his head to start drooping though, and he knew it was time to leave.

"Do you think they'll let me go?" he asked the grandmaster. "There was talk of arresting me, and I don't fancy coming across Vincent and his Enforcers again."

"Don't worry about it, that situation was resolved," Jye replied. "As for Vincent, you have nothing to fear, he is little better than a trained dog, he will only attack if his master gives the command."

Taj took one last look at the view, committing the sight to memory, and reluctantly walked away. He said brief farewells to the rest of his unit, receiving a few grunts and nods from the barely conscious men sprawled amongst the tattered remains of the tables.

Good luck getting this lot to leave.

Chapter Sixteen
The Boondocks

Taj exited the elevator at the base of the Spire and stepped out into the sunlight, his pale skin tingling in response. Under normal circumstances, he would have taken the time to enjoy his first experience with real sunlight, but the hulking figures of the two Enforcers on guard out the front left him with the distinct desire to leave immediately. Neither of them reacted to his presence as he walked by, but he still kept his rifle handy.

Regardless of the peace treaty, I don't think these Enforcers can be trusted.

A lean, wiry City Guard waited at the bridge, nervously playing with his short brown hair while his dark eyes switched between the Enforcers and Taj at regular intervals.

He doesn't have blond hair and blue eyes either, like General Valens, and that young woman from last night, I wonder if there is a reason?

"Greetings, I'm Sergeant Norrin," he said to Taj, saluting smartly. "Are you looking for passage back to the underground?"

"Yes," Taj replied, mimicking the gesture, which made Norrin's slight features twitch as he tried not to smile.

"There is one entrance back to the underground in each district, the closest one is in the fourth district at the Boondocks, we will head there. Stay close, and don't wander off."

On the other side of the water, a line of burly City Guard armed with six-foot-high rectangular plastic shields had formed a half circle around the lake, blocking a few thousand people from reaching the bridge. The crowd repeatedly surged, charging at the shields, but the men who wielded them were staunch, holding firm and preventing any of the civilians from getting past. The fierce melee came to a standstill as Taj approached, passing behind the protective formation.

Murderer," someone shouted at him.

"Filthy Subrat."

"You can't just let them leave, not after what they did."

"How can you protect that monster?"

Taj could only see distorted images through the plastic shields, but it was hard to mistake the glares and looks of contempt that every Surfacer held. A familiar wave of guilt quickly followed, clawing at his insides.

I wonder if any of the men we killed last night have family here.

"We need to go, now," Norrin advised. "If the mob get through, I can't guarantee your safety, there is a very real chance you'll be torn apart."

How did it come to this, we were only trying to save them from the Berserkers, now they hate us even more.

"Lead on sergeant," Taj sighed, ducking a glass bottle that flew over the line of guards and shattered behind him. As word spread about his presence, more projectiles quickly followed, and he was forced to hold his fists up over his head to protect himself from the small missiles. Norrin broke into a run, taking him around the lake, while the mob continued to charge, slamming into the shield wall with little regard for personal safety.

"Hold," A City Guard officer roared. "Push them back."

Taj kept going, keeping his eyes on Norrin's back, but the line began to crumble under the weight of so many bodies, several guards fell in his path, receiving swift kicks and knocks from improvised weapons as they tried to crawl away from the mob. He instinctively reached for his pistol, hesitating when his hand closed around the grip.

That's what started this mess in the first place, I need to stay out of this fight.

When Norrin reached the other side of the lake, he ducked into a street leading back into the city. Taj took a final glimpse back at the riot before following, the mob had breached the shield wall in four places but hadn't tried to get across the bridge yet. The two Enforcers had come to life, and were patiently waiting at the crossing for anyone foolish enough to go near them.

This is insane. How are the others going to get home now?

Norrin kept up the swift pace for another few hundred metres, finally slowing when they were sufficiently lost among the towering structures.

"Animals," Norrin breathed, shaking his head. "Little better than a rabble, they need to be put down before someone gets hurt."

"You wish your own people to be shot," Taj puffed, holding his aching sides with unsteady hands.

"We may share this city, and some common ancestry, but those people are not my kin," Norrin snarled. "I'm from the fourth district, under General Valens. Those sycophants are from this district, the third, under General Reinhart, they are among the loudest voices pushing for war."

"I thought he was a field marshal?"

"No that's the elder Reinhart, his younger brother is the general in charge of this district. Under normal circumstances, I wouldn't be caught dead here, but when your lot came topside last night, the field marshal ordered everyone to join the search. Valens nearly refused to come, he hates the Reinhart brothers with a passion."

"Is that allowed up here? Can you refuse orders?"

"It depends on who the orders come from, the field marshal is technically the highest ranked City Guard leader, but everyone knows it's the generals who have the real power, it's been at least a century since a field marshal held the allegiance of all four districts."

So, Alexandria isn't united under one banner. I wonder how deep the divide goes, if war breaks out in one district, would the others come to their aid?

"Will the rest of my unit be able to get home?"

"If the mob doesn't disperse, the Directors will most likely bring in a fleet of Sky Corps to ferry your friends' home, don't worry."

A pang of jealousy stirred inside Taj, and he suddenly had the urge to go back to the spire and face the fury of the mob for the chance to fly.

Dal will never let me forget it if the Sky Corps take them home.

Norrin didn't bother hiding the direct path to the Boondock's, forgoing the backtracking and changes of direction Valens had implemented to misdirect the Vanguards. Taj initially tried to memorise the way by looking for unique landmarks, just in case he got separated from his guide, but his attention was quickly diverted when the first vehicle shot past them in a blur of metal and screeching gears.

"What the hell was that," he shouted in alarm, ducking as another machine passed overhead in a flash.

"Hover train," Norrin said, "If you really push the throttle, a train can hit the speed of sound and travel across all of Alexandria in only a few minutes."

I wonder if Tig has been allowed to work on one of those yet.

The further they went into the city, the busier it got. Hover trains and flying machines frequently flew by, and Surfacers flooded the streets, going about their business. Unlike the people of Acropolis, who primarily wore plain, simple clothing, the Surfacers displayed a flare for extravagance. Taj saw more than a few bright coloured fur coats, blazers, leather vests, pants that shimmered in the light and dresses that changed colour when the wind hit the fabric. Nobody they saw was as overtly hostile as the mob outside the spire, but many still glowered at him, and before long he was forced to endure stares from more than a few onlookers.

"Move along," Norrin shouted at a particularly curious group who blocked the street and excitedly whispered to each other.

"That's him."

"I thought he'd be bigger."

Taj tried to smile, but everything suddenly started spinning. The sun had nearly risen to its peak, and the massive structures did nothing to block the heat and blinding light. His vison blurred, and his nausea came back with a vengeance, forcing him to hobble over to the shadow of a nearby alley.

What's wrong with me, is this because of the food, or is it sun sickness?

Images of fried skin, blisters and the screams of those afflicted with sun sickness flashed through his mind, prompting him to empty all the food left in his stomach on the ground, followed by yellow bile.

"Take a deep breath, drink this," Norrin said, handing him a metal bottle. "You're probably dehydrated, the sun can be deadly, especially when you're not used to it."

Taj didn't bother asking what was in the bottle and gulped down the contents. His dizziness and nausea lingered for a few more moments, before gradually receding as he drank more of the cooling tasteless liquid.

"Norrin, who is that?" a man in a fur coat and matching dark pants asked, breaking away from the passing crowd and interrupting Taj's misery. "Are you arresting him?"

"I'm taking him home," Norrin said. "We nearly didn't make it, just came from the third district, Reinhart's sycophants were waiting outside the Directors Tower to get a shot at our visitors.

"Looks like they will be too late to claim this one," the man cackled while walking away. "He's already half gone from the looks."

"Don't listen to that nonsense," Norrin said to Taj. "It's not much further, you'll be back home very soon."

Taj smiled weakly, handing the empty bottle back. "Thank you."

"Don't thank me," Norrin snapped. "General Valens ordered me to get you home safe, that's what I'm going to do, otherwise I would have left you to the mob. I knew some of the City Guard your people killed last night, they were good men, they didn't deserve to die."

A fresh wave of guilt hit Taj. "*I'm sorry*", he wanted to say. "*We were only defending ourselves.*" The words died on his tongue though.

Nothing I say will change anything.

"Let's cut through the alley," Norrin grunted, fastening the bottle to his belt. "The Boondocks are located on the next street over."

Taj nodded, following the sergeant. Unlike his previous experience in one of Alexandria's alleyways, it didn't reek with the stench of fresh urine, or have piles of garbage. It was also significantly wider, allowing them to travel side by side. His nausea was gone, but he had begun to notice another worrying side effect of being in the sun, all his visible skin had begun to turn a shade of pink, with his forearms boasting the brightest shade of colour. Panic shot through him like a super-heated piece of shrapnel, and he started prodding his arms, wincing as stinging pain radiated out from where he touched.

Is this how sun sickness starts? Is my skin going to blister and burn?

Norrin observed his discomfort, adopting a sly smile. "You'll be fine, it's just a little burn, should go away in a day or two," he told Taj.

Taj frowned. *I might still get Sai to have a look at it when I get*

199

home.

"I'll never understood you Vanguards," the sergeant continued. "You're happy to face down hordes of bloodthirsty beasts without a second thought, but a little sunburn makes you whimper like a kicked dog."

"Is that what you think?" Taj said. "I can assure you, my people don't relish battle with the creatures, or with anyone. We only fight to survive, nothing more."

Norrin grimaced but didn't bother replying. The alley spat them out into a street that angled upward to a large gateway where six City Guard were allowing a steady stream of Surfacers to pass through. Giant canvas shade sails were behind them, blocking what lay beyond from view, but the sound of hundreds of people talking came from within.

"That's the Boondocks entrance," Norrin said, pointing to the gateway. "Nobody should bother you from here, the lads might hate you, but they won't start anything. Tell the corporal I sent you, they will let you pass."

"Where are you going?" Taj asked.

"To make sure that riot in the third district doesn't spill over into the fourth. Last time this happened those idiots spent three days destroying their part of the city, then when they got tired of that, they started moving into the second district and laid waste to that too, I'd prefer they don't come here."

Taj was about to thank the man for his help, but he stopped himself, instead saluting to show respect.

Sergeant Norrin laughed at the clumsy attempt at etiquette, but still smartly saluted in return. "I wish you good fortune," he said before going back into the alley, his duty completed.

Taj went out into the street, wincing as the sun hit his tender skin again, and joined the queue of Surfacers waiting to get into the Boondocks. Some stared, but nobody bothered him as the line moved forward.

200

Nearly home.

When he reached the front of the line, a City Guard, who looked exactly the same as the other rank and file Taj had already seen, waved people through with little enthusiasm. A bright blue triangle stuck out proudly on his white chest plate.

That must be the corporal, Taj thought. *I wonder why they display their ranks like that, it would make it extremely easy to target their officers in a fire fight.*

"Hold," the corporal said when he spotted Taj. "What are you doing on this side of the gateway? You know the rules, you people aren't allowed in Alexandria without expressed permission from the Directors."

The other five City Guard surrounded Taj, their guns raised, while the people in line behind him dispersed, retreating back to a safe distance.

"Sergeant Norrin sent me, "I'm going back to Acropolis," Taj said, trying to appear at ease. is hands itched to grab his weapons as they often did when he was challenged, but he stopped himself, knowing the cost of giving into the temptation would no doubt be very high.

The corporal's strikingly blue eyes narrowed, and his companions visibly tensed. "You are a Vanguard?" he asked. "Were you involved in the incident last night?"

"Yes," Taj replied, raising his empty hands to show he wasn't holding any weapons. "I'm not looking for trouble, I just want to go home."

"There won't be trouble, just keep your guns holstered and stay where you belong," the corporal snapped. "Now, move along."

Taj nervously looked around at the five City Guard with their rifles pointed at him. *I'll be glad to be gone from here.* He kept his hands raised, and slowly walked through the gateway, entering the Boondocks trading quarter. The vast area buzzed with activity, hundreds of people scurried around the ramshackle stalls, while the many traders called out their wares, trying to snare potential buyers. The entrance back into the Labyrinth lay near the back of the space, a gaping black hole in the cobblestone protected by two units of stern looking Vanguards. Above him, the great shade sails flapped in the wind, held in place by thick steel poles scattered around the trading quarter.

I might as well look around before I go home.

He wandered into the crowd, navigating his way through the tight laneways in front of the stalls that allowed passage through the Boondocks. For the most part, the traders displayed their wares on tables with colourful signs to attract the eye, but he saw several that had only bothered to lay out an old blanket and haphazardly throw items over the top.

"Roll up, roll up for the finest in cuisine from the underground," a shirtless man in front of a table covered by a multi coloured patchwork quilt called out. "Made by chefs renowned around the underground for their talents, you won't believe your taste buds, these fine dishes are guaranteed to be a one of a kind dining experience."

Taj did a double take as he passed by, on top of the damp blanket were food packs, a plate of meat that had turned green, several of the sickly yellow mushrooms that grew in the Labyrinth, and vegetables that had lines and wrinkles on them. Despite the pathetic appearance, several Surfacers still came rushing forward, pushing past him without so much as an upward glance.

After last night, I would have thought this place would be empty, strange to see everyone interacting in peace.

"Can I get this, it's a genuine Vanguard warding necklace," A young Surfacer girl squealed to her elderly looking companion, catching Taj's attention. "It defends against attacks from beasts, dad, I need this."

The trader who owned the necklace stepped out from behind his stall, pulling up his brown cloth pants and fastening them with an electrical cord. He bowed, revealing a thin skeletal physique hidden underneath his hole ridden shirt.

"That's right, young miss, standard issue for all Vanguards," the trader said with a touch of theatrics. "Many in the underground have been saved by old Xan's warding necklaces."

Taj observed the necklace in the girl's small hands, a piece of scrap metal forged into a cross, fastened to a grimy silver chain. *If that protects against creatures, then I'm eight feet tall and can shoot lightning bolts out of my eyes. Maybe I should warn them it's a scam?*

"Very well my girl," the elderly man said to his daughter. "Xan, I shall trade you 30 kilograms of food, or your choice of medical supplies."

Even after he pays half to the council as a trade fee, that will be enough to feed Xan and his family for a month, easy.

Xan stroked his greasy goatee with his short sausage like fingers, muttering to himself. "30?" he suddenly yelled, causing a few nearby people to jump in alarm. "I can't believe my ears. Do you mean to insult me? Only 30 kilograms for such a powerful artefact. It's worth 50, at least."

The elderly Surfacer scowled and looked down at his daughter, who smiled sweetly, cradling the useless trinket as though it were the most valuable thing in the world.

"Fine," he sighed. "You have a deal Xan."

I doubt the man and his daughter will starve after paying for the necklace. A lot of needy families are being fed by the council using those trade fees, and I can't take food off Xan either, even if he is a liar.

After a moment's contemplation, he decided to leave the charlatan to his work and kept moving further into the trading quarter. A three-man Vanguard patrol crossed over the lane ahead, two nodded in Taj's general direction in greeting, while the third tried to wave and fell over, to the amusement of everyone who saw the ridiculous display of flailing limbs. Mal's companions didn't wait, and left him crawling on the ground, searching for his dropped rifle, which had flung only a metre or so away from him.

"Are you alright?" Taj said, offering his hand to help Mal back to his feet.

"Taj," Mal croaked. "Good to see you boy, I hear you were caught up in the battle last night, glad you didn't die."

Others weren't so lucky.

"What are you doing here?" Taj asked, changing the subject.

"Patrol, Jaz wanted us to keep a presence up here," Mal said. "She has pulled nearly everyone else off regular duty for a counterattack to re-establish the perimeter. Turns out those Berserkers broke through because the creatures made a push, breaking through the lines in several places, god knows how they managed it, never thought they were smart enough to organise a coordinated assault like that."

I'd wager the Husker played a key role. I hope Jaz knows what she's doing, that thing is far more dangerous than all the other creatures combined.

"Aha," Mal laughed, picking up his rifle triumphantly and holding it above his head like a trophy. "Found the little bugger." He planted the gun on the cobblestones and used it as a crutch to leverage himself back up with an efficiency that suggested he performed the action frequently.

"When is Jaz leaving?"

"Soon, briefly considered volunteering to go, but thought better of it," Mal mumbled while unclipping a metal flask from his belt and unscrewing the cap. The bitter smell of strong liquor wafted out, but the Vanguard still gulped the contents down like water, savouring every drop. "I've already got more than enough nightmares to haunt me, don't need anymore."

When his death finally comes, it will probably be a

204

kindness, Taj thought. *Is this my future? A broken-down old drunk, waiting for the sweet release of the grave.*

Mal emptied his flask and loudly burped. "That's better. Should probably go find those two gits I've been saddled with."

"Take care Mal," Taj said sadly. *May your death come swiftly*, he added silently.

Taj parted with Mal and wandered to the end of the laneway, reaching the limit of the Boondocks, a great uninterrupted wall of steel that circled the entire trading quarter, blocking off all access points to Alexandria except for the gateway. He leaned on the wall, gazing out at the bustling marketplace. Games of Knifepoint had sprung up in several places, along with a makeshift boxing ring, marked off with rope, two shirtless Vanguards fought inside while Surfacers cheered them on. Neither of the men were pulling their punches, and both their faces already bore dark bruising from multiple hits to the head. Old Ryn the storyteller sat just beyond the ring, perched on a box, regaling a captivated audience with one of her tales.

Then he saw another familiar face. She wasn't scowling like the last time he saw her, and her attire was far more modest, consisting of a plain pair of blue pants, a white top and a piece of elastic holding back her jet black hair. The green eyed woman from the Banquet Pyramid strolled at a sedate pace, stopping at every stall in her path, greeting the traders like they were old friends. General Valens, along with four other City Guard dogged her footsteps, watching everyone with careful scrutiny, they all carried dozens of green canvas bags, but were otherwise unarmed.

What are you doing here with a general? He pondered. Then he saw it, she was subtle, but it was clear what she was doing. Valens handed another bag to the green eyed Surfacer, and she moved on to the next trader. She casually waved hello to the middle aged woman with scraggy grey hair, and dropped the bag among the items arrayed on the bland white quilt. Valens handed her another bag, and she moved to the next trader.

What are you up to?

Taj forgot about everything else, and followed, keeping several steps behind to avoid suspicion. He passed the grey haired woman, glancing at the contents of the bag, spying fresh vegetables and clothing packed tightly inside.

Why is she giving out supplies? What's her goal?

He observed the young woman until she had given out her last bag to a couple selling old bronze weapons. She dropped the prize and started looking at the old weapons with keen interest. The City Guard stayed nearby, but their focus had shifted to the nearby boxing ring where the two Vanguards were still fighting for the amusement of the crowd.

I think it's time I found out what you are up to.

Taj joined the line of people marching through, slipping past Valens as he spat in disgust at the display.

"Savages," the general said to his men. "Beating each other up for sport is no way for civilised people to behave."

And yet you are watching them, so what does that make you, moron.

Taj left the line and approached the green eyed women. "Didn't realise you were the giving sort," he said to her while pretending to peruse a bronze sword.

Her face changed in an instant, and her scowl returned with a vengeance. "You again," she sighed. "Are you following me?"

Taj's face went warm.

She rolled her distinctive green eyes and crossed her arms. "Is there something wrong with you?" she snapped. "Don't bother me if you're not going to say anything."

General Valens spun around, muttering indecipherable words under his breath.

"Watch yourself, Vanguard; it would be a shame if I had to break the new peace treaty so soon after it was signed. Move on now, before somebody gets hurt."

Taj quickly recovered from his awkwardness and felt a familiar flash of anger overtake him. "I'm not worried," he snarled. "If what we saw last night is anything to go off, City Guard can't shoot straight, I doubt you could even hit me at this range. You should be embarrassed, even our small children are better fighters.

"Don't sass me, Subrat," Valens retorted. "You and your cutthroats got lucky last night, if you had faced the men from my district, rather than those barely competent fools from the third district, you wouldn't be standing here right now."

Before either of them could launch another insult, the green eyed Surfacer smacked them both over the head, prompting Taj to get flashbacks of his training.

"Settle, both of you," she demanded, glaring at them. "There are a lot of innocent people here, if you want to measure gun sizes, go do it somewhere else."

Taj's anger disappeared, and all the embarrassment and shame from the night before returned like an old friend.

I nearly caused another fight, so soon after the last one, what is wrong with me.

"Sorry," he eventually muttered.

"Apologies for my behaviour," Valens murmured.

"Shake hands," she ordered. "And let this be the last time either of you tries to pick a fight in my presence again."

Taj extended his hand, waiting for Valens. The general gritted his teeth in a pained smile and reluctantly engaged in a brief handshake.

"We should go now, before anyone else sees us here," Valens said to the young woman. "We can't afford to be seen here for much longer, if the Directors find out what you've been doing here, I'm not sure even I can protect you from their retribution."

She nodded. "Agreed, let's get out of here."

"What's your name," Taj blurted out, prompting her to frown

207

and Valens to take a step toward him, murderous intent in his gaze.

"Why?" she asked, her disdain still evident in every fibre of her being. "What purpose would my name serve?"

"Well what should I call you?"

She shook her head and walked away. Valens glared at him one last time, before following her.

Taj watched them go, his mind swimming with more questions that he would probably never get answers to.

Chapter Seventeen
An Unexpected Visitor

Five Weeks later...

"Throw your left jab and step out with your left foot at the same time," Taj explained to the group of thirty Vanguard recruits as he demonstrated the action. "Then throw the right cross and twist your hip into the punch." The movement shot stinging pains down his back, but he gritted his teeth and pushed through the pain. It had been weeks since his fight with the Alpha Berserker, but the injuries he'd suffered still hadn't healed properly.

The recruits in front of him attempted to mimic the basic striking combination with limited success, he counted only two who could do it with any proficiency. The rest either overextended themselves and fell over, or couldn't move their fists in sync with their feet.

"This is becoming harder every day, they just can't get it right," he muttered while walking along the line of enthusiastic, gangly teens. "That's what you get when the bar is lowered. None of them will be fit for duty anytime soon."

Upon returning to Acropolis a few weeks ago, he had learned the full extent of the damage caused by the Berserkers. After they had broken through the lines, a flood of creatures followed, twenty units were wiped out in the initial onslaught. Jaz's counterattack had been swift, but over three hundred lives were still lost before the defensive perimeter could be re-established. In response to their rapidly declining numbers, Jye stepped up the enlistment of more Vanguards, thousands of young hopefuls were accepted.

"What's the point of learning hand to hand combat?" A callow boy whined near the end of the line. "We use guns, what's the point of learning to fight like this?"

"Because lackwit," Taj yelled. "What happens when you run out of bullets and something is trying to kill you? Punching and kicking may not do much, but it's better than nothing."

The youth scowled and started throwing his left fist at an imaginary opponent, but his feet stayed planted to the ground, the exact opposite of what had just been instructed.

"Make no mistake," Taj shouted to the rest of the group. "Being a Vanguard is not easy, if you can't hack it, quit now, it's only going to get worse from here.

He grimaced at the familiar words. *I sound like my own teachers, now I understand why they were angry all the time, this is so frustrating.*

Two more recruits tumbled into the dirt, flicking mud into the air and knocking over several others around them. *Half of these kids will die in one of the four trials*, he decided. *At least the Watchers will take any who survive, they won't be forced to make The Sacrifice and be left out in the tunnels to die.*

He averted his gaze from the stumbling recruits and scanned the rest of the walled practice field. The dirt covered training area stretched fifty metres in each direction and had an imposing black Vanguard Barracks at the entrance where everyone took their meals. There were twenty compounds just like it around the rest of Acropolis, generally only a few were in operation, but times had changed, now all of them were full.

The rest of his unit were scattered around the field teaching their own students. Tre was showing his group how to shoot at the target range set up in front of a sand hill. Ren was in the middle demonstrating knife fighting; plastic knives were used, the recruits still flinched and cried out whenever they were tagged with a fake blade though. Wes was near the back teaching basic first aid, while the twins had combined their efforts and had their recruits cleaning rifles. Dal had left an hour earlier to take his group out on a run

210

around the city.

"Enough," Taj announced, rubbing his itching eyes in frustration. "Go get some food and water from the barracks."

The recruits were gone in a flash, sprinting back to the barracks with the enthusiasm of kids who don't often get to have full bellies. The training was difficult, but one of the main perks was virtually unlimited access to food and drink.

They better enjoy it while they can, even if they get through the trials, they will probably never get to eat like this again.

"Hard at work Pinky?" Dal cut into his thoughts.

"Shut up," Taj groaned. His skin had kept the pink hue from his time in the sun for several days after his return to the underground, it had since faded, but that didn't stop Dal from teasing him. The name Pinky wasn't overly hurtful or clever, but he still found it annoying, which only spurred Dal on.

Dal laughed and took a swig from his water bottle, before pouring the rest on himself to cool down. "You're just angry the Sky Corps flew us home in style, while you were burned walking through the streets like a schmuck."

"How was the run?" Taj sighed.

"Frustrating, most couldn't keep up," Dal replied. "I swear not even you were that bad when you first joined."

"Tre would disagree."

"You passed the trials; half of these kids will be gone after the first one."

"Probably for the best, thirteen died from my group before the end of training, not everyone is cut out to be a Vanguard."

"You're telling me, you should have seen..." Dal trailed off as his left eye twitched, and his mouth went limp, the episode only lasted a few seconds, but he was still visibly frustrated when it passed. His head wound hadn't taken long to heal, however, his speech and face muscles had somehow been affected from the collision with the wall, a lingering reminder of the injury caused by the Husker.

"You two get over here," Ren barked from the other side of the field. The others had dismissed their recruits and a steady stream of exhausted and hungry youths flowed towards the barracks.

"We have another three days of this," Tre said when Taj and Dal had come within earshot. "Then Unit 35 takes over at this field for their five week stint as babysitters, and we head back out into the Labyrinth."

"You mean to food packs, and killer creatures? Lovely," Dal quipped.

As was customary whenever Dal interrupted with his nonsense, Tre ignored him and kept talking. "We will patrol between checkpoints and ensure we don't have another incident like a few weeks ago. Jye doesn't want us clearing any new tunnels, our current orders are to hold the territory we have."

"What about riot control?" Wes asked. "Will we be on call to help with any further acts of violence in Acropolis? The Watchers are struggling to contain the fighting as it is."

The rest of the unit grumbled. A week earlier they were forced to help the Watchers stop a riot between pro and antiwar groups. Since seeing the Husker, Tre had ceased his advocacy for a conflict with Alexandria and publicly put his full support behind Jye, however, the seeds of dissent he had planted were alive and well.

"I think Jye is planning something big," Tre answered. "The Watchers will need to stand on their own for a while, because something tells me we will have our hands full over the next few months."

"I might help the Watchers one last time tonight," Ren said. "I've heard some of the Harvesters are planning to protest again late this evening, it could get messy, especially if anyone from our ranks joins them."

"Have they found anyone willing to challenge Jye for leadership yet?" Wes said. "Or are they just going to keep causing trouble in the streets? They need to either make a move, or back off. It's getting ridiculous, the other day I heard Cal calling that fight at the Banquet Pyramid the first battle in the Vengeance War."

"It was hardly a battle, more like a massacre," Dal said. "Only one of ours was killed, they lost over sixty, even if their Directors deny anyone was killed, we all saw the bodies for ourselves."

The discussion quickly descended into multiple conversations as they talked about the one Vanguard casualty, a youngblood named Sal, and the pro war groups demanding more fighting.

This could go on forever, Vanguards are the worst gossips in the whole damn city, Taj mused.

"What about Huskers?" he interrupted, putting a stop to all the idle chatting between his fellows. "Has there be any more sightings?"

Tre shook his head. "There haven't been any more reports of Husker activity since our encounter, I doubt they are done with us though. We need to be alert for any sign of them, I want us to be the first unit to bag one of those bastards."

Knowledge of the Huskers had spread through the ranks quickly, the reaction by most had been anger at being left in the dark about the new threat, then rivalries started to form; every Vanguard unit wanted to be the first to kill one of the monsters.

Tre waved them away. "Send your recruits home after they've filled their bellies, training starts again in twelve hours."

****

Taj fired his weapon until the Lurker in front of him stopped moving, but the tunnel section was full of them, hundreds of pale creatures fighting for the chance to feast on his flesh. He ran into their midst firing his weapon in an arc, the pack disappeared in a flash and was replaced by the young Surfacer woman with green

213

eyes.

"How did you get down here?" he asked her.

She growled, and her skin bubbled, melting off her slender frame and pooling on the concrete. He tried to look away, but he was transfixed, unable to move. When the last of her skin had gone, a grey monster emerged, its laugh like roars reverberating off the concrete walls.

Taj woke with a start, his body dripping with sweat, a familiar acrid taste burned in his mouth. *The nightmares are back, but why now?*

He lay back down, cursing the phantoms who were haunting his rest again. Bitter experience had taught him that once the nightmares started, they wouldn't stop for many hours. *I might as well go for a walk, see Jun, maybe he can give me some tips on teaching for tomorrow.*

Taj slowly got out of his bed and crossed the darkened room. Sai's shadowy form lay in a corner, her light breathing the only noise in the house. He opened the door slightly, wincing at the creak, light from the streetlamps flooded in, and he inched his way outside.

The street was alive with activity, Guild members were working on fluttering light fixtures, civilians were chatting in the streets and Harvesters trudged along to their shifts in the agricultural fields. Taj kept his head down and pushed his way past, his thoughts focussed on his frequent nightmares. *They are far too frequent, it can't just be from a restless mind, there is something else going on here.*

Upon reaching Doc's hut on the outskirts of the city, he was still unsure if there was any meaning behind the nightmares. *I don't even know who I can talk to about this without sounding like a lunatic.* He knocked on the door and waited.

"Oh, come in, you spectre," Doc cackled. "I pray your entry will stop you haunting me."

Taj entered and took his usual position on the opposite side of the fire to Doc. The old grandmaster tinkered with the various rifle parts arrayed in front of him. An old worn set of armour and several large knives were either side of him.

"Kai, I'm glad you are here," Doc said. "I'm trying to reassemble my gear; I fear I will need it again before long."

It wasn't the first time Doc had called Taj by his father's name, and he had learned to ignore the slip up and just move on with the conversation. "Why will you be fighting again? You're retired."

Doc stopped working and pointed a recently sharpened blade at Taj. "I was out in the Labyrinth long before you were born. I can fight whatever I want, except those yellow eyed Demons from Agora."

"The Huskers?"

"Yes, you should stay away from them, nasty, wretched things," Doc said in an unusual tone. "Seems even Unit 6 have struggled to best them."

Taj had heard him ramble many times, but it was the first time he had heard Doc sound worried. Only a select few knew Unit 6 had gone deeper into the Labyrinth in search of help to fight the Huskers, and Jye had told him recently they were long overdue to return.

If the old man is worried too, then things must be worse than I thought.

He spent the next few hours helping Doc assemble and clean his weapons, it was slow monotonous work, but it kept his mind occupied so he couldn't dwell on his nightmares.

Doc filled the silence with his usual incoherent chatter, occasionally he would recount stories of past catastrophes and how Acropolis always pulled through, or comedic tales of Jye and Tre's youth. Taj's favourite was by far when the two now legendary Vanguards had tried brewing alcohol out of beans, which turned volatile and blew up a house.

"They were both running up the street with their pants on fire," Doc explained with glee. "Their fathers gave them quite the hiding for that one. Good men, both died only a few months later, the boys were devastated, they'd never admit it though."

By the time Doc's weapons and armour were ready for use, Taj's head was drooping, and his eyes struggled to stay open. *I have to get to the practice field soon, but maybe I can get a little rest, hopefully it's safe to sleep now.* He was about to say his farewells to Doc, when the old man loaded his rifle and fired a quick burst into the roof, prompting people around them to shout in alarm.

"Dammit, not again, don't you ever sleep, lunatic," someone yelled from next door.

"Not to worry, it's all part of the plan," Doc replied.

"Never a dull moment," Taj chuckled. "I have to go now Doc, I'm not sure when I will be back, my unit is being sent back out into the Labyrinth again soon."

Doc visibly deflated at the news. "Yes, of course," he mumbled. "You have many things to do, be careful out there boy."

Taj took one last look at the hut, from the ever growing assortment of pots and pans in the corner, to the cook fire that was always alight. *I hope the old goat will be safe here while I'm gone.* He reluctantly stepped outside and found Docs bleary eyed neighbours gathering in a group on the doorstep.

"Come out here old man, we have a bone to pick with you," a young woman with a loose fitting nightshirt screamed.

Doc strolled out the door and lifted his arms as though he were preparing to perform for the crowd. "Welcome, can I interest anyone in my latest soup recipe, it's quite yummy."

Taj stifled a giggle and sidestepped the growing number of angry people. *I almost feel sorry for them, the wily old coot will talk them around in circles for hours before they realise he is toying with them.* He ducked into an alley and ran along the muddy trail until he reached the next street over.

Without looking, Taj jogged into the intersection, but failed to see the cloaked figure hurrying towards the outer wall in time. He collided with the figure and stumbled; gritting his teeth when his lingering injuries sent stinging reminders all through his body.

"Sorry about that…" He started saying before trailing off. *What's she doing here?*

The green eyed Surfacer fumbled with the folds of her black cloak, covering her face.

"You're a long way from home," Taj teased. "Just a tip, next time you sneak down here, maybe wear a less conspicuous outfit."

Her eyes widened, and she held up her hands in exasperation, "Quiet," she whispered. "Do you have any idea what your people will do to me if they catch me here, moron."

Taj reddened; he hadn't considered the consequences of a Surfacer being caught in Acropolis, he glanced around, nobody in the street was paying attention to them, yet. *She is right, if the wrong people find her, they will kill her, I need to get her out of here before anyone notices her.*

"What are you doing here?" he said, "It's not safe, you need to go."

"I know that," she snapped. "I was delivering antibiotics to some friends, their daughter is sick, without penicillin she would have died. We lost track of time, I meant to leave hours ago. I should be home right now."

"Why do you care?" Taj said without thinking. "Don't most of your people hate us?"

The woman lunged at him, grabbing his collar. "Because unlike you," she growled through clenched teeth. "I don't seek to murder everything I come into contact with."

A pleasant but unfamiliar scent tickled Taj's nose. *Why does she smell like that?* He wondered. *Smells like the flowers in that garden on the surface.* "You never did tell me your name," he

217

suddenly said, the words falling out of his mouth, apparently of their own accord.

Her tense features relaxed and she released him. "If you must know," she sighed. "Call me Valens."

"Isn't that the name of that idiot general?" Taj blurted.

"He's my brother, and I'll thank you not to call him an idiot," she scolded. "It's our family name, first names are kept for close friends and family."

"You don't find that confusing?"

"No more confusing than your people only using first names."

What a strange custom, but I suppose she is right; our traditions must seem odd to her as well.

"What's this then," a gravelly voice interjected. "Looks like some Surfacer has gotten lost on her travels."

Taj groaned as three middle-aged men slinked towards them, their dirt-covered clothing and grey overalls identifying them as Harvesters. *Probably just knocked off from work, or come back from the protest Ren mentioned, either way this is bad.* Even at the best of times, the food pickers were notoriously ill-tempered.

"How dare you call me a Surfacer," Valens exclaimed in mock outrage. "I have lived In Acropolis all my life. This is my close friend Taj, he can vouch for me."

How did she come up with a lie so fast? She didn't even need to think about it.

"I can assure you, she isn't from above," Taj said awkwardly. "Go about your business, have a drink, I'm sure you've earned it."

"Don't smell right," The smallest of the men wheezed, his muscled frame quivering as he sniffed around Valens like a hound chasing a scent. After doing a complete circle, he patted his balding head and mumbled to himself. "My nose never lies."

His two larger companions were similarly brawny from a lifetime of hard labour, but they sported disfiguring injuries. One had a piece of brown canvas sack partially covering his left eye

218

socket, while the other had a metal plate bolted onto his face where his nose used to be.

"Smelling clean, sticks out down here," the man with a missing eye said in his gravelly voice. "You made a big mistake coming here."

"Maybe I just bathe regularly," Valens retorted. "What are you doing smelling people? Your odd suspicions about my scent hardly seem pertinent; in fact, they are downright rude."

The three men frowned, confusion crossing their weathered faces as they tried to make sense of what was said.

"She doesn't talk right either," The man without a nose insisted. "Our people don't use words like that."

"Well, excuse me for learning how to communicate in ways other than mumbled grunting," Valens chided. "If you are done insulting me, my friend and I will be on our way."

The small man held up his dirt-covered hand. "No, I don't think so," he bellowed. "Your lot think you can go where you please, that you're better than us. You are the reason my family goes hungry; you are the reason I've spent my life bent over in the muck. Jye might have stopped us from going to war, that doesn't mean we can't put a nosy Surfacer invading our city in her place."

"Back off, before you get hurt," Taj cautioned, he didn't like threatening his own people, but he couldn't allow them to hurt her, especially when she had come to help a sick girl.

"You would side with her over your own?" The man with no nose whined, pointing his long-gnarled finger at Valens. "She is probably a spy gathering information on us. What if she has found a weakness in the outer defences, there could be an army marching here as we speak, ready to take advantage."

If they won't listen to reason, I will have to give them a beating to get out of this. Taj readied for the inevitable fight and assessed his foes. *They are strong,* he surmised. *I doubt they know how to fight properly though. If I knock one of them out, the other two might run.*

The small man jabbed Taj in the chest with his thick thumb. "Careful boy," he threatened. "We don't want to hurt you, step aside."

Taj's fist connected with the Harvester's stomach, turning the man's legs to jelly and dropping him to the ground. He turned focus to the other two, raising his clenched fists to his head, ready to block the inevitable retaliation.

"This won't do at all," Valens said. "Hurry up and deal with them Taj, Jye is expecting us, he will be most displeased at the delay."

The other two Harvesters recoiled at the mention of the grandmaster.

"Why are you meeting Jye?" the man with one eye stuttered. "Do you know him?"

Valens laughed, "Quite well actually, Taj is a Vanguard; he is escorting me to the nearest compound to meet with the grandmaster and discuss a private matter."

She's playing a dangerous game, Taj mused. Jye still commanded great respect in the city, however, his popularity and influence had taken a massive hit recently because of his refusal to start a war. *Let's just hope their fear of him outweighs their hatred of Surfacers.*

"Vic, he is a Vanguard," the man with one eye whined to his smaller companion. "I've seen this kid before."

Vic slowly got back up, gingerly rubbing his stomach, calculation and distrust in his gaze.

"You sure, Sid?" Vic demanded. "There are thousands of young punks like this in the city."

"Seen him with Tre," Sid confirmed. "The boy was mixed up in the battle a few weeks ago, he is definitely a Vanguard. I don't care who this girl is, no way I'm crossing Jye on my own, you saw what that crazy bastard did to former Grandmaster Hal."

Vic crumbled, swearing under his breath as he stormed past, his two relieved friends in tow. "You best not linger then," the Harvester murmured. "There are plenty of others in Acropolis who would be willing to risk the wrath of the grandmaster to get a shot at a Surfacer."

"Thank you, gentlemen," Valens called after them in an overly sweet voice. "It's been a pleasure." She linked her arm with Taj's and led him back towards the inner city.

"You are an excellent liar," Taj whispered. "What are we doing now?"

"I don't know, I just reacted," she muttered. "I didn't want anyone getting hurt because of me. I don't think I'll have time to sneak out now, those three louts will probably tell everyone who will listen about this, I need to lie low for a little while."

"How did you get in here anyway? The Watchers patrolling the walls should have seen your approach, people rarely gain entry to Acropolis unnoticed."

"I'll tell you about it another time. For now, we should go somewhere safe before somebody else tries to attack me."

I doubt I can get her through the gate unnoticed right now, especially if the Harvesters are still protesting. If they catch us, we will be lucky to escape being ripped apart by furious hands.

"Home," he decided. "We can figure out a way to sneak away later, let's just get inside."

Taj set a sedate pace to avoid arousing suspicion, but made sure to keep scanning the area for potential threats. His heart thundered every time they passed other people, even though most didn't even give them a second glance.

Despite the danger, Valens stopped to marvel at an agricultural pen, and a Guild factory as though they were the most interesting thing in the world. He had to gently pull her away each time, reminding her of the urgency to get somewhere safe.

"Every time I come here; I see something new," she remarked.

221

"It's fascinating the way your people have adapted to life down here."

"You come here often?" Taj said in disbelief. "Why would you willingly leave the wonders in Alexandria?"

"There is nothing wonderous about Alexandria, it was built as a monument to vanity and corruption, the city is an illusion, fake. Acropolis is so alive and genuine, I'd live down here in a heartbeat if I could."

"You're crazy," Taj declared as they dodged two Watchers on patrol and entered his street.

Nearly there.

When they reached his home, he quickly opened the door and ushered Valens inside.

"Sai, you home?" Taj shouted as he shut the door. "Sai?" His sister often went to check on their elderly neighbours when she awoke, and it appeared that today was no different.

"She'll be back soon," he told Valens. "Take a seat anywhere you like."

Despite the invitation, she took some time to walk the perimeter of the room, her green eyes darting from the pile of dirty clothes on the floor to the rusted roof.

Taj suddenly felt more than a little self-conscious at the chaotic state of his home. "Sorry for the mess," he said sheepishly. "Probably not what you're used to."

"It's fine, this place has some real character, you should see my apartment; it's stupidly big and boring, I much prefer this."

"Is that why you come here, because you're bored?"

"Maybe a little," she conceded. "But the main reason is to help, the Boondocks gave me a firsthand look at the state of your people; your health care is atrocious. You shouldn't have to suffer just because you were unlucky enough to be born down here. Whatever your ancestors alleged crimes, your people have more than paid for them."

222

"Are you a Healer then?"

"Sometimes, I do possess some of the same skills as your Medics and Healers, but I also delve deeper, research disease, create vaccines. My work is very boring to most people, but I find it fascinating."

Taj nodded politely even though he didn't understand what had been said. Normally he would pester for more information to learn everything he could, but he didn't want to appear foolish in front of his guest.

Valens didn't seem to notice his ignorance though and kept talking. "If I discover a new treatment, or vaccine, after testing, the Directors distribute it to the population through the air filters, potential health problems are averted before they begin."

"Air filters?" Taj enquired, sitting down with his back to the wall that allowed a view of the front door. "I think Tre mentioned something about that once."

"You didn't notice the clean air when you were up top?" Valens asked him. "There are devices all around Alexandria that keep the air clear of smog and other toxic particles, they really are quite remarkable."

"Taj," Sai exclaimed as she walked in. "You're back, there is something I need to tell you, I've joined the…"

"Sai," Taj said, springing to his feet. "This is Valens, a friend."

Sai glanced from Valens to Taj, a small smile ghosting her lips. "Taj, why is there a Surfacer girl in our house?"

How did she know? Taj quickly tried to think of a lie, but his sister knew him all too well.

"Don't try and mislead me, little brother," she giggled. "You have always been awful at it, I still remember the time you tried convincing me the hicky on your neck was from a stray punch during training, last time I checked, fists don't have teeth."

Taj's face went warm, and he suddenly had the desire to run away and hide. *Why did she have to bring that up now?*

"I think we've met before Valens," Sai continued. "At Sam's house a few weeks ago, her parents are very grateful you saved her from the lung sickness. What brings you here?"

"Trouble with the Harvesters," Taj explained. "They were going to attack Valens, so I brought her here, she can sneak out of the city later."

"I'm not surprised, those brutes aren't known for their tolerance," Sai said, rolling her eyes. "I wouldn't take it personally, they don't like anyone smarter than them, which is everyone."

Valens laughed. "I do remember you, Sai, you punched that man with the wandering hands. What was his name?"

"Opi, he's a harmless old perve, just needs the occasional reminder to keep his hands to himself."

Sai and Valens started talking at a lighting fast pace, Taj lost track of the conversation immediately. *Maybe I can get a few hours' sleep while they chat.*

"Taj, aren't you supposed to be meeting Tre and the others?" Sai reminded him. "You had better hurry, I saw Ash and Ace on my way home."

I completely forgot, Tre is going to kill me if I'm late.

"What did you want to tell me Sai, what have you joined?" he asked.

"Don't worry about that now," she said. "We can talk later."

More secrets. I hope she hasn't done anything rash.

Taj ran to the other room and gingerly got dressed in his armour, the normally simple process becoming several minutes of agony as his back ached, shooting pains down his spine. He picked up his weapons and went to grab his spare ammunition when a loud high-pitched siren thundered through Acropolis, blocking out all thought and reason. His stomach dropped, *that's the perimeter alarm, the city is under attack.* The steady drum--beat of the big guns shaking the foundations started a moment later.

Chapter Eighteen

The Outer Barricades

"Get to the vaults," Taj shouted, running back into the main room of the house. "No time to waste, go now."

Sai shook her head, "No, the whole city will be headed there, it will be safer to stay here and wait this out. I can protect us." She went over to the back wall and pulled an unassuming panel off, revealing a cavity with a two-barrelled gun the size of a standard rifle.

"What is that?" Taj asked. "Since when do you have weapons in the house?"

Sai turned the gun over, showcasing her handy work. "I made it myself, haven't figured out a name yet. It has better stopping power than a rifle, but the range leaves much to be desired."

"Where did you learn to make something like that?" Taj said incredulously. "How long has it been in the wall?"

"Never you mind, little brother," she replied with a twinkle in her eye. "Valens and I will stay here, there is no point in arguing, you're just wasting time, get out there."

Taj gave them a weak smile and started toward the door. *She won't listen to me, she never does.* "Ok, stay in the house though, don't leave here until it's over." He went outside, making sure to firmly close the door behind him. *Please be safe.* In the few minutes since the perimeter alarm had sounded, dozens of families with bleary eyed children and other non-combatants had flooded the streets. As per Jye's directive, the vaults near the Amphitheatre had been cleared and refurbished to house the city's population in case of emergencies, but this was the first time they had reason to use them.

Acropolis turned to chaos as he ran toward the main gate, common sense giving way to fear as thousands pushed to reach safety by any means necessary. Violence broke out almost immediately, with dozens of angry and scared people venting their frustrations by beating each other bloody. Taj avoided getting involved in most of the fights, but he was left with little choice when a member of the Guild sporting a slash across his face fell in front of him. The two attackers, one brandishing a small knife and the other a table leg he wielded like a club, bared down on the fallen man as he held up his hands in a plea for mercy.

Where are the Watchers when you need them? I don't have time for this, if the wall falls, whatever petty quarrel they're having won't matter.

"Enough," Taj shouted, firing a few shots in the air, prompting hysterical screams from the surrounding people.

"Back off Vanguard, this isn't your concern," The knife wielding man spat. "This traitor is getting what he deserves."

"Help me," the Guild member pleaded. "These two.."

"Quiet, traitor," the man with the table leg roared as he struck his helpless victim over the head.

"I said enough," Taj growled. "Leave him, get to the vaults, now."

"Or what boy, you going to shoot us?" The man with the knife laughed. "Do you know who you're messing with here?"

"I don't care," Taj said. "Whatever this is, it's done, get out of here, now."

"This isn't over, I will remember your face," the man with the table leg yelled.

The two thugs glared at him but didn't push the issue, disappearing back into the crowd.

Taj hauled the injured Guild member to his feet, his grey jacket was dripping with blood and torn in several places, but he didn't appear to have any injuries except the cut to his face.

"Thank you, truly," he stammered. "My name is Hec, I just returned from the surface after being traded a few months ago, a lot of people are calling me a spy."

"Are you alright? Can you get to the Vaults?" Taj said. "You should be safe there."

"I don't think anywhere is safe anymore," Hec replied sadly as he stumbled away.

Taj watched him go, everyone gave him a wide berth, and more than a few people shot dirty looks in the injured mans direction.

The Huskers won't need to destroy the city, we might kill each other for them.

****

By the time he reached the gate, at least thirty units of Watchers, and a handful of Vanguards were making their way down the dirt track to the outer barricades. Tre was at the front of the procession, screaming orders, most of his words were lost amongst the sound of the big guns and the perimeter alarm, which still blared from every corner of the city.

Taj followed, nervously checking if his rifle was still loaded and ready. *Here we go.* When he reached the barricades, he jumped up the nearest stairs two at a time. The defensive structure circling the city stood over twenty metres tall, blocking what lay beyond from view. At the summit, he found a mix of Vanguards and Watchers thinly spread in both directions along the fortifications.

There are so few of us still in Acropolis, the Watchers are scattered, we might not have enough fighters to defend the city.

Taj ran to an empty spot across from the stairs, a big gun thundered next to him, spitting a near constant wave of gunfire at what lay below. He gazed down, his body froze, hundreds of Lurkers filled his vision, with even more pouring in from the tunnels.

Run, hide, a voice whispered in the back of his mind. *Death has come, flee before you're caught in its wake.*

"*If they take the walls, it will be like Agora, Sai, Valens, Dal, Jye, everyone will die*," he told himself. He bared his teeth and opened fire, cutting down a line of creatures before he had to reload. The bodies were gone in a heartbeat, swallowed by the rest of the pack as they surged forward. The massing swarm of flesh heaved and flowed like a great wave, breaking against the wall and sending small shockwaves along the battlements.

He grabbed the stone crenelations with one hand to steady himself, then rained another hail of bullets on the enemies below. A routine quickly set in, shooting, reloading and his rapidly thumping heart was all he knew. Creatures fell in droves, and the tide slowly receded, until Taj couldn't find any more targets, all that was left of the pack was a dead carpet of unmoving bleach white flesh.

"Cease fire." The cry went along the barricades and everything went deathly still all at once. The perimeter alarm stopped, and the big guns fell silent.

Taj rubbed his ringing ears. *We did it, they didn't get through.* A cheer went up, and the Vanguards and Watchers celebrated their victory. He went along the wall, looking for anyone he knew among the smiling faces. Tre was easily recognisable, while everyone around him laughed or hugged each other, the commander remained stern faced.

Something is wrong.

"Get back to the city, Jye is gathering reinforcements," Tre told him. "We can't use grenades so close to the wall, we will need more guns to hold them back until he gets here, grab anyone you can, be quick about it."

Taj frowned, waving his hand at the mass piles of dead. "What for Tre? We killed them all, it's over."

"No, Taj, it's not over yet. That was only the first attack lead by the Omega, it was probing our defences with the other disposable members of the herd. I suspect the Alpha is about to send the entire pack against us."

The Vanguard pointed to the tunnel just as a Lurker charged out, hurtling towards the wall, howling as it ran over the motionless forms of its brethren. Hundreds more followed, spewing out of the Labyrinth in an unceasing tide.

"Go now, make…" Tre said as the big guns exploded back to life, drowning out the rest of his order.

Taj cursed, and bounded down the stairs, breaking into a full sprint as he climbed back up the dirt track to the city. The main gate was still open, twenty Watchers blocked the entrance.

"Help. Down. Now," he stammered to them. *That makes no sense.* He took a deep breath.

"Think, then act," he murmured, repeating a doctrine his father had told him once. "Who's in charge here?" he said, his voice going hoarse.

A man only a few years older than Taj raised his hand, he wore the red armour of a Watcher, but his empty eye socket and the thick white scar tissue that covered his face and neck bespoke a life of combat.

"I am," he rasped. "Name's Fin."

"Attacks not over," Taj explained. "We need more fighters to help hold them back or the outer barricades will fall."

"Watcher Grandmaster Lee has sent word that he will be here shortly with all of the Watchers from our main barracks," Fin reported. "I've also sent runners to collect others who are patrolling the city. Where is Jye?"

"On the way, he should be here soon."

I hate this, I know what I have to do, but I don't have the right to ask them for this.

"Fin, how many Watchers have you got here?" Taj inquired.

"Can they fight?"

The disfigured man grimaced, his remaining eye raking over those under his command. "I have twenty here and another eighty nearby in reserve, they are capable, but very inexperienced in real combat."

It's not enough, but it will have to do.

"Most will die if we send them to fight," Fin added in a barely audible whisper.

Taj glanced back at the outer barricades, the fortifications were glowing from the muzzle flash of hundreds of weapons firing at once. "More will die if the creatures reach the city walls, another few dozen guns could be the difference."

Fin swore but didn't argue the point. "Alright," he said. "Lads, you heard him, we need to get down there. Gaz, go get the others, hurry."

A gangly youth whom Taj assumed was Gaz ran off to do Fin's bidding, returning a few moments later with another eighty Watchers in tow.

"Gaz, Fil, Jes," Fin said to the group. "You three wait here, send down anyone else who arrives, let Grandmaster Lee know where we've gone."

"If the barricades fall before reinforcements arrive," Taj added. "Close the gate, don't wait for us to fall back." He didn't know whether he had the authority to give the order, but the images of Agora's ruptured walls and the bone-choked streets refused to leave his head.

It can't happen here; I refuse to let them inside Acropolis.

Taj led his haphazard reinforcements through the gate and down to the barricades, when they reached the stairs, Tre was waiting for them. "Half of you go left, the other half right," the commander shouted. "Don't stop shooting until you're dead or out of bullets."

The Watchers did as they were told, and Taj returned to his

spot on the wall. *I just brought a hundred people to their deaths.* In his absence, thousands of Lurkers had spilled into the chamber, filling the plain in front of the city. There were four gates that allowed access through the outer barricades, he had been taught they were the weak point of any defences, but from what he could see, the creatures didn't appear to be interested in trying to batter the gates down. Many were bunching in large clumps at the base of the fortifications, creating towers of flesh and bone that steadily grew as more writhing bodies were added to the construction.

"In a siege, the attackers should hit the gates first, what are they doing?" he pondered. "Is there some master strategy here I'm missing?" He sprayed a nearby tower until his rifle was empty, dislodging a dozen or more creatures, but it failed to slow the growth.

Why aren't the big guns helping?

The nearest big gun was silent, its barrels glowing red as the two operators carefully poured water over the metal, trying to cool the weapon. All along the barricades, gun emplacements went quiet, and the Lurker towers grew mostly unhindered.

We can't hold them for much longer, if Jye doesn't hurry, he'll arrive to a wall full of dead men.

Taj eyed his own gun barrel with apprehension, the hot metal glowing an angry red, he had seen a rifle explode from overuse before and had no desire to experience it firsthand. *If I don't cool my rifle soon, it will explode too.* A Lurker jumped up on the precipice, he fired three shots into its head, but another quickly followed. He jammed his superheated barrel into its face, cooking the flesh and forcing it back over the wall.

The towers peaked above the battlements and hundreds more Lurkers leapt over, knocking down anyone in their path, tearing into armour and flesh. Savage close quarters fighting erupted, with knives and fists versus teeth and claws, the howls of dying creatures and men drowning out all other noise.

Taj dropped to a knee, with clumsy hands he reached for one of his knives just as an airborne creature slammed into him, knocking them both to the ground. He instinctively grabbed his pistol, jamming the weapon between the creature's snapping jaws, pulling the trigger.

He rolled the corpse off his stomach and used his other hand to draw one of his curved knives. Another Lurker sprang over, he rammed his knife upwards through its skull, pushing the blade until it found the brain. He took a few steps back, using his boot to push the body off his knife A few metres away, Ash whirled his blades in an arc, keeping at least a dozen enemies at bay. Ace was on top of the battlements carefully sniping, Tre and Ren were just beyond in front of a tower with four other Vanguards, killing any creatures unfortunate enough to land near them, a carpet of pale bodies already lay at their feet, but more flooded toward them in an unceasing tide.

Hurry up Jye.

A loud roar caught his attention, a Lurker larger than most grown men scaled the tower above him, standing atop the structure of flesh and bone like a king watching over his subjects. Its skin bore haphazard patterns of scars and fresh wounds, each one a testament to the leadership challenges it had faced.

"The Alpha," he decided. *If I can kill that thing, it should buy us some time while the Beta takes control.*

Taj fired his pistol, every shot found the mark, tearing into the unsuspecting Alpha's flesh. The Alpha roared in rage and surprise, then launched itself off the tower, landing near him. He fumbled for another clip, his shaking hands slow from adrenalin and fear. The creature charged, slashing at him with claws and teeth in a rapid flurry that sent him back peddling. A glancing blow struck his chest plate, the force of the hit making him stumble. The Lurker saw its chance and leapt forward, bowling him over.

Snapping jaws came flying toward his exposed throat, he

232

angled his blade upward to deter the attack. Undaunted by the feeble defence, the Alpha impaled itself on the knife and kept driving forward, pushing the weapon deeper into its torso, while its jaws inched closer to the soft flesh they were seeking. Taj grabbed the blade handle with both his hands, pushing with all his might to keep the creature back.

The Alpha convulsed, and he braced himself for the next lunge, but the Lurker's eyes glazed over, and it collapsed, a fresh bullet hole in the back of its head. Without checking to see who had fired the lifesaving shot, he pulled his second knife free from its sheath, repeatedly driving the weapon into his downed foe, each blow rattling his arms.

A collective shiver went through the rest of the pack, they stopped in their tracks, unable to continue until the Beta took control. None of the defenders needed any instruction on what to do next, a mass slaughter of the docile creatures began. Taj wiped his blood soaked hands on his undershirt. *Another close call.* He dropped to his knees, rummaging among the carpet of dead for his lost rifle, most of them were Lurkers, but every so often, he would find one of his own people, savaged beyond all recognition.

His hands brushed up against metal and he grabbed what lay beneath, extracting a rifle from the pile. *I don't think this is mine, but it will have to do.* A deep rumbling started, and he saw a Lurker tower crumble, raining bodies along the battlements, forcing everyone in the vicinity to duck for cover. A high-pitched howl came from below, and the pack mimicked the cry of their new Alpha.

Taj tensed, *that wasn't nearly long enough.* He looked around and saw a sea of white on the barricades. *Still too many, even if we kill this Alpha, another will take control and we will be no better off.*

The pack awoke, and the frenzy began anew, he shot a creature point blank in the side of the head, then turned to blast another that came towards him. Ace and Ash were fighting nearby, back to back with two Watchers, Wes was just beyond, trying to help a man who had lost an arm, then Tre filled his vision, screaming and pointing back toward Acropolis.

Taj leaned closer, his ears ringing from the sounds of battle. "Fall… back," he discerned among the yelled expletives.

Fall back to what? he thought, turning and seeing that Lee, Jye and hundreds of reinforcements had arrived unnoticed, setting up a defensive line of bodies behind the barricades that followed along the wall and out of sight in both directions.

Taj didn't hesitate and jumped off the battlements, rolling as he hit the ground. Dozens of other fighters landed with him, and they sprinted back to the line of reinforcements, taking up a crouch at their feet, aiming their rifles back at the barricades. The few who remained on the wall were quickly overwhelmed.

"Open fire," Jye roared.

Gunfire erupted in a slow trickle outward as word passed along the battle lines to start shooting. It looked to Taj like there were still a few of their comrades fighting among the creatures, but he pushed the thought from his mind. *We can't save them.*

Everything on the barricades was killed in a hail of bullets, and even the fresh Lurkers who stormed over the wall were quickly dispatched. Unable to gain a foothold, the tide of creatures ceased for a second time and the remaining towers crumbled.

Some of the bodies on the barricades still writhed and twitched, but none were still standing. *Was the new Alpha killed?* Taj wondered. *Or is this a trap?*

"Cease fire," Jye ordered, stepping out in front of the battle lines with his rifle over his shoulder. "Front line, take back the barricades, the rest of you hold here." The grandmaster didn't wait to see if anyone was with him and trudged back toward the wall.

Taj stood back up and followed the other Vanguards, his eyes trained on the barricades, for any sign the creatures were making another push. *If this is an ambush, we won't have time to fall back again*. He reached the steps and hesitated for a second, afraid of what he might see above. *I just want this to be over*.

"Hurry up boy," a Vanguard grunted behind him. "Best to just get it over with."

Taj took a breath and joined the line of men slowly making their way back up to the barricades. *The Beta should have taken control by now, the next wave should be hitting us any second now.*

"Send back word to Acropolis, get more people down here, now. I don't care if you have to grab Harvesters or Guild," Jye yelled.

That's probably not a good sign. At the top, Taj found the view of the plain blocked by Watchers, gazing out at the vast expanse in wonder. He walked along the battlements and found an open spot where he could see what lay below, his jaw dropped.

Chapter Nineteen
Clearing the Field

Jye perched on the precipice of the outer barricades, his cold hard eyes darting back and forth as he scanned the area. The massive Lurker pack had disappeared, leaving nothing but piles of their dead. Many Watchers and Vanguards lay with them, their mangled bodies and crimson blood the only colour among the pale white creatures.

Taj waited patiently with Tre, while the grandmaster decided what he wanted to do next. Around them, Watchers and Vanguards, assisted by Harvesters, disposed of the Lurkers by throwing them over the walls, while members of the Guild attempted to fix the heavily damaged big guns. Medics hovered around, checking injuries and trying to find any who were calling for help, the dead far outweighed the living though.

Jye suddenly fired a shot at the nearest Labyrinth tunnel, catching everyone's attention and causing the work to halt while they waited to see what he was shooting at.

Taj saw it immediately, two great big yellow eyes glared at them from the safety of the tunnels. The monster roared, sending a chill down the collective spine of everyone who heard.

"Should we go after it?" Tre asked Jye. "If we hurry, maybe we can catch it before the damn thing disappears."

"No," Jye replied. "We need to secure the city, make it safe before we can sally forth, its lackeys failed to take the walls this time, but it wasn't from lack of trying, we are vulnerable right now."

So, it's true, Taj mused. *They really can control the lesser creatures, how many attacks have they instigated, I wonder?*

"What was their plan here?" he said out loud. "If they were trying to wipe us out, then why didn't they send Slammers, along with some of the other creatures to support the attack, like they did at Agora."

"I don't know," Jye admitted. "This could have been a test, so they could observe how we react to threats. From what I remember, there was a massive Lurker assault on Agora days before it was destroyed. Perhaps they will return in in a few days with an army of other creatures, like they did before."

It wasn't a comforting thought, even Tre appeared unnerved at the revelation. The creatures had never been anything but mindless animals, with the Huskers leading them though, it appeared they were capable of anything, even destroying a fortified city.

The Husker returned a moment later, walking out of the tunnel with a newly crowned Alpha Lurker struggling in its grasp, whinnying in fear. The monster lifted its victim high enough for everyone to see, then with an effortless twist of its hands, snapped the Alpha's neck with an audible crack. The body was cast aside like an old piece of trash, and the monster vanished in a flash.

"It's gone," Jye told them. "Everyone back to work," he said loud enough for everyone to hear. "We need those big guns working, and the walls cleared."

"If they were able to strike Acropolis, the wall of light must have fallen," Tre said. "Once the city defences are repaired, I will take everyone we have left and investigate."

"Agreed," Jye said. "We will need to meet with the council first, we might need to keep them in the vaults until further notice. In the meantime, let's find Lee and get a count of our casualties."

The two men left without acknowledging Taj and he awkwardly waited for a few seconds until he was sure they weren't coming back. *Why did he ask me to wait with Tre if they were just going to leave without me?*

He went back along the outer barricades and joined a small

group throwing Lurker corpses over the battlements. One of them took the time to kick each body before he threw it over the edge. Two identical men watched him with bemused interest.

"It's already dead, Dal," Taj chuckled. "Ease off, it will take twice as long if you waste time kicking each one."

"Can't be too careful," Dal said as he effortlessly lifted a creature with one hand. "An uncle of mine was killed because he was careless after a battle, I won't make that mistake."

Taj slung the new rifle he had acquired, and grabbed a dead Lurker, recoiling at the touch of its coarse rubbery skin.

Dal noticed his reaction and smiled, "Smell your hands," he advised. "You haven't even noticed the best part yet."

Taj put his hand over his nose and inhaling deeply, an overpowering damp, mouldy scent filled his nostrils. His stomach churned and he dry heaved, his whole body convulsing as it reacted to the stench.

"That's the worst thing I've ever smelt," he coughed, reluctantly bending down to grab the creature by the head and hurl it over the wall.

Dal laughed, "Dirty little fuckers aren't they, no matter how much you wash yourself, that smell will linger on your skin for the next few days."

Great.

"Has anyone seen Ren and Wes," Taj wondered out loud.

"Saw them over there," Ash said, pointing behind them. "They are fine, it looks like Ren got a few new wounds, but the old goat is still alive and yelling."

"I feel like Ren was born yelling," Dal murmured. "I don't think the man knows there are other ways to communicate."

"That's because you irritate him," Ace stated. "You're lucky he doesn't shoot you."

Dal held a hand over his chest in a display of mock outrage, his eye twitched slightly, but the episode quickly passed. "How could you say such a thing, he loves me, like a son."

Ren limped over and slapped Dal over the back of the head, along with the limp, the second captain had a newly stitched gash on his forehead, and his undershirt was soaked with blood. "If you were my son," he growled. "I would have left you out in the Labyrinth with a bloodied pork chop tied around your neck long ago."

Dal and Taj burst out laughing; the twins quickly followed suit, Ren tried his best to keep a straight face, but the grizzled old veteran lost his composure and allowed a rare smile to play over his lips.

"Enough nonsense," Ren barked. "Let's clear this mess before I die of old age."

"That means we don't have long then," Dal quipped.

****

The next few hours saw the barricades cleared of the dead, the work was monotonous which prompted Taj and Dal to start a game and see who could throw the dead creatures the furthest. The game quickly caught on, and before long, more than a few others had started their own competitions, cries of triumph at good throws became commonplace along the fortifications.

I'll get him this time, Taj thought as he spun around and hurled a dead Lurker over the side by its head. The corpse fell a good metre in front of Dal's previous shot.

"That makes 60 wins to me, and 55 to you," Taj said. "Maybe you should give up now, before you embarrass yourself."

"You got lucky with those last few shots," Dal groaned. "I guarantee you won't win another game."

Taj bent down picked up another body, he had a suitable insult ready to tease his friend, but his mind went blank when he saw what the dead Lurker had been hiding. His throat closed over, and a familiar deep feeling of guilt welled in his chest. *So, he died after all*. They had found quite a few dead Vanguards and Watchers while clearing the wall, but he hadn't had the misfortune of seeing anybody he knew, until now.

Fin's armour had been cut open in several spots, leaving deep wounds on his chest and legs, his left arm had also been torn off at the elbow. Taj had never been in command before, never brought someone to their death, but found it left a bitter taste in his mouth. "I'm sorry," he breathed.

Fin was safe in Acropolis. A voice in the back of his mind said accusingly. *You brought him here.* "Those Watchers were necessary, without them, the outer barricades would have fallen before Jye got here," he countered. *Liar, you didn't even try to find other help, you just grabbed the first people you saw.*

"That's a shame," Ren said, temporarily banishing the voices of doubt in Taj's head. "Fin was one of the most promising Vanguard recruits when he joined, until he was mauled by a Harpy, he was demoted to the Watchers because of the injuries."

Ren sensed his mood and gave Taj a tap on the shoulder, it wasn't much, but to a hardy man like Ren, it was the equivalent of an affectionate, comforting hug.

"Now you know why I never rose above the rank of second captain," he explained. "There were opportunities of course; you don't get to my age without fielding a few offers. I could never get right with knowingly sending people to their deaths, making the decision of who lives and dies. The burdens of command are harsh; many people don't realise that. I have a little bit of responsibility, but thankfully there are very few deaths on my conscience."

"Those two," Ren pointed to Tre and Jye who were in a deep conversation with Watcher Grandmaster Lee on the path leading up to Acropolis, "send thousands of our people to their deaths every year. It's a hard job, but somebody has to do it, you will need to make peace with that, sooner rather than later."

"What are you on about, Ren?" Taj growled with a little more aggression than was necessary.

"There are rumblings about you, boy, the powers that be have seen something in you," Ren explained. "You're smarter than most and are prone to the occasional good idea, it didn't go unnoticed how quickly you managed to gather up reinforcements and lead them back here. You might find yourself in charge of your own unit one day. Why do you think Jye told you to listen in on his conversation with Tre before? The best way for you to learn is to listen and watch, so pay attention."

"I'm not cut out for leadership."

"Few are, if there is one thing I've learnt in all my years, it's that what you want is rarely taken into consideration, especially in Acropolis, sometimes you are forced to step up."

Ren called over Wes and another medic to collect Fin for formal identification at the makeshift triage set up behind the barricades. There were already many awaiting treatment by the medics, and even more dead laid out awaiting identification by family or friends.

Taj returned to his game with Dal, but discovering Fin had drained him of all desire to play. *I hope Valens and Sai are alright.*

****

Once the outer barricades were cleared of the dead, and most of the big guns were back in usable condition, teams of Harvesters and Guild were tasked with burning off the Lurker bodies in front of the outer barricades. Vanguards were stationed at intervals along the perimeter to ensure their safety, Watchers kept a vigil on the outer barricades.

Taj stood guard near a tunnel entrance with the rest of his unit, watching over the hundred or so people they had been assigned to protect. They were two men down, with Tre gathering more fighters for a sortie to retake the ring of light, and Wes still helping with the wounded. Harvesters dragged the corpses into piles and the Guild members doused them with a blue liquid the tinkerers had invented to create an intense flame capable of eating through steel, stone, bones and flesh. From what he had heard, the concoction didn't have a name yet, having only been created a month prior.

He shuddered, observing the process of flesh burning away, the pale skin turned black collapsing in on itself, before erupting in intense blue flames. Several piles were already alight, clogging the air with thick smoke that smelt like rotten eggs and burnt hair. The teams of workers had rags tied around their faces, the Vanguards hadn't bothered.

"This is a shit job," Dal coughed, covering his nose to the foul smelling smoke. "What's the point of this?"

"It has to be done," Ren growled. "The flesh will be rotting soon, if we don't clear the field, it could spread disease, or attracts rats, or maybe more creatures looking for an easy meal."

Seems a shame to waste all this meat.

"Can we eat it?" Taj suggested. "I'm sure it wouldn't taste great, but if it's cooked well, and we add some spices or something, it could feed a lot of people."

Ren grimaced and spat on the ground. "Have you ever heard of Hat the Mad?"

Taj hummed, racking his brain. "The name does sound familiar, is that one of old Ryn's stories?"

Ren shook his head, "Most of the old bats stories are about times long past, Hat the Mad is a far more recent tragedy. He was one of us, a mountain of a man, broad shouldered and limbs as thick as the pillars in the Amphitheatre. It was said his strength allowed him to knock out Berserkers with one punch."

Taj snorted, *I seriously doubt that, punching one of those things would break your hand,* he would never dare to question

242

Ren like that, Dal on the other hand had no qualms about voicing his doubt.

"That sounds like bullshit," he chuckled. "You're just making this up, aren't you?"

Ren shot Dal a dirty look, but otherwise ignored the display of scepticism and continued recounting his story. "During a culling mission, Hat went missing, his unit searched for him of course, they found no trace though. A year later, long after his presumed death, his unit discovered him wandering the Labyrinth, a hunched husk of a man. From what little sense they could make of his muttering lunacy, apparently, he had survived by eating creature meat, and it had slowly poisoned him. Eating creatures makes you violently ill, and eventually rots your brain, many have tried it over the centuries, no matter how well the meat is prepared, the end result is always the same."

"I heard the Terror Twins eat their kills," Ace said, "Some weird ritual about absorbing their strength?"

"Didn't Marauders used to do that?" Taj asked, half remembering something Doc had told him once.

"I've never met a Marauder," Ren said. "I think they would be far more reasonable than Jye's pet psychopaths."

"Movement," came a cry from atop the walls. The Watchers fired a few shots at the nearest tunnel, prompting a halt to all work in the vicinity. Ren signalled for everyone to follow him, and the Vanguards converged on the tunnel entrance, adopting a lined formation so everyone had a clear shot at whatever was coming.

"Hold fire, wait for my word," Ren said. "The Watchers might just be jumping at shadows again."

Has it returned? Is the Husker back for another attempt on the city?

Taj stared into the infinite blackness, waiting for the tell-tale flash of yellow eyes that would signal their doom. *If that thing is back with another wave of Lurkers, we are dead.* In the background, Harvesters and Guild members abandoned the field, trickling back behind the safety of the walls. Footsteps echoed out from the Labyrinth, everyone tensed, waiting for the word to start shooing again. The noise steadily got closer, and still Ren stayed silent.

What's he waiting for? Taj wondered. *It only sounds like one, but we can't take any chances, there might be more.*

A shadowy figure appeared at the mouth of the tunnel, just outside the light, and every gun swivelled around to aim directly at it. Taj rested his finger on the trigger, ready for the command. *Here we go again.*

"Hold fire," Ren ordered. "Lower your weapons. Ace, go get a medic, find Wes, if you can."

The scout didn't question why a medic was needed and sprinted back to the outer barricades. Taj looked to Ren for an explanation, when a man stumbled into their midst, his Vanguard armour and clothes hung from his muscular frame, revealing bloodied wounds over nearly every visible piece of skin.

"They are coming, fall back," the man cried, falling to his knees and waving a severed hand around. "They are coming, fall back, there are too many."

"Battle sickness," the phrase was whispered by everyone present, the dreaded affliction they had seen affect so many of their comrades. After witnessing one too many horrors, men could break down with the disease, none were ever the same again, there was no cure. Most of the sufferers were regulated to new less stressful jobs or left in the tunnels to die as part of The Sacrifice, there could be no invalids in Acropolis.

"They are coming," the man screamed hysterically. "Their mark is on me, kill me before it consumes us all."

Ace returned with Wes a few minutes later, and the medic slowly approached the ranting man with his hands in the air, trying to show he meant no harm. The man lashed out, lunging at Wes with the severed hand he clutched like a talisman, forcing the medic back.

"Ash, Ace, grab his arms," Wes instructed. "We need to get him to the Healers, whatever has happened to him, it's far beyond my abilities to help."

The man screamed as he was carried away, his babbled cries of anguish and pain stabbing at the heart of all who heard.

****

Work steadily resumed, and the Harvesters and Guild returned to the field. A short time later, Tre and Jye passed through the outer barricades at the head an army of Vanguards over a hundred strong. The grim-faced men and women gathered at the mouth of the tunnel the injured man appeared out of, Taj and the rest of his unit joined them at Tre's instruction.

"We need to retake the ring of light," Jye announced. "I'm not sure what we are walking into, the main pack appears to have gone, but with our defences down, who knows what else could have walked in, stay alert."

Jye and Tre went first, and the rest of the Vanguards shuffled after their leaders in a loose skirmish formation. Taj walked side by side with Dal near the front, their rifle torches adding to the beams that were lighting the way. The few Lurkers they came across were feasting on the remains of defenders caught in the path of the pack, they were easily dealt with, a hundred bullets tearing into the surprised creatures before they could flinch.

At end of the tunnel, Jye increased the pace, running to the other side. After a moment's hesitation, the frontrunners followed, entering the chamber that held the ring of light. The ten foot tall continuous ring of steel and lighting circled all the passages around the city, acting as a barrier between the creatures and the outer barricades. Barbed wire snaked along the battlements, while a makeshift rampart nestled underneath allowed units to patrol the perimeter in relative safety. All the visible sections had been ruptured in at least twenty places, the breaches filled with the corpses of creatures and defenders alike, locked together in death. Nearly all the lights were dark, and the handful that were still working flickered intermittently.

The defensive structure already had at least a hundred Vanguards patrolling along the wreckage, with even more watching the three tunnels that lead into the chamber. The Terror Twins were at a breach on the other side, surrounded by other captains, who were all shifting uncomfortably from the proximity to the notoriously unstable brothers.

"Fan out, coordinate with the other units, make sure this area is secure," Jye ordered. "Tre, come with me, we need to talk with Jax and Taz."

The other Vanguards spread out, trampling through the wreckage. Tre gave Ren a nod and the two had one of their silent conversations. It was never clear how exactly they communicated without any words or visible signs, but when they were done, Ren always knew exactly what Tre wanted him to do.

"Alright lads, we are going with the commander," Ren said. "Hang back and shut up, that means you Dal."

Dal cackled but didn't make any more unwise comments to provoke Ren, much to the surprise of everyone. Tre and Jye took them through the aftermath of the battle, all around them their fellows cleared the rubble and looked for survivors. When they got closer to the captains meeting, it was clear Jax and Taz were in charge.

"Is there any word from anyone in the Labyrinth?" Taz asked the captains as he eyed off Tre and Jye, who waited outside the circle.

"No, we need to send out more patrols, who knows how many creatures have slipped through," one of the captains replied.

"Jye, nice of you to join us," Jax said to the grandmaster. "Bit late, nothing left here but the dead."

"What happened Jax?" Tre asked. "Did you see where the pack went?"

"No idea," Jax admitted. "We heard the commotion when they broke through, by the time we got here, all that remained was the tail end of the horde, our scouts report that this is the only place they've breached."

"We sent out runners, calling everyone back, thought you were still under siege," Taz added, lifting his wrist mounted blades. "It looks like you won't need reinforcements after all, shame, was looking forward to some more close quarters fighting."

Their blades were bloodied and broken in half, prompting Taj to imagine the level of violence they must have unleashed to break their weapons. *The creatures didn't stand a chance.* Taz caught him staring and pointed to the artery in his neck, then his eyes.

The meaning was clear, Taj looked away, fearful of the man trying to show him how to kill an enemy with a knife again.

"Tre, re-call the units we just brought with us, take them back to Acropolis, they aren't needed," Jye said. "You all have a day's rest, then get ready for active duty again, training is cancelled, we will need fresh troops for what comes next."

"Taz and I will head out after the Lurkers" Jax announced, "A pack of that size can't be allowed to roam so close to the city."

"Very well, report back in a day," The grandmaster said. "The rest of you" he addressed the other captains, "Take your units and secure the surrounding area, the Guild is needed to fix the ring of light, they will need safe conditions to work in."

The Vanguards dispersed, their orders clear, Taj was about to follow the rest of his unit, when Jye grabbed him by the shoulder.

"I hear we have a visitor in the city," Jye whispered. "I've told her many times to be more careful, but she doesn't listen, a trait you both share, you need to take her home, soon. Do you understand?"

Of course he knows, the man seems to know everything that happens in Acropolis.

Chapter Twenty
Intruders

Valens was still in the house when Taj came home, she sat in a corner with a piece of his drawing paper and charcoal, busily working. He stomped through the door, feeling every footstep radiate through his weary bones.

"Your sister left to help with the wounded," Valens said without looking up. "Are you okay?"

"Still alive," he replied, dropping to the floor and staring at the rusted ceiling.

"I helped myself to your paper and charcoal," she said slyly. "Your drawings are quite good by the way, who knew you had a talent for creating rather destroying."

Taj's heart skipped a beat; he had never shown anyone other than Sai his pictures before, he had always been too fearful of criticism.

"What are you doing?" he asked, changing to a safer subject.

"I'm writing down a story I heard a few days ago," she explained. "I meant to do it when I went home, but I was bored after your sister left, so now seemed like as good a time as any. This charcoal isn't the best writing implement, but I've always enjoyed a challenge."

"What story?"

"About a man called Han, apparently, he founded your Vanguards. A strange fellow at the Boondocks told me about it. I found him underneath a table; he seemed rather unhinged to tell you the truth, he kept talking about a witch who was trying to poison him."

Taj burst out laughing and instantly regretted it, pain shot through his entire being, "That sounds like Doc," he winced.

"He didn't tell me his name, then I heard the same tale from a woman in the street, they say Han killed all the warlords one by one, defeated the Marauders in a great battle, and founded the Vanguards, it sounds fanciful, almost like a child's bedtime story."

"That's how most of our history is recorded, in stories, Han was very real, we are told he was the first Grandmaster of the Vanguards."

Valens looked up from her work. "How very strange, there might be…" Her voice droned on and Taj found his eye lids drooping as sleep threatened to overtake him. She sounded far away, but he was able to catch snippets of what was said.

"They live on a continent far to the east, their technology rivals that of our own, the only problem is they…"

Normally, he would be intrigued by the prospect of learning about the wild and strange civilisations across the sea, but fatigue refused to leave him alone, and instead he just mumbled a few words in response. *Just a few hours of rest*, he decided before nodding off. *Then I need to get her home.*

****

Alexandria was silent as a bright light shone down from above, lighting up the bone-filled streets. Taj spun around, looking for something, but he couldn't remember what. He tried to call out, the words died in his throat. Suddenly all light disappeared, and the familiar set of yellow eyes appeared in front of him. "See you soon," a voice hissed out of the dark.

Taj woke with a start, his old back wound burning as though it had been freshly opened. He still lay where he had dropped earlier, Valens had curled up in a corner to sleep, an old blanket covering her lithe form.

It not safe here anymore, I need to get her home.

He went over to her sleeping form and woke her with a jab of his finger. If it were Dal, he would just kick him, but something told him Valens wouldn't appreciate being struck.

"You awake?" he whispered. "Valens, wake up." He prodded her a few more times and she groaned.

"That's very annoying," Valens said through a yawn. "What do you want? Is Sai back?"

"She might be gone for days, our Healers were already stretched pretty thin with so many wounded coming back from the Labyrinth. After the attack, I expect they will be flat out for a while."

"Then what do you want?"

"It's probably time you go back home, before anything else happens. The path to the closest surface entrance should be clear of enemies, but we should get Dal, just to be safe."

"Oh, how delightful," she said sarcastically. "Your gentlemanly friend should make things go so much smoother."

"Dal is the only one who will help us without asking too many questions."

"He's a jerk, I don't need his help to find a way out, I've been sneaking in here for months without an issue."

"With things as they are, it's too dangerous for you out there on your own. Especially after the assault on the city, and the incident with the Harvesters."

"Fine," she sighed. "Let's get this over with then."

****

"Why exactly do you need me?" Dal whined as the three of them walked the well-lit tunnel to the nearest of the four surface entrances. "I was having the best dream; we were back at the Director's Tower; the whole courtyard was made of chocolate."

They had reached Dal's home without arousing suspicion and Taj had managed to sneak into the house to wake him without alerting Dal's family. However, persuading the stubborn Vanguard to accompany them proved more difficult than Taj anticipated. He knew his friend was stringing them along before he said yes, but Dal still made every effort to refuse.

"I didn't want you to come at all, Taj insisted we need you," Valens said. "I'm not convinced though, the only use I can see you serving is throwing you at a beast and escaping while it feasts upon you."

"That's funny, my plan was very similar," Dal countered. "Except Taj and I would leave you out here to be eaten, then storm your city and rule the place like kings."

Is this how Tre feels when I argue with Dal all the time?

After leaving Dal's house, they passed through the gates by saying they were delivering a message to the Boondocks for Jye. The same trick worked at the ring of light, although the Vanguards on duty gave them suspicious looks and took a bit more persuading. In the end, they were allowed though, the repairs were already underway and everyone at the defensive fortification had far more important things to worry about.

"You think because your ancestors were mistreated that gives you the right to demand everything," Valens shouted. "I do something every day to make life better for your people, while all you do is complain like a selfish child. If you devoted even half that energy to helping, then maybe things would improve."

"That's so easy to say," Dal said menacingly. "When you're not the one who's watching your family starve half to death every other day for the actions of long-dead men."

"That's not my fault."

"Well, it's not mine either, Taj why does she need an escort? If she runs into any trouble, she can just freeze everything with her icy heart."

"It's too dangerous for her to travel alone," Taj replied breathlessly. "So soon after the city was hit, there might still be creatures around."

"Why didn't you ask one of the others for help?" Dal

mumbled.

"The less people that know about Valens sneaking into Acropolis, the better. Besides, I would have thought you'd enjoy the challenge, you must be losing your edge."

Dal grimaced, baring his teeth at the crude insult. "Let's just get this over with," he grumbled.

Taj hid a knowing smile, Dal was argumentative at the best of times, but question his bravery and he would rise to meet any challenge. *Maybe Ren should give that a try sometime, perhaps Dal would listen more.*

"Where are the patrols?" Dal remarked. "We should have seen another unit by now."

Taj didn't get a chance to reply, twenty City Guard walked into view and immediately raised their guns.

"What do you want to do?" Dal asked. "If we are going to fight, we should strike first."

"Relax," Valens said, casually strolling out from behind Taj. "There is no need for things to escalate."

"Arrest them," General Valens roared as he stormed out from among his City Guard. "Or shoot them, I don't care which."

"Wait, brother, please," Valens said with her hands up.

"Selene," the general thundered. "What are you doing with these Subrats? Some of your friends at the Boondocks said you were down here. Did they hurt you?"

"Lysander," Selene snapped. "Calm down, these are my friends; they were taking me home."

Taj wasn't sure if the use of their private first names was a good or a bad sign, but the look of red-faced fury on Lysander Valens face made him think it was the latter. He had already seen how quickly fiery tempers and guns could result in violence, and had no desire to revisit the experience.

We can't allow this to turn deadly, not again.

The City Guards began to creep forward, Dal fired a warning

shot at the ground just in front of them, narrowly missing the Valens siblings.

"Take another step, and you'll never see a sunrise again," he said fiercely.

"Careful whom you threaten," spat the front City Guard, a stocky man with a squashed nose. "We won't miss at this range, and you are heavily outnumbered."

"That's not what happened last time," Dal laughed. "You people are all talk, why don't we save you from embarrassing yourselves again and settle this with fists, I bet I could fight you all at once without getting a scratch."

The Surfacers angry reply was drowned out by howls of pain coming from a man near the back of the squad, he clutched a severed stump that used to be his right hand while his comrades recoiled in fear and disgust.

Taj spotted the culprit immediately; a section of air was shimmering nearby.

They're back, he realised, a chill shooting down his spine. *How did they get through the lines again?* Without voicing a warning, he fired at the camouflaged monster, the towering Husker let out a roar as it became visible.

Lysander recovered from the shock quickly, screaming orders to his men, but it was far too late. Four more Huskers appeared, and the monsters wasted no time in carving through the stunned Surfacers. The first Husker charged toward the Vanguards, taking a swipe at General Valens as it passed, forcing him to roll out of the way. Taj wordlessly handed his sidearm to Selene, a voice in his head was screaming to take her and run, he knew with a cold certainty they wouldn't get far.

In a heartbeat, the Husker loomed over them, Taj struck out with his rifle, hitting the monster with all his strength. The assault sent crippling shockwaves up his arms as it bounced off the rock-hard skin, before he knew what was happening, he was swatted away by a heavy shot to the chest. He had a few seconds of dizzying vertigo, before slamming into the ground.

Taj's vision clouded, and he groggily got back to his feet. The Husker appeared in front of him in a flash, and he quickly drew his curved blades. The monster lashed out with its long-fingered hand, fastening it around his throat and lifting him into the air. He reacted by kicking and slashing at the arm that held him up, but the blows bounced uselessly off its rock hard skin.

The vice like grip tightened, Taj gasped as his eyes threatened to pop out of his skull and he desperately tried to breathe. He dropped one knife, using two hands to furiously stab at the Husker. Each strike got steadily weaker as his strength faded and his lungs cried out for air, until eventually, he couldn't hold his arms up anymore, and they fell uselessly to his side.

The monster leered, bringing its other hand up, extending five claws that glistened with a liquid that Taj suspected would hungrily eat away any flesh it touched. He defiantly stared into the big yellow eyes that had been haunting his dreams, waiting for the monster to tire of the game and kill him, when Taz's advice about killing a superior foe decided to float back into his oxygen-addled brain. *I can't hit its artery, but he did say there was a second option available.*

Taj lifted the blade, his arms straining as though the weapon weighed a ton. The Husker turned its head, smiling at his feeble struggles with grim amusement. *I'll give you something to smile about you bastard.*

He lined it up and struck out with a slow clumsy thrust, the monster didn't react, failing to see the intended target until it was far too late. The blade pierced straight through the soft tissue of the Husker's left eye and buried itself up to the hilt. The monster howled, a deep throaty noise that sounded like a hundred voices crying out in pain. The grip on his throat loosened, but Taj's eyes were heavy, he couldn't keep them open anymore, they closed and he drifted into the abyss.

THE END OF BOOK ONE

Look out for Book 2 of the Acropolis series:
Extinction, available soon

Acknowledgements

Writing this two part book series has taken the better part of the last five years and has seen more edits and changes than I'd care to mention. I only showed the manuscript to a handful of people but all of them helped improve it.

Thanks to Yasmin, who was the first person I showed a draft too. Her early editing saw many errors eliminated, and she also spent countless hours discussing possible plot points and storylines with me.

Thanks to Annie, who has helped me for the last three years, offering guidance and editing to help make a book far better than anything I could have done on my own. Thanks to Kristen, who proofread and polished one of the final drafts into a finished state.

Finally, thanks to Jye, whose name and partial likeness helped inspire one of Vanguards best characters.

About the Author

Stephen Novak lives on the coast of Australia where he works as a journalist and freelance writer. When not recording the real-life stories of people, he works on fantasy and science fiction novels spanning multiple series, with Vanguard being the first.

The decision to start writing didn't come until much later in life, but Stephen has been around storytelling all his life. From a young age, family members often recounted tall tales that stretched the truth far into the realms of fantasy.

After a few years spent at university, where he eventually left with a Bachelor of Writing and a dislike of cities, he moved to the coast where he engages in a healthy mix of skateboarding, Brazilian jiu-jitsu and travelling.